The New

PILGRIM'S
PROGRESS

Given as a gift in
November 1993
by "Dad".

P U B L I S H E R S
BOX 3566 · GRAND RAPIDS, MI 49501

*PUBLISHING BOOKS THAT FEED
THE SOUL WITH THE WORD OF GOD.*

The New

PILGRIM'S
PROGRESS

John Bunyan's Classic Revised for Today

with notes by Warren W. Wiersbe

The New Pilgrim's Progress
Text copyright © 1989 by Discovery House Publishers
Revised notes copyright © 1989 by Warren W. Wiersbe
The annotations were previously published in another form under
the title *The Annotated Pilgrim's Progress* by Moody Press,
copyright © 1980 by The Moody Bible Institute.

Discovery House Publishers is affiliated with Radio Bible Class,
Grand Rapids, Michigan.
Discovery House books are distributed to the trade by
Thomas Nelson Publishers, Nashville, Tennessee 37214.

Library of Congress Cataloging-in-Publication Data
Bunyan, John, 1628–1688.
[Pilgrim's progress]
The new pilgrim's progress / by John Bunyan ; with notes by Warren
Wiersbe.
p.   cm.
ISBN: 0-929239-13-X
I. Wiersbe, Warren W. II. Title.
PR3330.A2W54   1989
828'.407—dc20
                           89-36626
                              CIP
Printed in the United States of America.
       93 / CHG / 10 9

Contents

Introduction

Since it was published in 1678, John Bunyan's *The Pilgrim's Progress* has been an inspiration to millions of readers. This magnificent work is still a classic and always will be a classic. But over the centuries Bunyan's readers have changed, and many people who want to enjoy this work and profit from it are baffled by some of the archaic language, symbols, and allusions. Bunyan's original readers were better taught in the Bible than the average reader today, and some of Bunyan's personal life that shows up in the text was better known to them than to us.

I suggest that you keep a copy of the King James Version of the Bible at hand while reading this book. Where Bunyan quotes a verse or phrase, paraphrases, or makes an allusion to Scripture, I have given the reference and, if necessary, explanation to help you to understand what he is saying.

There are also references to Bunyan's personal Christian experience, as well as to political and religious circumstances of his day. I have indicated these in the appropriate places, either in introductory sections or in the notes.

The original work contained no chapter or other divisions. For readability, we have broken it at natural places throughout both to give the reader a place to pause and to give an opportunity to introduce supplementary material or information for better understanding of the text.

At the end you will find "The Author's Apology for His Book," the extended poem with which Bunyan originally began his work and which was an explanation of why he used allegory. There are also sections on "The Life and Times of John Bunyan" and "The Puritans," which set this work in its proper historical and cultural framework.

It is possible to read *The Pilgrim's Progress* and benefit from it while knowing nothing about Bunyan himself or the historical circumstances of his life. But knowing these extra facts will give greater meaning to what he has written.

If you have never read this classic work, we suggest that you read it through and enjoy it, using the marginal notes only where you actually need help in understanding the text. Then, after you have read it, go back and read it again, using the marginal notes and your Bible. Take your time, read carefully, and think about both the text and the Scriptures. You will discover new truths that will make both this enduring classic and your Bible new books to you.

If you are not "a pilgrim," I trust that using this book will help you become one. If you are already on that pilgrimage to Glory, I trust that this book will make the pathway brighter and more victorious.

The Pilgrim's Progress

In the Similitude of a Dream

The Pilgrim's Progress *begins with a wilderness and ends with the crossing of a river, which parallels the history of the nation of Israel. The Israelites wandered as pilgrims in the wilderness for forty years, then crossed the Jordan River to enter the Promised Land.*

In the first paragraph, Bunyan says that the narrator (himself) laid down in a "Den." This refers to the Bedford jail where Bunyan was confined for several months in 1675. It was during this imprisonment that he wrote The Pilgrim's Progress.

Pilgrim's name is Christian, which means "belonging to Christ." Before he begins his pilgrimage to the Holy City, his name is Graceless. Grace is God's favor to undeserving sinners, and Christian has been without that grace.

Christian will journey from the City of Destruction to the gates of heaven, and Bunyan introduces a description of the heavenly city early in his book for several reasons. The glories of heaven are an encouragement to Christian to keep on his difficult journey and to invite others to share the pilgrimage with him. These glories also help Christian keep in perspective the trials he endures along the way because the glory to come more than compensates for the sufferings (Rom. 8:18; 2 Cor. 4:16–18; 1 Peter 5:10). For Christian, the expectation of heaven is a proper motive for godly living and sacrificial service.

And so let us begin our journey with Bunyan's pilgrim.

s I walked through the wilderness of this world, I came upon a certain place where there was a den, and I laid down in that place to sleep: and as I slept I dreamed a dream. In my dream I saw a man dressed in rags standing with his face turned away from his own house; he held a book in his hand and carried a great burden upon his back.[1] I saw the man open the book and read; and as he read,[2] he wept and trembled and cried out mournfully, "What shall I do?"[3]

In this distraught condition the man went home, determined not to say anything to his family, for he did not want them to see his distress; but he could not be silent long because he was so greatly troubled. Finally he told his wife and children what was on his mind: "O my dear wife and children," he said, "I am greatly troubled by a burden that lies heavy upon me. Moreover, I have been informed that our city will be burned with fire from heaven; and in this fearful destruction both myself and you, my wife and my sweet children, shall perish, unless we can find some way of escape or deliverance, which presently I cannot see."[4]

His family was amazed at his words. Not because they believed what he said, but because they thought he was mentally deranged. Since it was almost night, and they hoped that sleep might settle his mind, they got him to bed as quickly as they could. But the night was as troublesome to him as the day; instead of sleeping, he lay awake sighing and crying, so

---

[1] His sense of sin. Later he tells Worldly Wiseman that he got the burden by reading the book. By revealing our sinfulness, the Bible increases the burden. The Puritans called this conviction. As a traveling tinker, Bunyan carried a sixty-pound anvil on his back.

[2] The book is the Bible (Hab. 2:2). In his autobiography *Grace Abounding* he said, "I was then never out of the Bible ... still crying out to God, that I might know the truth and way to heaven and glory."

[3] The cry of the convicted sinner (Acts 2:37; 16:30; Hab. 1:2–3).

[4] The city is named "City of Destruction," fashioned after the wicked cities of Sodom and Gomorrah, which were destroyed by fire (Gen. 19:23–28). Bunyan wrote this in 1675. The great London fire was in 1666.

that when morning came and they asked him how he felt, he told them, "Worse and worse." He began talking to them in the same vein again. Thinking they could drive away his madness with harsh behavior, they began to make fun of him, to scold him, and sometimes even to ignore him. Because of this, he began to retire to his room to pray for and pity them, as well as grieve over his own misery; he would also walk alone in the fields, sometimes reading and sometimes praying. For several days he spent his time this way.

Now in my dream I saw that one day when he was walking in the fields, he was reading his book and was greatly distressed; and as he read, he cried out, as he had done before, "What shall I do to be saved?"

> *Christian no sooner leaves the world but meets*
> *Evangelist, who lovingly him greets*
> *With tidings of another; and doth show*
> *Him how to mount to that from this below.*

He looked this way and that, as if he wanted to run but did not know which way to go. Then I saw a man named Evangelist [5] coming toward him. "Why are you crying?" Evangelist asked.

The man answered, "Sir, this book tells me I am condemned to die, and after that to come to judgment, and I find that I am not willing to do the first, nor able to do the second."[6]

Then said Evangelist, "Why are you not willing to die, since this life is filled with so many evils?" The man answered, "Because I fear that this burden that is upon my back will sink me lower than the grave, and I shall fall into hell.[7] And, sir, I

---

[5] "Evangel" is the good news that Christ died for the sins of the world, was buried, and rose again (1 Cor. 15:1–4). "Evangelist" tells this good news to others to bring them to Christ (Acts 21:8; Eph. 4:11). Bunyan was probably depicting John Gifford, his pastor, who helped lead him to salvation.
[6] Heb. 9:27; Job 10:21–22; Ezek. 22:14
[7] Bunyan used the term "Tophet," an Old Testament name for hell (Isa. 30:33). Tophet was an area outside Jerusalem where some of the wicked

am not fit to go to judgment, and from there to execution; and the thought of these things makes me cry."

Then said Evangelist, "If this is your condition, why are you standing here?" The man answered, "Because I don't know where to go." Then Evangelist gave him a parchment roll, upon which was written, "Flee from the wrath to come."[8]

The man read it and, looking at Evangelist very carefully, said, "Where shall I go?" Evangelist pointed across a very wide field, "Do you see that wicket-gate over there?"[9] The man said, "No." Then said Evangelist, "Do you see that shining light over there?"[10] The man said, "I think I do." Then said Evangelist, "Keep your eyes on that light and go directly to it; then you will see the gate. Knock on it, and you will be told what you should do."

So I saw in my dream that the man began to run. Now, he had not run far from his own door when his wife and children saw him and began to cry for him to return; [11] but the man put his fingers in his ears and ran on, crying, "Life! Life! Eternal life!"[12] So he did not look behind him, but fled toward the middle of the plain.[13]

The neighbors also came out to watch him run; some mocked him, others threatened, and some called for him to

---

kings practiced idolatrous worship (Jer. 7:31). The word probably comes from an Aramaic word that means "to burn."

[8]Another picture of the Bible. As a young man seeking salvation, Bunyan was under a constant fear of judgment (Matt. 3:7).

[9]A small gate on a footpath that leads into a field or a road. In *Paradise Lost* Milton calls the gate of heaven "Heaven's wicket" (published in 1667). Matthew 7:13 –14 refers to the "strait" gate; "strait" means "narrow."

[10] Evangelist points away from himself and uses the Word of God to guide the burdened sinner. God's Word is "a light that shineth in a dark place" (2 Pet. 1:19, also Ps. 119:105). If people will follow the light God gives, He will lead them to salvation.

[11]Our desire for God and salvation ought to be so great that even the closest ties on earth cannot hold us (Luke 14:26).

[12] This is God's life shared with those who trust Christ (John 3:16).

[13] Lot's wife looked back and was judged (Gen. 19:17, 26). "Middle of the plain" connects this scene with the destruction of Sodom and Gomorrah.

return. Among those who called to him were two men who resolved to fetch him back by force. The name of the one was Obstinate, and the name of the other was Pliable.[14]

Now by this time the man had gotten a good distance from them; but they were resolved to pursue him, which they did, and in a little while they overtook him. Then said the man, "Neighbors, why have you come?" They said, "To persuade you to go back with us." But he said, "You cannot do that. You dwell in the City of Destruction, the place where I was born; and if you die there, sooner or later, you will sink lower than the grave into a place that burns with fire and brimstone.[15] Be content, good neighbors, and go along with me."

OBSTINATE: What! And leave our friends and our comforts behind us?

"Yes," said Christian (for that was the man's name),[16] "because ALL that you shall forsake is not worthy to be compared with a little of that which I am seeking; and if you will go with me, you shall fare as I do, for where I go there is enough and more to spare.[17] Come with me and see that I speak the truth."

OBSTINATE: What are you seeking, since you leave all the world to find it?[18]

CHRISTIAN: I seek an inheritance that can never perish, spoil, or fade, and it is kept in heaven, to be bestowed, at the

---

[14] When the sinner begins to seek salvation, well-meaning friends often try to stop him. "They that fly from the wrath to come are a gazing-stock to the world," Bunyan wrote. See Jer. 20:10.

[15] This destroyed Sodom and Gomorrah. Also describes hell (Rev. 21:8).

[16] The word "Christian" is used only three times in the New Testament: Acts 11:26; 26:28; and 1 Peter 4:16. Bunyan himself did not approve of denominational labels. He wrote, "I tell you I would be, and hope I am, a Christian, and choose, if God should count me worthy, to be called a Christian, a believer, or other such name which is approved by the Holy Ghost."

[17] The Prodigal Son said this when he came to himself (Luke 15:17). God has more to offer than the world does (see also 2 Cor. 4:18).

[18] Matt. 16:26

time appointed, on those who diligently seek it. Read about it in my book.[19]

OBSTINATE: Nonsense! I don't care about your book.[20] Will you go back with us or not?

CHRISTIAN: No, I will not, because I have put my hand to the plow.[21]

OBSTINATE: Come then, neighbor Pliable, let us turn back and go home without him. Crazy fools like this are so conceited that they think they are wiser than seven men who can give good reasons why they are wrong.[22]

PLIABLE: Don't be unkind. If what the good Christian says about the things he seeks is true, I am inclined to go with him.

OBSTINATE: What! Another fool! Take my advice and go back. Who knows where such a mad fellow will lead you? Be wise and go back home.

CHRISTIAN: No, come with me, Pliable.[23] The things I have told you about are waiting, as well as many more wonderful things. If you don't believe me, read here in this book; and the truth of what is said here is confirmed by the blood of him who wrote it.[24]

PLIABLE: Well, neighbor Obstinate, I believe I will go along with this good man and cast in my lot with him; but, my good companion, do you know the way to this desired place?[25]

CHRISTIAN: I have been told by a man whose name is Evangelist to go to a little gate that is before us, where we shall receive instructions about the way.

---

[19] 1 Pet. 1:4–6; Heb. 11:6, 16

[20] Obstinate's mind is made up; do not confuse him with facts (1 Cor. 2:14).

[21] Luke 9:62

[22] Prov. 26:16

[23] Some sinners must struggle to decide for Christ.

[24] Old Testament Law was sealed by the blood of sacrifices; the New Covenant of grace was sealed by the blood of Christ (Heb. 9:17–22; 13:20–21).

[25] Pliable is more concerned with the blessings at the destination than the steps of obedience along the way. He is a picture of many people who want to enjoy the blessings of heaven but want to get there the easy way.

PLIABLE: Come then, good neighbor, let us be going.

Then the two went on together.

OBSTINATE: And I will go back home. I will not be a companion to such misled, foolish fellows.

Now I saw in my dream that when Obstinate had left, Christian and Pliable went across the plain together talking.

CHRISTIAN: Neighbor Pliable, I am glad you have decided to go along with me. Had Obstinate felt what I have felt of the powers and terrors of what is yet unseen, he would not have turned his back on us so lightly.

PLIABLE: Come, neighbor Christian, since there are only the two of us here now, tell me now about where we are going and the things we will enjoy there.[26]

CHRISTIAN: I can better imagine them with my mind than speak of them with my tongue; but since you want to know, I will read to you from my book.

PLIABLE: And do you think that the words of your book are really true?

CHRISTIAN: Yes, certainly; for it was written by him who cannot lie.[27]

PLIABLE: Well said. So tell me more about this place.

CHRISTIAN: There is an endless kingdom to be inhabited, and we will be given everlasting life so we may inhabit that kingdom forever.[28]

PLIABLE: Well said. And what else?

---

[26] Pliable receives the Word with joy, but he has no room, like the "shallow soil" (Matt. 13:1–9, 18–23).

[27] Titus 1:2

[28] Bunyan introduces this description of the heavenly city early in his book for several reasons. The glories of heaven are an encouragement to Christian to keep on his difficult journey and to invite others to share the pilgrimage with him. These glories also help him to keep in perspective the trials that he endures along the way because the glory to come more than compensates for the sufferings (Rom. 8:18; 2 Cor. 4:16–18; 1 Pet. 5:10). Jesus Christ was able to endure the cross because of the "joy that was set before him" (Heb. 12:2). For the Christian, the expectation of heaven is a proper motive for godly living and sacrificial service.

CHRISTIAN: We will be given crowns of glory and garments that will make us shine like the sun.

PLIABLE: This sounds very pleasant. And what else?

CHRISTIAN: There shall be no more crying nor sorrow in that place where we are going; for he who is owner of the place will wipe all tears from our eyes.

PLIABLE: And who else will be there?

CHRISTIAN: There we shall be with seraphim and cherubim, creatures that will dazzle your eyes. There also you shall meet with thousands and ten thousands who have gone before us to that place. None of them are unkind, but are loving and holy; every one walks in the sight of God and stands in his presence with acceptance forever. There we shall see the elders with their golden crowns; the holy virgins with their golden harps; and the men and women who by the world were cut in pieces, burnt in flames, eaten by beasts, drowned in the seas, because of the love that they have for the Lord of that place. All of them will be well and clothed with immortality.[29]

PLIABLE: Just hearing about this is enough to delight one's heart. But how shall we get to share in these things and enjoy them?

CHRISTIAN: The Lord, the Governor of the country to which we are going, has recorded that in this book. The substance of it is that if we are truly willing to have all this, he will bestow it upon us freely.[30]

PLIABLE: I am glad to hear these things. Let us hurry.[31]

---

[29] See Isa. 65:17; John 10:27–29; Matt. 13:43; 2 Tim. 4:8; Rev. 3:4; 22:5; Isa. 25:8; Rev. 7:16–17; 21:4; Isa. 6:1–8; Exod. 25:17–22; Ezek. 1:4–14; Rev. 4:4; Heb. 11:33–34. "Holy virgins" refers to the 144,000 dedicated Jews described in Rev. 7:1–8; 14:1–5, and refers to their purity of life and devotion to God. "Clothed with immortality" refers to the new body the believer receives at the resurrection and the return of Christ (2 Cor. 5:2–4; John 12:25).

[30] God is willing to save if we are willing to receive His gift of eternal life (John 6:37; 7:37; Rev. 21:6; 22:17; Isa. 55:1–8).

[31] Pliable is in a hurry to get to heaven. Unlike Christian, he has no burden for sin to hold him back. He is a picture of the person who has never felt conviction for sin.

17

CHRISTIAN: I cannot go as fast as I would like because of this burden on my back.

Now I saw in my dream, that just as they had finished this conversation, they came to a very miry swamp[32] that was in the middle of the plain; and because they were not paying attention to where they were walking, they both fell into a bog called the Swamp of Despond.[33] Here they floundered for a time, covered with mud; and Christian, because of the burden on his back, began to sink in the mire.

PLIABLE: Ah! neighbor Christian, where are you now?

CHRISTIAN: Truly, I do not know.

At that Pliable began to be displeased and angrily said to Christian, "Is this the happiness you've been telling me about all this time? If we're having this much trouble at the start, what can we expect between here and our journey's end? If I get out of this place alive, you can go on without me." And with that Pliable gave a desperate struggle or two and got himself out of the mire on the side of the swamp that was nearest to his own house, and Christian saw him no more.[34]

Now Christian was left to flounder in the Swamp of Despond alone. But still he managed to make it to that side of the swamp that was farthest from his own house and next to the wicket-gate, although he could not get out because of the burden upon his back. [35]

Then I saw in my dream that a man, whose name was Help, came to him and asked him, "What are you doing there?"

---

[32] There was such a swamp (Bunyan's original word was "slough") near his birthplace in Bedford, England. Rain would turn the area into mire.

[33] Pliable got Christian so interested in things to come that he became careless about things present. Christian's burden made him sink, picturing the despair that can come with conviction of sin, something Bunyan experienced in great measure.

[34] Pliable had no true conviction to become a Christian. He endured for a while, then became offended when trouble came (Matt. 13:20–21). People who want salvation to avoid trials will always be disappointed.

[35] People who do not feel a burden for their sins find it easy to escape conviction. Christian's burden made it difficult for him to get out.

CHRISTIAN: Sir, I was told to go this way by a man called Evangelist, who directed me also to yonder gate, that I might escape the wrath to come; and as I was going toward it, I fell in here.

HELP: But why did you not look for the steps?[36]

CHRISTIAN: I was so afraid that I wasn't paying attention and I fell in.

Then said Help, "Give me your hand." So Christian gave him his hand, and Help drew him out and set him upon firm ground and told him to go on his way.

---

[36] The promises of God found in the Word. Later when Christian finds himself in the dungeon of Doubting Castle, it is the "key of promise" that opens the door and sets him free.

When the sinner begins to seek salvation, well-meaning friends often try to stop him. Such are Obstinate and Pliable. They are two opposite characters. Obstinate has great strength of will, but he lacks the insight and values to put it to work in the right way. Pliable seems to have some insight, but he lacks the willpower to act and continue to the end. Bunyan himself was a very stubborn man prior to his conversion, so perhaps he saw himself in this scene.

Pliable is interested only in enjoyment; he wants to hear nothing about terror. He is in a hurry to get to heaven, but he has no burden for sin to hold him back. He illustrates the "shallow soil" in Christ's parable of the sower (Matt. 13:1–9). He receives the Word with joy but has no roots. He has never felt conviction and does not want to face the fact that salvation involves more than the pleasures of heaven. When he comes to the Swamp of Despond, he decides to turn back.

Before he leaves, Pliable asks, "What may we expect?" The rest of the book answers that question, but Pliable never experiences the journey's end. Like many people, he makes a brave beginning outwardly, but he lacks inward conviction. He cannot keep going.

Pliable gets Christian so interested in things to come that he becomes careless about things present. Christian's burden makes him sink, and here Bunyan is picturing the despair that can come with conviction of sin, something he himself experienced.

Christian's name means "belonging to Christ." Before he started on his pilgrimage to the Holy City, his name was Graceless. Grace is God's favor to undeserving sinners, and Christian had been without that grace.

Christian is assisted by Help, who is neither an ordained minister nor an evangelist. He represents any believer who assists others in getting out of despair. Note, however, that Help does not do all the work for Christian. Christian has to give him his hand. To sit and do nothing is the best way to stay in despair.

In this section, we reach a point where for a few paragraphs Bunyan uses the pronoun "I" to identify with Christian, thus ceasing to be a spectator.

At this point he meets up with Mr. Worldly Wiseman, a character who was not in the original edition of The Pilgrim's Progress; *but we are glad Bunyan later added him, for he pictures the man of this world who really has no understanding of spiritual things. He wants to deal with the symptoms, not the causes. His counsel is, "Get rid of your burden!" not, "Deal with the sins that cause your burden." He condemns Evangelist for his counsel and even condemns the Bible because it helped to give Christian his burden. His only solution to Christian's problem is morality: obey the Law of God and you will lose your burden. He does not understand the deeper meaning of sin, that mere outward obedience is no guarantee of an inward change.*

hen I stepped to Help, who had pulled Christian out, and said, "Sir, since this is the way from the City of Destruction to yonder gate, why is it that this piece of ground is not repaired so that poor travelers might go this way with more security?"

And Help said to me, "This miry swamp cannot be repaired. It is where the scum and filth of the conviction of sin collects, and therefore it is called the Swamp of Despond; for as the sinner becomes aware of his lost condition, many fears and doubts and discouraging apprehensions arise in his soul; and all of them together settle in the depths of this place. And this is the reason for the bad condition of this ground.

"It is not the desire of the King that this place should remain in such a state. For over sixteen hundred years his laborers have, at the direction of his Majesty's surveyors, been working on this patch of ground. Yes, and to my knowledge," said Help, "at least twenty thousand cartloads—yes, millions of wholesome instructions—have been swallowed up here. They that are knowledgeable say they are the best materials to make good ground of the place. But it is still the Swamp of Despond, and will be when they have done what they can.[1]

"True, at the direction of the Lawgiver, certain good and substantial steps have been placed through the very midst of this swamp. But during the times when this place spews out its filth, these steps can hardly be seen; or if they are, men beome confused and overstep them and become mired down, even though the steps are there. But once they get to the gate, the ground is good."[2]

Now I saw in my dream that by this time Pliable had returned to his home, where his neighbors came to visit him; and some of them called him a wise man for coming back,

---

[1] God has provided a right way, and no man need fall into the Swamp of Despond. Stick to God's highway! (Isa. 35:3–4).

[2] These steps are God's promises of forgiveness and acceptance when we trust Christ (1 Sam. 12:23).

and some called him a fool for hazarding himself with Christian. Others mocked him for his cowardliness, saying, "Surely, since you began the venture, you should not have turned back because of a few difficulties. I would not have done so." So Pliable sat cringing among them. But eventually, when he gained more confidence, they all changed their tune and began to deride poor Christian behind his back. And thus we leave Pliable.

Now as Christian was walking by himself, he spied someone afar off coming across the field toward him, and before long their paths crossed. This gentleman's name was Mr. Worldly Wiseman, and he lived in the town of Carnal Policy, a large town located near where Christian had come from.[3]

Thus, this man knew about Christian, for there had been much talk about his setting forth from the City of Destruction, not only in that place where he had lived, but in nearby towns. Master Worldly Wiseman, therefore, having some ideas about him after observing his difficult path and his sighs and groans, began to converse with him.[4]

WORLDLY WISEMAN: Hello, my good man, where are you going in this burdened manner?

CHRISTIAN: A burdened manner indeed, and as great as any poor creature ever had! And since you ask me where I'm going, I tell you, sir, I am going to yonder wicket-gate; for there, so I have been told, I shall be able to get rid of my heavy burden.

WORLDLY WISEMAN: Have you a wife and children?[5]

CHRISTIAN: Yes, but this burden loads me down so that I cannot enjoy them as I once did; it is as if I had none.[6]

---

[3] Read 1 Cor. 1:18–31 for Paul's estimate of the wisdom of this world, for this is where Bunyan got his idea.

[4] Worldly wise persons find it easy to jump to conclusions.

[5] To the man of this world, leaving a family behind in order to find salvation is a foolish thing. In the second part of *The Pilgrim's Progress,* published in 1684, Bunyan tells how Christian's wife, Christiana, and his children made their journey to the Heavenly City.

[6] 1 Cor. 7:29

WORLDLY WISEMAN: Will you listen to me if I give you some advice?

CHRISTIAN: If it is good, I will, for I stand in need of good counsel.

WORLDLY WISEMAN: I would advise you, then, to get rid of your burden quickly, for until you do, you will never be settled in your mind, nor will you be able to enjoy the benefits of the blessing which God has bestowed upon you.

CHRISTIAN: That is what I am seeking: to get rid of this heavy burden. But I cannot get it off myself, nor is there any man in our country who can take it off my shoulders. Therefore I am going this way, as I told you, to get rid of my burden.

WORLDLY WISEMAN: Who told you to go this way to get rid of your burden?

CHRISTIAN: A man who appeared to me to be a very great and honorable person. His name was Evangelist.

WORLDLY WISEMAN: I condemn him for his advice, for there is no more dangerous and troublesome way in the world than that to which he has directed you, and that you will find if you heed his counsel.[7] You have met with something already, I perceive, for I see the dirt of the Swamp of Despond upon you. But that swamp is just the beginning of the trouble that awaits those who go that way. Hear me! I am older than you. If you continue on, you are likely to meet with weariness, pain, hunger, perils, nakedness, sword, lions, dragons, darkness, and, in a word, death![8] These things have been confirmed by many testimonies. So why should you carelessly throw your life away on the word of a stranger?

CHRISTIAN: Why, sir, this burden upon my back is more terrible to me than all those things you have mentioned. No, I don't care what I encounter on the way if I can be delivered from my burden.

---

[7] The man of the world has no understanding of the Gospel and no appreciation for those who tell it to others.
[8] 2 Cor. 11:26–27.

WORLDLY WISEMAN: How did you get this burden in the first place?

CHRISTIAN: By reading this book in my hand.

WORLDLY WISEMAN: I thought so! It has happened to you as it has to other weak men, who, meddling with things too high for them, do suddenly fall into confusion as you have.[9] Such confusion not only unnerves men, as it has done with you, but sends them on desperate paths seeking they know not what.

CHRISTIAN: I know what I seek: it is ease for my heavy burden.

WORLDLY WISEMAN: But why do you search for ease along this dangerous path? Especially since, if you have patience to hear me out, I can direct you to what you desire without the dangers that you will run into in this way. Yes, the solution is at hand, and it does not involve those dangers. Instead, you will meet with much safety, friendship, and content.

CHRISTIAN: Pray, sir, tell me this secret.

WORLDLY WISEMAN: All right. In that village over there called Morality lives a gentleman named Legality, a very judicious and honorable man who has the skill to help men rid themselves of such burdens as yours.[10] To my knowledge he has done a great deal of good in this way and has the skill to cure those who are somewhat crazed with their burdens. You can go to him for help. His house is not quite a mile from this

---

[9] Worldly Wiseman suggests that the desire to read and understand the Bible is an evidence of pride. This, of course, was the attitude Bunyan's judges had toward him when he was tried for preaching illegally. They could not understand how an untrained tinker could understand the Bible and preach it to others. See Ps. 131:1.

[10] In his early life, Bunyan went through a period of intense legalism, during which he thought he could be saved by morality. He wrote in *Grace Abounding*: "Wherefore I fell to some outward reformation, both in my words and life, and did set the commandments before me for my way to heaven; which commandments I did also strive to keep .... Thus I continued about a year; all which time our neighbors did take me to be a very godly man, a new and religious man, and did marvel much to see such a great and famous alteration in my life and manners."

place, and if he should not be at home himself, his handsome young son, Civility, can help you as well as the old gentleman himself.

There you can be eased of your burden. And if you do not want to go back to your former habitation, as indeed I would not wish you to, you may send for your wife and children to join you in this village, where there are houses available at reasonable rates. Everything you need for a happy life will be provided there, and you will live among honest neighbors. [11]

Now Christian was somewhat at a standstill; but soon he concluded that if what this gentleman said was true, then the wisest course was to take his advice.

CHRISTIAN: Sir, which way do I take to this honest man's house?

WORLDLY WISEMAN: Do you see that high hill over there?[12]

CHRISTIAN: Yes, I see it clearly.

WORLDLY WISEMAN: Go past that hill, and the first house you come to is his.

So Christian turned aside to go to Mr. Legality's house for help. But when he was close to the hill, it seemed so high and hung so far over the path that he was afraid to venture further, lest the hill should fall on his head. Therefore he stood still, not knowing what to do. Also his burden now seemed heavier to him than it had before, and there were flashes of fire coming out of the hill that made Christian afraid he should be burned.[13] He began sweating and quaking with fear.

---

[11] There is no price to pay for worldly morality. But outward conformity to laws does not change the heart.

[12] This is Mount Sinai, where God gave the Law to Moses (Exod. 19:16–25; Heb. 12:21). This is the first of several hills that Christian will encounter: the Hill Difficulty, the Hill Error, Mount Caution, the little hill Lucre, the high hill Clear, and the Holy City set on a high hill.

[13] Christian's burden became heavier because the Law does not remove sin; it only makes our guilt worse. The Puritans made much of the work of the Law to bring sinners to conviction and repentance.

When Christians unto carnal men give ear
Out of their way they go, and pay for it dear;
For Master Worldly Wiseman can but show
A saint the way to bondage and to woe.[14]

Now Christian began to be sorry that he had taken Mr. Worldly Wiseman's counsel. And with that he saw Evangelist coming to meet him and began to blush with shame. Evangelist drew nearer and nearer; and when he came up to Christian, he looked at him with a severe and fearsome expression. Then he began to reason with Christian.

EVANGELIST: What are you doing here, Christian?

Christian didn't know what to say, so he stood speechless before him.[15]

EVANGELIST: Aren't you the man I found crying outside the walls of the City of Destruction?

CHRISTIAN: Yes, dear sir, I am the man.

EVANGELIST: Didn't I tell you the way to the little wicket-gate?

CHRISTIAN: Yes, dear sir.

EVANGELIST: How is it, then, that you have so quickly turned aside? For you are now going the wrong way.[16]

CHRISTIAN: As soon as I got out of the Swamp of Despond I met a gentleman who persuaded me that I might find a man who could take off my burden in the village before me.

EVANGELIST: Who was he?

---

[14] Carnal means "fleshly." It is a New Testament word that describes the old nature of the sinner. Mr. Worldly Wiseman was a carnal man; he thought like a mere man, not like a Christian.

[15] See 1 Kings 19:9, where Elijah is asked the same question. Christian is out of God's will and is caught, speechless. What could he say? See Matt. 22:12 and Rom. 3:19.

[16] See Gal. 1:6. The Galatians letter was written by Paul to refute the idea that sinners can be saved by keeping the Law of Moses. Evangelist is also referring to Exod. 32:8, where God spoke to Moses when Israel, because of Moses' absence, made an idol and worshiped it. The Law did not make Israel obedient!

CHRISTIAN: He looked like a gentleman, and talked much to me, and got me at last to yield, so I came here. But when I saw this hill and how it hangs over the path, I suddenly stopped, lest it should fall on my head.

EVANGELIST: What did that gentleman say to you?

CHRISTIAN: Why, he asked me where I was going, and I told him.

EVANGELIST: And what did he say then?

CHRISTIAN: He asked me if I had a family, and I told him I did. But I told him I was so loaded down with the burden on my back that I cannot take pleasure in them as I did formerly.

EVANGELIST: And what did he say then?

CHRISTIAN: He told me to get rid of my burden quickly,[17] and I said I wanted to and was going to yonder gate to receive further direction on how I may get to the place of deliverance. He said that he would show me a better and shorter and less difficult way than that which you told me about, sir. He said he would direct me to a gentleman who has skill to take off these burdens; so I believed him.[18] But when I came to this place and saw things as they are, I stopped because I was afraid it was dangerous. Now I don't know what to do.

Then Evangelist said, "Stand still for a bit so I may show you the words of God."[19]

So Christian stood, trembling.

Then said Evangelist, "See that ye refuse not him that speaketh. For if they escaped not who refused him that spake on earth, much more shall not we escape, if we turn away from him that speaketh from heaven."[20] Moreover, he said, "Now the just shall live by faith: but if any man draw back, my

---

[17]Salvation is not quick and easy, as Mr. Worldly Wiseman suggested. The Puritans spoke of "heart work"— the deep working of God in the heart to bring the sinner to the light. Salvation is instantaneous, but preparation takes time.

[18]Christian had faith, but not in Christ. Faith is only as good as the object. Faith in worldly wise religion cannot save the sinner.

[19]1 Sam. 9:27.

[20] Heb. 12:25.

soul shall have no pleasure in him."[21] Then he concluded with this application: "Thou art the man who is running into this misery. You have begun to reject the counsel of the Most High and to draw back from the way of peace, almost to the point of perdition."[22]

Then Christian fell down at Evangelist's feet, crying, "Woe is me, for I am undone!"[23]

At the sight of this, Evangelist caught him by the right hand, saying, "All manner of sin and blasphemies shall be forgiven men. Be not faithless, but believing."[24]

Then Christian recovered somewhat and stood up, trembling as he had before, and Evangelist continued speaking.

EVANGELIST: Heed seriously the things that I shall tell you, for I will now show you who it was that deluded you and who it was to whom he was sending you. The man who met you is one Worldly Wiseman, and he is rightly named; partly because he enjoys only the doctrine of this world, which is why he always goes to the town of Morality to church, and partly because he loves that doctrine best, for it saves him from the cross. And because he is of this carnal nature he seeks to pervert my ways, though they are right. Now there are three things in this man's counsel that you must utterly abhor.[25]

---

[21]Bunyan is quoting from Hebrews 10:38. This statement is found originally in Hab. 2:4 and is also quoted in Rom. 1:17 and Gal. 3:11. It is an important concept in the Bible, that a person is justified (declared righteous by God) by faith in Christ and not by obeying laws. This was a cardinal doctrine in Puritan theology.

[22] This is a reference to 2 Sam. 12:7, where Nathan the prophet, speaking for God, faced King David with his sins. In listening to the Worldly Wiseman, Christian rejected God's counsel given him by faithful Evangelist (Luke 7:30; Ps. 1:1). "Perdition" (judgment) refers to Heb. 10:38–39.

[23] Isaiah's response to the vision of God (Isa. 6:1–8).

[24] Matt. 12:31; John 20:27

[25] Heb. 2:1; 1 John 4:5; Gal. 6:12; 1:7. The false teachers that Paul describes taught that a person becomes a Christian by faith in Christ *plus* keeping the

First, he turned you out of the way; second, he tried to make the cross odious to you; and third, he set your feet on a path that leads to death.[26]

First, you must abhor his turning you out of the way—yes, and your own consenting to do so — because to do this is to reject the counsel of God for the counsel of a Worldly Wiseman. The Lord says, "Strive to enter in at the strait gate," the gate to which I sent you, for "strait is the gate that leadeth unto life, and few there be that find it."[27] This wicked man has turned you from your pilgrimage to the little wicket-gate, and in doing so has brought you almost to destruction. Hate, therefore, his turning you out of the way, and abhor yourself for listening to him.

Second, you must abhor his attempts to make the cross repugnant to you, for you are to desire the cross more than "the treasure of Egypt." Besides, the King of Glory has told you that he who "will save his life shall lose it" and he who comes after him "and hates not his father, and mother, and wife, and children, and brethren, and sisters, yea, and his own life also, he cannot be my disciple."[28] Therefore, you must abhor any doctrine that would persuade you that this truth, without which you cannot have eternal life, shall be your death.

Third, you must abhor his getting you to take the path that leads to death. And in this regard you must consider to

---

Law of Moses. Circumcision was the "sign of the covenant," proof that a person was seeking to obey the Law. These teachers held to the Law so that they could avoid persecution from the Jews. But there is no salvation apart from the cross. Morality avoids the cross and clings to the Law. Mixing the Law with the Gospel perverts the truth.

[26]Another name for the Law (2 Cor. 3:1–9). The Law can never give life because it can only reveal sin, not remove it.

[27]Luke 13:24; Matt. 7:13–14

[28]Moses gave up the treasures of Egypt to "suffer affliction with the people of God" (Heb. 11:25–26). People who depend on religious morality avoid the doctrine of the cross because it reveals the sinfulness of sin and the necessity for a Savior. See also Ps. 24:7–10; Matt. 10:37–39.

whom he sent you and how unable that person was to deliver you from your burden.

You were sent to Legality, the son of the bond-woman who now is in bondage with her children.[29] This is a mystery,[30] this Mount Sinai, which you feared would fall on your head. Now if she and her children are themselves in bondage, how can you expect them to free you? Legality, therefore, is not able to set you free from your burden. No man has ever yet been relieved of his burden by Legality, nor ever is likely to be. You cannot be justified by works of the law; for the law cannot release any man from his burden.[31] Therefore, Mr. Worldly Wiseman is an alien, and Mr. Legality is a cheat; and his son Civility is nothing but a hypocrite and cannot help you. Believe me, what you have heard from these stupid men is nothing but a design to deceive you by turning you from the way I had sent you.[32]

---

[29] Worldly Wiseman promised life, but the Law only brings death. The Law can put a man in bondage, but it cannot deliver him (Gal. 2:21). See also Gal. 4:21–31; Gen. 18, 21:1–21. Abraham ran ahead of God's will and married Hagar, his wife's maid, hoping to beget the son God had promised him. Ishmael was born, and he brought nothing but trouble. Hagar represents the Law; she was a bond-woman. Ishmael represents the flesh, the old nature, because he was born out of Abraham's disobedience. Sarah represents God's grace, and Isaac pictures the true believer, born out of promise by the power of God. Ishmael was a slave because his mother was a bond-woman. Isaac was free because his mother was free. There is no salvation through the Law: Hagar and Ishmael were cast out!

[30] A symbol, a "sacred secret" hidden in the Old Testament and explained in the New Testament.

[31] Justification is the act of God whereby He graciously declares righteous all who trust Jesus Christ. It is a legal term and has to do with our standing before God. We cannot justify ourselves; only God can declare us righteous, and He does this on the basis of the work of Christ on the cross. See Gal. 2:16; 3:11. The fact that Martin Luther's *Commentary on Galatians* greatly influenced Bunyan's life helps to explain his many references to this New Testament letter.

[32] Satan is the great deceiver (2 Cor. 11:1–3).

After this, Evangelist called aloud to the heavens for confirmation of what he had said, and with that there came words and fire out of the mountain under which poor Christian stood that made his hair stand up: "As many as are of the works of the law are under the curse; for it is written, Cursed is every one that continueth not in all things which are written in the book of the law to do them."[33]

Now Christian expected nothing but death and began to cry out mournfully, even cursing the moment he had met up with Mr. Worldly Wiseman and calling himself a thousand fools for listening to his counsel. He also was greatly ashamed to think that this gentleman's arguments, flowing only from the flesh, had prevailed with him, causing him to forsake the right way. This done, he applied himself again to Evangelist's words.

CHRISTIAN: Sir, what do you think? Is there hope? May I now go back and go up to the wicket-gate? I am sorry I have heeded this man's counsel, but may my sin be forgiven?

EVANGELIST: Your sin is very great, for by it you have committed two evils: you have forsaken the way that is good and you have taken forbidden paths.[34] Yet the man at the gate will receive you, for he has goodwill for men.[35]

Then Christian prepared to go back, and Evangelist, after he had kissed him, smiled and wished him a successful journey. So Christian hurried on, speaking to no one on the way.[36] He traveled quickly, like one who knows he is on dangerous ground, until he once again reached the place where he had left to follow Mr. Worldly Wiseman's counsel. Thus, in time, Christian got up to the gate, over which was written, "Knock, and it shall be opened unto you."[37]

---

[33]Gal. 3:10

[34]Jer. 2:13

[35]Goodwill turns out to be the name of the man at the gate (Luke 2:14).

[36]See Christ's commands to His disciples in Luke 10:4.

[37]Matt. 7:7–8

He that will enter in must first without
Stand knocking at the gate, nor need he doubt
That is a knocker but to enter in,
For God can love him and forgive his sin.

He knocked, therefore, several times, saying:

May I now enter here? Will he within
Open to sorry me, though I have been
An undeserving rebel? Then shall I
Not fail to sing his lasting praise on high.

At last an authoritative person named Goodwill came to the gate and asked who was there, and where he had come from, and what he wanted.[38]

CHRISTIAN: I am a poor burdened sinner. I come from the City of Destruction, but am going to Mount Zion[39] so I may be delivered from the wrath to come. Since I have been informed that this gate is the way to that place, I want to know if you are willing to let me in.[40]

GOODWILL: I am willing with all my heart.

And with that he opened the gate.

---

[38]Christian will answer these questions several times during his pilgrimage. The Puritans carefully questioned new converts and candidates for church membership to make certain they were truly converted (1 Pet. 3:15).

[39]Mount Zion is another name for the heavenly city, applied to the earthly city of Jerusalem (Heb. 12:22ff.; Ps. 2:6; 48:2; 1 Chron. 11:4–9). See also Matt. 3:7; 1 Thess. 1:10.

[40] "Am I one of God's elect? Is He willing to save me?" These questions plagued the Puritans. See 1 Tim. 2:3–4; 2 Pet. 3:9. Bunyan's marginal note here is: "The gate will be opened to broken-hearted sinners," referring to Ps. 51:17.

There is no salvation that is "quick and easy" as Mr. Worldly Wiseman suggests. The Puritans spoke of "heart work"— that is, the deep working of God in the heart to bring the sinner to the light. This takes time.

At this point, Christian has faith, but not in Christ. Faith is only as good as the object. Faith in worldly wise religion cannot save the sinner. In listening to the counsel of Mr. Worldly Wiseman, Christian rejects God's counsel, as given to him by the faithful Evangelist.

Mr. Worldly Wiseman promises life through Morality and Legality, but the Law only brings death. The Law can put a man in bondage, but it cannot deliver him. When Christian at last recognizes this, his feet are once more set on the path and he finally reaches the wicket-gate of salvation.

After he knocks at the gate, Goodwill asks him, "Who is there? Where have you come from? What do you want?" Christian will answer these questions several times during his pilgrimage. In this way the Puritans carefully questioned new converts and candidates for church membership to make certain they were truly converted.

Christian also asks, "Are you willing to let me in?" Questions like this plagued the Puritans: "Am I one of God's elect? Is He willing to save me?" Bunyan's marginal note here says, "The gate will be opened to broken-hearted sinners," referring to Psalm 51:17.

s Christian was stepping through the gate, Goodwill gave him a pull. Then Christian said, "Why did you do that?"

"A little distance from this gate," said Goodwill, "there is a strong castle, of which Beelzebub is the captain; he and his cohorts shoot arrows at those who come up to this gate, hoping they may die before they can enter in."[1]

Then said Christian, "I rejoice and tremble."[2] And when he was in, Goodwill asked who had directed him there.

CHRISTIAN: Evangelist told me to come here and knock. He said that you, sir, would tell me what I must do.

GOODWILL: An open door is before you, and no man can shut it.[3]

CHRISTIAN: Now I begin to reap the benefits of my hazards.

GOODWILL: But how is it that you came alone?

CHRISTIAN: Because none of my neighbors saw their danger, as I saw mine.

GOODWILL: Did any of them know you were coming?

CHRISTIAN: Yes. First my wife and children saw me and called after me to return; also some of my neighbors did the same. But I put my fingers in my ears and kept going.

---

[1]To get him in quickly before Beelzebub could attack and hinder him, Goodwill did not pull Christian in against his will; nor did Christian force his way in. Here Bunyan reconciles God's divine election and man's responsibility to believe (John 6:37). Beelzebub is one of several names for Satan in the Bible (Matt. 10:25; 12:24–27), and speaks of his filthiness of character and works. It may mean "lord of the flies" (2 Kings 1:2) or "lord of the house" (Matt. 10:25). It could also mean "the dung god." See Eph. 6:16, on shooting arrows.

[2]See Ps. 2:11. Later, Christian will experience "hope and fear." The Puritans sought to maintain proper balance in their spiritual emotions. If they rejoiced, they also realized the greatness and holiness of God and therefore trembled. Their hope was balanced by godly fear. There is a false joy that is shallow and a false hope that lacks reality.

[3]Rev. 3:8

GOODWILL: But did none of them follow you and try to persuade you to go back?

CHRISTIAN: Yes, both Obstinate and Pliable. When they saw that they could not prevail, Obstinate went back, reviling me, but Pliable came with me a little way.

GOODWILL: But why did he not come through the gate?

CHRISTIAN: We traveled together until we fell into the Swamp of Despond. Then my neighbor Pliable became discouraged and would not venture further. Wherefore, getting out again on that side nearest to his own house, he told me I should go without him. So he went his way, and I came mine—he after Obstinate, and I to this gate.

GOODWILL: Alas, poor man, is the celestial glory of such little value to him that he figures it is not worth risking a few difficulties to obtain it?

CHRISTIAN: Indeed. I have told the truth about Pliable, and if I should tell the truth about myself, I am no better than he. For while it is true that he went back to his own house, I also turned aside to go in the way of death, being persuaded to do so by the carnal arguments of one Mr. Worldly Wiseman.

GOODWILL: Oh, did he find you? And he would have had you seek the easy way with Mr. Legality. Both of them are deceitful. But did you take his advice?

CHRISTIAN: Yes, as far as I dared. I went to find Mr. Legality, until I thought the mountain that stands by his house would fall on my head; wherefore, I was forced to stop.

GOODWILL: That mountain has been the death of many and will be the death of many more; 'tis well you escaped being dashed in pieces by it.

CHRISTIAN: Why, truly, I do not know what would have become of me there, had not Evangelist met me again in the midst of my gloomy state of mind. It was God's mercy that he came to me again, for otherwise I would never have gotten here.[4] But now I am here—I who deserve death by that moun-

---

[4]God in His mercy does not give us what we deserve; in His grace He gives us what we do not deserve—salvation.

tain rather than to stand thus talking with my Lord; oh, what grace this is to me, that I am still admitted entrance here!

GOODWILL: We make no objections against any, notwithstanding all that they have done before they came here. They "in no wise are cast out."[5] Therefore, good Christian, come a little way with me, and I will teach you about the way you must go. Look before you! Do you see that narrow way?[6] That is the way you must go. It was formed by the patriarchs, prophets, Christ, and his apostles, and it is as straight as a rule can make it. That is the way you must go.

CHRISTIAN: But are there no turnings or windings by which a stranger may lose his way?

GOODWILL: Yes, there are many ways that border upon this, and they are crooked and wide.[7] But you can always distinguish the right way, for it is always straight and narrow.

Then I saw in my dream that Christian asked him if he could not help him take off the burden that was upon his back; for as yet he had not got rid of it, nor could he by any means get it off without help.

GOODWILL: As to your burden, be content to bear it until you come to the place of deliverance, for there it will fall from your back by itself.

Then Christian began to prepare himself for his journey, and Goodwill told him that when he had traveled some distance from the gate, he would come to the house of the Interpreter, at whose door he should knock and who would show him excellent things.[8] Then Christian said good-bye to his friend, and he bid him Godspeed.

Christian went on till he came to the house of the Interpreter, where he knocked over and over; at last someone came to the door and asked who was there.

---

[5] John 6:37
[6] Matt. 7:13–14
[7] Christian will discover some of these detours!
[8] This is the Holy Spirit of God, who interprets the things of God to seekers (John 16:13).

CHRISTIAN: Sir, I am a traveler, who was told by an acquaintance of the good owner of this house that it would be to my benefit to call here; I would therefore speak with the master of the house.

So he called for the master of the house, who after a little time came to Christian and asked him what he wanted.

CHRISTIAN: Sir, I am a man who has come from the City of Destruction, and am going to Mount Zion; and I was told by the man that stands at the gate, at the head of this way, that if I called here, you would show me excellent things that would be a help to me in my journey.

INTERPRETER: Come in. I will show you that which will be profitable to you.

So he commanded his man to light the candle and bid Christian follow him. [9] He led him into a private room and bid his man open a door. When he had done so, Christian saw the picture of a very grave person hanging upon the wall.[10] He had eyes lifted up to heaven, the best of books in his hand, the law of truth written upon his lips, and the world behind his back. He stood as if he pleaded with men, and a crown of gold hung over his head.

CHRISTIAN: What does this mean?

INTERPRETER: The man who is pictured there is one of a thousand; he can beget children, travail in birth with children, and nurse them himself when they are born.[11] And you see him with his eyes lifted up to heaven, the best of books in his hand, and the law of truth upon his lips to show you that his work is to know and unfold dark things to sinners; even as

---

[9]"Thy word is a lamp unto my feet, and a light unto my path" (Ps. 119:105). The Holy Spirit uses the Bible to show us God's truth.

[10] The picture is that of the ideal pastor, and Bunyan certainly had his own pastor, John Gifford, in mind. The Puritans held their pastors in great respect and condemned the careless pastors. See also Mal. 2:4–7 for a description of God's ideal servant.

[11]Puritan pastors diligently cared for their "spiritual children" (1 Cor. 4:15; Gal. 4:19; 1 Thess. 2:7).

you also see him standing as if he pleaded with men; and you see the world cast behind him and a crown over his head to show you that because he despises the things that are present, for the love he has for his Master's service, he is sure to have glory for his reward in the next world.

Now, I have showed you this picture first because this man pictured here is the only man whom the Lord of the place where you are going has authorized to be your guide in all the difficult places you may encounter on the way; wherefore, heed what I have showed you and bear in mind what you have seen, lest on your journey you meet with some who pretend to lead you right, but whose way only leads to death.[12]

Then he took Christian by the hand and led him into a very large parlor that was full of dust because it was never swept. After a little while the Interpreter called for a man to sweep, and when he began to do so, the dust flew about so abundantly that Christian almost choked on it. Then said the Interpreter to a young woman who stood nearby: "Bring water here and sprinkle the room"; and when she had done this, it was pleasantly swept and cleansed.

CHRISTIAN: What does this mean?

INTERPRETER: This parlor is the heart of a man who was never sanctified by the sweet grace of the Gospel; the dust is his original sin and inward corruptions that have defiled the whole man.[13] He that began to sweep at first is the Law; but

---

[12] The officials of the established church told Bunyan he was not authorized to preach, and this is why they put him in jail. It was necessary for a man to have a license from the government before he could preach and pastor a church. The Puritans were careful to ordain men called of God, and they warned their people about false prophets (Matt. 7:15, also see verses 13–20; Prov. 14:12).

[13] *Sanctified* literally means "set apart for God's exclusive use." To the Puritans it meant the process of becoming a holy person. When a sinner trusts Christ, he is *justified* (declared righteous by God), and he should be *sanctified* (reveal that righteousness in daily living). The Law can never sweep the parlor clean; it can only "raise the dust" and reveal how sinful the human heart is. The Gospel is like water that keeps the dust down. We are

she that brought water and sprinkled it is the Gospel. Now you saw that as soon as the first began to sweep, the dust flew about the room so that it could not be cleaned, and you were almost choked with it; this is to show you that the Law, instead of cleansing the heart (by its working) from sin, does revive, strengthen, and increase sin in the soul, even as it does discover and forbid it, for the Law does not give power to subdue sin.[14]

Again, you saw the young woman sprinkle the room with water, upon which it was cleansed with pleasure; this is to show you that when the sweet and precious influence of the Gospel comes into the heart, then sin is vanquished and subdued and the soul made clean and consequently fit for the King of Glory to inhabit.

Moreover, I saw in my dream that the Interpreter took Christian by the hand and led him into a little room where sat two little children, each one in his chair. The name of the eldest was Passion, and the name of the other Patience.[15] Passion seemed to be very discontented, but Patience was very quiet. Then Christian asked, "Why is Passion discontented?" The Interpreter answered, "Their Governor would have him wait for his best things until the beginning of next year; but

---

born with *original sin* by nature because we are children of Adam. Note that the water does not completely wash away the dust; it merely keeps it under control. Salvation does not remove the old sinful nature; rather, it gives us a new nature within. This new nature enables us to conquer sin and obey God. Perhaps Ezek. 36:25–27 is what Bunyan had in mind. However, do not read baptism into this sprinkling. Bunyan did not believe that baptism was essential to salvation.

[14]God did not give the Law to save people, but to reveal to us that we need to be saved (Rom. 5:20). In Rom. 7:7–11 Paul describes how his trying to keep the Law only increased his desire to sin! Rather than weaken sin, the Law actually gives strength to sin. This explains why Morality and Legality can never save. See also John 14:21–23; 15:3; Acts 15:9; Rom. 16:25–26; 1 Cor. 15:56; Eph. 5:26.

[15] The Christian does not receive everything here and now; he must exercise patience and wait for the promised blessings (James 5:8). The citizens of this world must have everything now.

Passion wants them all now. Patience, however, is willing to wait."

Then I saw that one came to Passion and brought him a bag of treasure and poured it down at his feet, which Passion then took up rejoicingly and laughed Patience to scorn. But I watched, and it was not long before he had spent it all lavishly and had nothing left but rags.

CHRISTIAN: Explain this matter to me more fully.

INTERPRETER: These two lads are figures: Passion represents the men of this world, and Patience the men of that which is to come. As you have seen, Passion will have all now, this year—that is to say, in this world; so are the men of this world, who must have all their good things now. They cannot wait until next year, that is, until the next world, for their portion of good. That proverb, "A bird in the hand is worth two in the bush," is of more authority with them than are all the Divine testimonies about the good of the world to come.[16] But as you saw, he quickly wasted all and had nothing left except rags; so will it be with all such men at the end of this world.

CHRISTIAN: Now I see that Patience is the wiser in many ways. First, because he waits for the best things. And second, because he will have the glory when the other has nothing but rags.

INTERPRETER: And you may add another, and that is that the glory of the next world will never wear out, whereas the good things of this world are suddenly gone. Therefore, Passion did not have as much reason to laugh at Patience, because he had his good things first, as Patience will have to laugh at Passion, because he had his best things last;[17] for first

---

[16] The ancient Greek author Plutarch wrote, "He is a fool who lets slip a bird in the hand for a bird in the bush." But martyred missionary Jim Elliot wrote, "He is no fool to give what he cannot keep to gain what he cannot lose." Bunyan would have agreed with Elliot.

[17] At the judgment, those who are first in the eyes of men, or in their own eyes, will be last; while those who are last will be first (Matt. 20:16).

must give place to last because last will have his time to come; but last gives place to nothing, for there is not another to succeed. He, therefore, who has his portion first must have a time to spend it; but he that has his portion last must have it lastingly; therefore it is said of Dives, "Thou in thy lifetime receivedst thy good things, and likewise Lazarus evil things: but now he is comforted, and thou art tormented."[18]

CHRISTIAN: Then I perceive that it is not best to covet things that are now, but to wait for things to come.

INTERPRETER: You speak the truth. "For the things that are seen are temporal; but the things that are not seen are eternal."[19] Since things present are such near neighbors to our fleshly appetite, and since things to come are such strangers to our carnal sense, therefore the first of these suddenly fall into amity, and a distance continues between the second.

Then I saw in my dream that the Interpreter took Christian by the hand and led him into a place where there was a fire burning against a wall, and someone standing by it, continually casting water upon it to quench it; yet the fire burned higher and hotter.

CHRISTIAN: What does this mean?

INTERPRETER: This fire is the work of grace in the heart, and he who casts water upon it, trying to extinguish it, is the Devil.[20] But let me show you why the fire continues to burn higher and hotter.

---

[18]See Luke 16:19 –31. "Dives" is the traditional name for the rich man, although he is not named in the account Jesus gave.

[19]See 2 Cor. 4:18.

[20]See Luke 24:32; also, 2 Tim. 1:6. Bunyan writes in *Grace Abounding:* "Then hath the tempter come upon me with such discouragements as these: You are very hot for mercy, but I will cool you; this frame shall not last always; many have been as hot as you but I have quenched their zeal. Though you be burning hot at present, yet I can pull you from this fire; I shall have you cold before it be long."

So he took Christian around to the backside of the wall, where he saw a man with a vessel of oil in his hand, which he also continually cast, secretly, into the fire.[21]

CHRISTIAN: What does this mean?

INTERPRETER: This is Christ, who continually, with the oil of his grace, maintains the work already begun in the heart; by the means of which, notwithstanding what the Devil can do, the souls of his people prove gracious still.[22] And you saw the man standing behind the wall to maintain the fire, teaching you that it is hard for the tempted to see how his work of grace is maintained in the soul.

I saw also that the Interpreter again took Christian by the hand and led him into a pleasant place, where there was a stately palace, beautiful to behold, and Christian was delighted at the sight.[23] He saw also, upon the top thereof, certain persons walking, clothed all in gold.

Then Christian said, "May we go in there?"

Then the Interpreter led him up toward the door of the palace. At the door stood a great company of men who desired to go in, but dared not; while at a little distance from the door, at a table, with a book and his pen before him, sat a man taking down the name of any who should enter there.[24] He saw also that in the doorway stood many men in armor to protect it, ready to do what hurt and mischief they could to the men that would enter. Now Christian was amazed.

At last, when every man stayed back for fear of the armed men, Christian saw a strong and determined-looking man come up to the man that sat there to write, saying, "Set

---

[21] This image comes from Zech. 4:11–14. The oil symbolizes the grace of God given through the Holy Spirit (Phil. 1:6).

[22] See 2 Cor. 12:9. Satan attacked Paul, but God's grace sustained him.

[23] This seems to symbolize the rewards God has for those who "fight the good fight of faith" (1 Tim. 6:12). Although salvation is by grace, the rewards are given only to the faithful; and faithfulness involves fighting a battle.

[24] The image comes from Ezek. 9, except that the recorder here wrote down the names instead of putting a mark on the persons.

down my name, sir." And when he had done this, the man drew his sword and put an helmet upon his head and rushed toward the armed men, who attacked him with deadly force; but the man, not at all discouraged, cut and hacked fiercely.[25] So after he had received and given many wounds to those that attempted to keep him out, he cut his way through them all and pressed forward into the palace, at which there was a pleasant voice heard from those who walked upon the top of the palace, saying:

Come in, come in;
Eternal glory thou shalt win.[26]

So he went in and was clothed with garments like theirs. Then Christian smiled and said, "I think I know the meaning of this. Now, let me go from this place."

"No, stay," said the Interpreter, "till I have showed you a little more, and after that you shall go on your way." So he took him by the hand again and led him into a very dark room, where there sat a man in an iron cage.[27]

Now to look at him, the man seemed very sad; he sat with his eyes looking down to the ground, his hands folded together, and he sighed as if his heart was breaking. Then said Christian, "What does this mean?" At which the Interpreter told him to talk with the man.

Then said Christian to the man, "What are you?" The man answered, "I am what I once was not."

CHRISTIAN: What were you once?

---

[25] See Matt. 11:12; Acts 14:22. The man in armor balances the picture of Patience given previously. In the Christian life, patience is not merely waiting; it is also bravely enduring and keeping going when things are difficult.
[26] The New Testament letters often use military figures of speech to picture the Christian life. Bunyan himself was in the army at one time. Keep in mind that Christian is being shown the difficulties and demands of the pilgrim walk. He will fight many enemies before he reaches the Holy City.
[27] A picture of despair, in contrast to the valiant soldier who pressed through to victory.

MAN: I once professed to be a Christian, both in my own eyes and also in the eyes of others; I once was, as I thought, set for the Celestial City, and had then even joy at the thoughts that I should get there.[28]

CHRISTIAN: But what are you now?

MAN: I am now a man of despair and am shut up in it, as in this iron cage. I cannot get out. Oh, now I cannot!

CHRISTIAN: But how came you to be in this condition?

MAN: I stopped watching and being sober. I allowed my lusts to control me; I sinned against the light of the Word and the goodness of God; I have grieved the Spirit, and he is gone;[29] I tempted the Devil, and he has come to me; I have provoked God to anger, and he has left me; I have so hardened my heart that I cannot repent.

Then said Christian to the Interpreter, "But is there no hope for this man?" "Ask him," said the Interpreter. "No," said Christian, "pray, sir you ask him."

INTERPRETER: Is there no hope, that you must be kept in the iron cage of despair?

MAN: No, none at all.[30]

INTERPRETER: Why, the Son of the Blessed is full of pity.[31]

MAN: I have crucified him afresh, I have despised his person, I have despised his righteousness, I have counted his blood an unholy thing, I have "done despite to the spirit of

---

[28] Bunyan refers to Luke 8:13, from the parable of the sower. Feelings alone are no guarantee of salvation.

[29] See Eph. 4:30. When the sinner trusts Christ, he receives the gift of the Holy Spirit and his body becomes God's temple (1 Cor. 6:19–20). To grieve the Spirit is to sin repeatedly against God.

[30] The man is convinced that he has no hope. In *Grace Abounding* Bunyan states that he "was persuaded that those who were once effectually in Christ ... could never lose him forever." The Interpreter does not say that the man's case is hopeless, nor does Bunyan. It is the man who condemns himself because he is in such despair.

[31] See James 5:11. The Interpreter assures the despairing man that Christ is ready to forgive and restore him.

grace."[32] Therefore I have shut myself out of all the promises, and there now remains nothing for me but fearful threats of certain judgment and fiery indignation, which shall devour me as an adversary.

INTERPRETER: Why did you bring yourself into this condition?

MAN: For the enjoyment of the lusts, pleasures, and profits of this world. But now every one of those things gnaws me like a burning worm.

INTERPRETER: But can't you repent and turn from these things? [33]

MAN: God has denied me repentance. His Word gives me no encouragement to believe otherwise; yea, he himself has shut me up in this iron cage; nor can all the men in the world let me out. O eternity! eternity! how shall I grapple with the misery that I must meet with in eternity!

INTERPRETER: Remember this man's misery and let it be a warning to you.

CHRISTIAN: Well, this is fearful! God help me to watch and be sober and to pray that I may shun the cause of this man's misery! Sir, is it not time for me to go on my way now?

---

[32]Quoted from Heb. 6:4–6; 10:28–29. These passages in Hebrews have long been a battleground for theologians. Do they describe the condition of the believer who has abandoned faith in Christ? Or do they describe a professed Christian who was not truly converted? Bunyan's previous reference to Luke 8:13 suggests that the man in the cage was not saved at all because he did not produce the necessary fruits. In any case, the man in despair is a warning that we should "watch and be sober." See Luke 19:14.

[33] To repent means to change your mind. True repentance results in an act of the will that causes the sinner to turn from sin and trust Christ. The man in the cage believed that the gift of repentance had been denied him and it was too late. Bunyan may be referring here to Heb. 12:16–17, the experience of Esau, who begged his father Isaac to give him a blessing. Isaac had already given the blessing to Esau's brother, Jacob, and Isaac could not change his mind. It is Isaac's change of mind that is referred to, not Esau's. See Gen. 27.

INTERPRETER: Wait until I show you one more thing, and then you shall go on your way.

So he took Christian by the hand again and led him into a chamber, where there was someone rising out of bed; and as he put on his clothing, he shook and trembled.[34]

Then said Christian, "Why does this man tremble like that?" The Interpreter then asked the man to tell Christian the reason. So he began and said, "This night, as I was asleep, I dreamed, and behold the heavens grew very black and it thundered and lightninged so fearfully that it put me into an agony.[35] So I looked up in my dream and saw the clouds rushing and colliding at an unusual rate, upon which I heard a great sound of a trumpet and saw a man sitting upon a cloud, attended by the thousands of heaven; they were all in flaming fire, and the heavens were in a burning flame.[36] Then I heard a voice saying, "Arise, ye dead, and come to judgment." And with that, the rocks were torn apart, the graves opened, and the dead that were in them came forth.[37] Some of them were very glad and looked upward; and some tried to hide themselves under the mountains.[38] Then I saw the man that sat upon the cloud open the book and order the world to draw near. Yet there was, because of a fierce flame issuing out before him, a proper distance between him and them, like the distance between the judge and the prisoners at the bar.[39] I

---

[34]Caused by the fear of judgment. Bunyan wrote, "Even in my childhood the Lord did scare and affright me with fearful dreams, and did terrify me with dreadful visions." During his period of conviction, he greatly feared God's wrath. "My sins also came into my mind, and my conscience did accuse me on every side."

[35] The dream of judgment is a composite of several "judgment passages" in the Bible. See John 5:28–29; 1 Cor. 15:51–58; 2 Thess. 1:7–10; Jude 14–15; and Rev. 20:11–15.

[36] 1 Thess. 4:16; Matt. 26:64

[37] Matt. 27:50–53

[38] Ps. 50:1–3, 22; Isa. 26:20–21; Micah 7:16–17; Rev. 6:12–17

[39] Fire is a symbol of the holy judgment of God. See Dan. 7:10; Mal. 3:2–3.

heard it also proclaimed to them that attended the man who sat on the cloud, 'Gather together the tares, the chaff, and the stubble, and cast them into the burning lake.'[40] And with that the bottomless pit opened, just about where I stood, and out of it came an abundance of smoke and coals of fire, with hideous noises.[41] He also said to the same persons, 'Gather my wheat into the granary.' And with that I saw many caught up and carried away into the clouds, but I was left behind.[42] I tried to hide myself, but I could not, for the man that sat upon the cloud kept his eye upon me; my sins also came into my mind, and my conscience accused me on every side.[43] Upon this, I awoke from my sleep."

CHRISTIAN: But what made you so afraid of this sight?

MAN: Why, I thought that the day of judgment had come and that I was not ready for it; but what frightened me most was that the angels gathered up several and left me behind; also the pit of hell opened up just where I stood. My conscience, too, afflicted me; and I thought the Judge had his eye upon me, looking at me with indignation.

Then said the Interpreter to Christian, "Have you considered all these things?"

CHRISTIAN: Yes, and they give me both hope and fear.[44]

---

[40]See the parable of the wheat and tares in Matt. 13:24–30, 36–43. The wheat pictures the true children of God; the tares picture imitation believers or counterfeits. You cannot distinguish them until the harvest. At the judgment, the tares will be burned. See also Mal. 4:2; Matt. 3:12; Luke 3:17.

[41]See Rev. 9:1–2,11; 11:7; 17:8; 20:1, 3. "Abyss" is the correct word, and it seems to be a pit within the confines of hell.

[42] This is the "rapture" of God's people when Jesus Christ returns. It is described in 1 Thess. 4:13–18. Christians will suddenly be caught up to meet Christ in the air.

[43]See Rom. 2:14–15. Conscience is the inner judge, given by God, that accuses us when we have done wrong, and approves when we have done right. The word "conscience" was important in the Puritan vocabulary. If a man was right with God, he was also right with himself and others, and had a good conscience that did not disturb him.

[44]See note 2.

INTERPRETER: Well, keep all these things in mind that they may prod you forward in the way you must go.[45]

Then Christian began to prepare himself for his journey, and the Interpreter said, "May the Comforter always be with you, good Christian, to guide you in the way that leads to the City."[46]

So Christian went on his way, saying:

Here I have seen things rare and profitable;
Things pleasant, dreadful, things to make me stable
In what I have begun to take in hand;
Then let me think on them, and understand
Wherefore they showed me were, and let me be
Thankful, O good Interpreter, to thee.

Now I saw in my dream that the highway up which Christian was to travel was fenced on either side with a wall, and that wall was called Salvation.[47] Up this way, therefore, did Christian run, but not without great difficulty because of the load on his back.

He ran until he came to a hill, and upon that hill stood a cross, and at the bottom was a sepulchre.[48] So I saw in my dream that just as Christian came up to the cross, his burden was loosened from his shoulders and fell from his back and began to tumble, and continued to do so until it came to the mouth of the sepulchre, where it fell in, and I saw it no more.

Then Christian was glad and lighthearted and said with a merry heart, "He has given me rest through his sorrow, and

---

[45] This image of the sharp stick used to prod or goad oxen comes from Eccl. 12:11. All that Christian had seen in the house of the Interpreter should motivate him to continue his pilgrimage, no matter the cost. See Acts 9:5.

[46] The Comforter is one of the names of the Holy Spirit. See John 14:16–26. The Greek word means "one called to your side to help." The English word comes from the Latin, meaning "with strength." The Holy Spirit gives us the strength we need to do God's will.

[47] See Isa. 26:1; 35:8.

[48] The death of Christ and His resurrection are the heart of the Christian Gospel (1 Cor. 15:3–4).

life through his death."[49] He stood still a while to look and wonder, for it surprised him that the sight of the cross should thus ease him of his burden. He looked and looked, until the tears streamed down his cheeks.[50]

And as he stood looking and weeping, three Shining Ones came to him and said, "Peace to you." And the first said to him, "Your sins are forgiven"; the second stripped him of his rags and clothed him with a clean garment; and the third placed a mark on his forehead and gave him a roll with a seal upon it, which he told him to look at as he ran, and hand it in at the Celestial Gate.[51] Then they went their way.

> *Who's this? the Pilgrim. How! 'tis very true,*
> *Old things are passed away, all's become new.*[52]
> *Strange! he's another man, upon my word,*
> *They be fine feathers that make a fine bird.*

Then Christian jumped for joy three times and went on, singing:

> *Thus far did I come laden with my sin;*
> *Nor could aught ease the grief that I was in*
> *Till I came hither: What a place is this!*
> *Must here be the beginning of my bliss?*
> *Must here the burden fall from off my back?*
> *Must here the strings that bound it to me crack?*
> *Blest cross! blest sepulchre! blest rather be*
> *The Man that there was put to shame for me!*[53]

---

[49] The paradox of the Christian faith: Christ dies that we might have life; Christ sorrows that we might have joy and rest.

[50] See Zech. 12:10, a description of true repentance.

[51] The Shining Ones are angels. This scene is one of the most important in the book, for it presents Bunyan's beliefs about salvation. When he trusted Christ at the cross, Christian received peace (Rom. 5:1); forgiveness (Mark 2:5); a clean garment, representing salvation (Isa. 64:6; Zech. 3:4); a mark on his forehead — the seal of God (Eph. 1:13); and a roll or scroll (the assurance of salvation). The three angels symbolize the Trinity: the Father forgives, the Son clothes, the Spirit seals and gives assurance. See Eph. 1:3–14.

[52] 2 Cor. 5:17

[53] Bunyan's emphasis is on Christ, not on "religious places" such as the cross and the empty tomb.

Christian loses his burden of sin because he trusts Christ. This had been Bunyan's own experience, as he relates in Grace Abounding: *"I remember that one day, as I was musing on the wickedness of my heart ... that Scripture came into my mind. He hath 'made peace by the blood of His cross,' by which I was made to see both again and again that God and my soul were friends by His blood. This was a good day to me; I hope I shall never forget it." It is worth noting that there was a stone cross at Elstow, near which Bunyan often played games. The stump of the cross remains today.*

Now Christian goes from the three Shining Ones to three careless ones. Filled with the joy of his salvation experience, Christian wants to witness to them and try to help them. Bunyan wrote that he would have told God's love and mercy "even to the very crows that sat upon the ploughed lands." The three men in the following scene represent different kinds of religious indifference. Simple and Sloth depend on false security and false peace, and Presumption depends on false self-reliance.

 saw then in my dream that Christian went on joyfully until he came to a low-lying place, where he saw, a little out of the way,[1] three men fast asleep with chains upon their feet. The name of the one was Simple, the second Sloth, and the third Presumption.

Christian went to see if perhaps he might wake them, and cried, "You are like those who sleep on top of a mast, for the Dead Sea is under you—a gulf that has no bottom.[2] Awake, therefore, and come away; and if you are willing, I will help you take off your shackles." He also told them, "If he that goes about like 'a roaring lion' comes by, certainly you will become prey for him."[3] With that they looked at him and began to reply in this manner.

Simple said, "I see no danger"; Sloth said, "Let me sleep a little more"; and Presumption said, "I can make it myself without any help from you!"And so they lay down to sleep again, and Christian went on his way.

Yet he was troubled to think that men in such danger should think so little of his kindness in freely offering to help them, both by awakening them, counseling them, and offering to help them remove their chains. And as he was troubled about that,[4] he spied two men come tumbling over the wall on the left side of the narrow way; and they hurried to catch up to him. The name of the one was Formalist, and the name of the other Hypocrisy.[5] So, as I said, they drew up to him, and he entered into conversation with them.

---

[1]The first of the dangerous "detours" that run off of the true way. See note 7 [page 37].

[2]Prov. 23:34

[3]Satan. See 1 Peter 5:8.

[4] The new believer has a concern for those who are lost and cannot understand their ignorance.

[5]A "formalist" is a person who practices religious forms but does not possess real salvation. He may be very sincere, but his religion is vain (2 Tim. 3:5). A hypocrite, however, deliberately deceives. At one time, Bunyan was quite taken up with the rituals of the church and thought that, through them, he would find salvation.

CHRISTIAN: Gentlemen, where do you come from and where are you going?

FORMALIST AND HYPOCRISY: We were born in the land of Vain-glory and are going to Mount Zion for the purpose of doing a praiseworthy thing.[6]

CHRISTIAN: Why didn't you enter at the gate which stands at the beginning of the way? Don't you know that it is written that he who does not come in by the door "but climbs up some other way is a thief and a robber"?[7]

FORMALIST AND HYPOCRISY: To go to the gate for entrance is considered too far by all our countrymen. Therefore, the usual way is to take a shortcut and climb over the wall, as we have done.

CHRISTIAN: But won't it be considered a trespass against the Lord of the city where we are going, to thus violate his revealed will?

FORMALIST AND HYPOCRISY: As for that, don't trouble yourself about it; for what we did is according to custom, and we can produce, if need be, testimony that would attest that it has been so for more than a thousand years.[8]

CHRISTIAN: But will your practice hold up in a court of law?

FORMALIST AND HYPOCRISY: That custom, being of so long a standing—over a thousand years, would doubtless now be admitted as legal by an impartial judge; and besides, if we get

---

[6] The glory of man is empty (vain) because it does not endure (1 Peter 1:24). Their motive for going to Mount Zion is all wrong. Both ritualists and hypocrites enjoy the praise of men.

[7] John 10:1

[8] Ancient customs were the authority for their religion. The Puritans rejected tradition and held that only the Bible could dictate to their conscience. Bunyan wrote in *Grace Abounding:* "Because I knew no better, I fell in very eagerly with the religion of the times.... I was so overrun with the spirit of superstition that I adored ... even all things, both the high place, priest, clerk, vestment, service, and what else belonged to the church." Formalist and Hypocrisy depended only on ancient tradition to support their approach to the Heavenly City.

into the way, why does it matter which way we get in? If we are in, we are in. You came in at the gate, and we came tumbling over the wall. In what way is your condition better than ours?

CHRISTIAN: I walk by the rule of my Master; you walk by the ignorant working of your own imagination. You are considered thieves already by the Lord of the way; therefore I doubt that you will be found true men at the end of the way. You come in by yourselves without his direction, and shall go out by yourselves without his mercy.[9]

To this they had little to say, only to tell him to mind his own business. Then I saw that they went on, each in his own way, without much conversation between them, except that these two men told Christian that as far as laws and ordinances were concerned, they thought they should abide by them as conscientiously as he; therefore, they didn't see how he was any different from them except for the coat on his back, which was, they thought, given to him by some of his neighbors to hide the shame of his nakedness.[10]

CHRISTIAN: You will not be saved by laws and ordinances, since you did not come in by the door.[11] And as for this coat on my back, it was given me by the Lord of the place where I am going; and that, as you say, to cover my nakedness with. And I take it as a token of his kindness to me; for I had nothing but rags before. And besides, I comfort myself with this thought as I travel: Surely, I think, when I come to the gate of the city, the Lord will know me since I have his

---

[9] If we do not make the right beginning, we cannot expect the right ending. To come into the way by some other entrance than the right door is to be a thief and a robber. Again, the reference is to John 10.

[10] The coat symbolizes the righteousness of Christ received by faith. There is a difference between God's righteousness and mere morality that is religious. Christian goes on to explain that there are other differences: he bears God's mark on his forehead, and he possesses the scroll which assures him of his salvation. Formalist and Hypocrisy have none of these things.

[11] Gal. 2:16

coat on my back—a coat he gave me freely in the day that he stripped me of my rags. I have, moreover, a mark on my forehead, which perhaps you have not noticed, which one of my Lord's most intimate associates placed there on the day that my burden fell off my shoulders. Moreover, at that time I was also given a scroll, sealed, which I can comfort myself by reading as I go on the way; I was also told to turn it in at the Celestial Gate, to assure my admittance. But, I suppose, it is unlikely that you want any of these things because you did not come in at the gate.

They didn't reply to his comments, except to look at each other and laugh. Then I saw that they all went on, but Christian kept in front of them, talking only to himself, sometimes with a sigh and sometimes with assurance; also he often read the scroll that the Shining Ones had given him, and was refreshed by it.

They all went on till they came to the foot of the Hill Difficulty, at the bottom of which was a spring.[12] There were also in the same place two other paths besides that which came straight from the gate; one turned to the left and the other to the right at the bottom of the hill; but the narrow path went right up the hill, and it was called Difficulty. Christian now went to the spring[13] and drank to refresh himself, and then began to go up the hill, saying:

> *The hill, though high, I covet to ascend,*
> *The difficulty will not me offend;*
> *For I perceive the way to life lies here.*
> *Come, pluck up heart, let's neither faint nor fear;*
> *Better, though difficult, the right way to go,*
> *Than wrong, though easy, where the end is woe.*

---

[12] This is the second of seven hills named in the book. Early in the Christian life difficulties come to test our faith and to prove the reality of conversion. The true way leads up the hill; the false ways lead around the hill and end in judgment.
[13] Isa. 49:10–11; Ps. 110:7

The other two also came to the foot of the hill; but when they saw that the hill was steep and that there were two other ways to go, and figuring that on the other side of the hill these two paths would meet up with the one Christian had taken, they decided to take those paths.[14] Now the name of one of those ways was Danger, and the name of the other was Destruction. So the one took the way called Danger, which led him into a great wood, and the other took the way to Destruction, which led him into a wide field full of dark mountains, where he stumbled and fell and rose no more.[15]

> *Shall they who wrong begin yet rightly end?*
> *Shall they at all have safety for their friend?*
> *No, no; in headstrong manner they set out,*
> *And headlong will they fall at last, no doubt.*

I then watched Christian go up the hill, where I saw him go from running to walking, and from walking to climbing on his hands and knees, because it was so steep. Now about halfway up the hill was a pleasant shelter covered with trees and vines, provided by the Lord of the hill for the refreshing of weary travelers; and when he got there, Christian sat down to rest.[16] Then he pulled his scroll out and read it for comfort; he also began to think about the coat that was given to him as he stood by the cross. This was all very pleasant, and at last he dozed off, lightly at first and then into a deep sleep, which detained him in that place until it was almost night; and in his sleep his scroll fell out of his hand. Now as he was sleeping, one came to him and woke him, saying, "Go to the ant, thou sluggard; consider her ways, and be wise."[17] And with that Christian suddenly got up and hurried on his way until he came to the top of the hill.

---

[14] Prov. 14:12

[15] Jer. 13:16

[16] Isa. 32:18; 40:31

[17]Times of spiritual refreshment are to prepare us for the demands of life, not to lead us into careless lethargy. Bunyan quotes Prov. 6:6.

Now when he got up to the top of the hill, two men ran into him at full speed; the name of the one was Timorous and the other Mistrust.[18]

"Sirs, what's the matter?" said Christian. "You are running the wrong way."

"We are going to the City of Zion, and managed to get as far as this difficult place," answered Timorous. "But the further we go, the more danger we meet; so we are turning back."

"Yes," said Mistrust, "for just ahead lie a couple of lions, whether asleep or awake we don't know, but we are certain if we come within their reach they will tear us to pieces."[19]

CHRISTIAN: Your words frighten me, but where can I flee for safety? If I go back to my own country, which faces fire and brimstone, I shall certainly perish there.[20] If I can get to the Celestial City, I am sure to be safe there. I must go forward, facing the risks and dangers. To go back is nothing but death; to go forward is fear of death, and life everlasting beyond it. So I will go forward.

So Mistrust and Timorous ran down the hill, and Christian went on his way. But, thinking again about what he had heard from the men, he reached inside his coat to take out his scroll, that he might read and be comforted; but it was not there. Then Christian was greatly distressed and did not know what to do; for he wanted the scroll that relieved him and that should have been his pass into the Celestial City. Therefore, he became very perplexed about what he should do. At last he remembered that he had slept in the shelter on the side of the hill; and, falling down upon his knees, he asked God's forgiveness for that foolish act, and then he went back to look for his scroll.[21] But all the way back his heart was sorrowful.

---

[18] Fear and unbelief usually go together and try to escape difficulty and danger.

[19] Satan is pictured as a lion (1 Peter 5:8), but he does not sleep. These men are imagining the worst because they cannot trust God for the best.

[20] Heb. 11:14–16

[21] Christian's sin was forgiven because he confessed it to God (1 John 1:9). He did not need to return to the cross and be converted over again.

Sometimes he sighed, sometimes he wept, and often he chided himself for being so foolish as to fall asleep in that place which was erected only for a little refreshment for his weariness. Therefore he went back, carefully looking on both sides all the way, hoping he might find the scroll that had been his comfort so many times on his journey. But when he came within sight of the shelter where he had sat and slept, his sorrow was renewed, for he was reminded again of his wrongdoing. "O wretched man that I am!" he cried. "That I should sleep in the daytime![22] That I should so indulge the flesh and use that rest to ease my body which the Lord of the hill provided only for the relief of the spirits of pilgrims! How many steps have I taken in vain! (Thus it happened to Israel for their sin; they were sent back again by the way of the Red Sea.)[23] And now I must tread those steps with sorrow, which I might have trod with delight, had it not been for this sinful sleep. How far might I have been on my way by this time! Instead, I must tread those steps three times over, instead of only once; yes, now also I will probably be deprived of light, for the day is almost over. Oh, that I had not slept!"[24]

Now by this time he had come to the shelter again, where for a while he sat down and wept; but at last, as God would have it, Christian looked down and saw his scroll underneath a wooden bench, and he quickly picked it up and put it into his coat. But how can words express the joy this man felt when he had gotten his scroll again! For this scroll was his assurance of life and his acceptance at the desired haven. Therefore, he gave thanks to God for directing his eye to the place where it lay, and with joy and tears returned to his journey.

---

[22] Rom. 7:24; 1 Thess. 5:7–8; Rev. 2:4–5

[23] The nation failed at Kadesh-barnea, did not enter the Promised Land, and wandered for the next forty years in the Wilderness. See Num. 14.

[24] He had to go through dangerous places in the darkness because of his disobedience. Though God forgives the sin, He does not always change the consequences.

How nimbly he climbed the rest of the hill! Yet before he reached the top, the sun had gone down; and this made him recall the foolishness of his sleeping, and he again became sorrowful. "O thou sinful sleep: because of you, I am deprived of light for my journey! I must walk without the sun; darkness covers the path I must walk; and I must hear the noise of the night creatures because of my sinful sleep."[25] Now he remembered the story that Mistrust and Timorous had told him, how they were frightened by the sight of the lions. Then Christian said to himself, "These beasts range in the night, searching for prey; and if they should meet with me in the dark, how should I escape being torn to pieces?" But while he was bewailing his dangerous situation, he looked up, and behold there was a stately palace before him. The name of it was Beautiful, and it stood right beside the highway.[26]

So I saw in my dream that he hurried forward to see if he might get lodging there. Before he had gone far, he entered a very narrow passage,[27] which was about a furlong from the porter's lodge,[28] and looking very closely at the path ahead, he spied two lions. Now, thought he, I see the dangers that Mistrust and Timorous were driven back by. (The lions were chained, but he did not see the chains.)[29] Then he was afraid, and thought he should go back also, for it seemed nothing but death was before him. But the porter at the lodge, whose

---

[25] Isa. 13:21

[26] Bunyan's picture of the church (Ps. 48:2, 13). Note that the palace is beside the highway and not on the highway itself. It is not necessary to be a member of a church to be a Christian, but fellowship in the church strengthens the Christian for his difficult pilgrimage. Bunyan himself was not a denominationalist, although several groups would like to claim him.

[27] The Puritans did not make church membership an easy thing. A person had to give evidence of true salvation before he was received into fellowship.

[28] A furlong is about 220 yards.

[29] Timorous and Mistrust had run from lions that were already chained! Christian is afraid, but he keeps going. It is this spiritual perseverance that proves he is a true believer. See Prov. 22:13; 26:13.

name was Watchful,[30] seeing that Christian had stopped as though he might go back, cried out, saying, "Is your strength so small? [31] Do not fear the lions, for they are chained, and are placed there as a trial of faith, and to discover those that have none.[32] Stay in the middle of the path, and no harm shall come to you."

Difficulty is behind, fear is before,
Though he's got on the hill, the lions roar;
A Christian man is never long at ease,
When one fright's gone, another doth him seize.

Then I saw that he went on, trembling for fear of the lions, but heeding carefully the directions of the porter. He heard them roar, but they did him no harm. Then he clapped his hands and went on till he stood before the gate where the porter was. Then said Christian to the porter, "Sir, what house is this? And may I stay here tonight?" The porter answered, "This house was built by the Lord of the hill, and he built it for the relief and security of pilgrims." The porter also asked where he had come from and where he was going.

CHRISTIAN: I come from the City of Destruction and am going to Mount Zion; but because the sun has now set, I would like to stay here tonight if I may.

PORTER: What is your name?

CHRISTIAN: My name is now Christian, but my name used to be Graceless; I came from the race of Japheth, whom God will persuade to dwell in the tents of Shem.[33]

---

[30] The porter illustrates the work of the faithful pastor in watching for souls and helping them enter the fellowship. See Heb. 13:17; Rev. 3:2.

[31] Mark 4:40; Prov. 24:10

[32] James 1:3; 1 Peter 1:7

[33] Noah had three sons: Shem, Ham, and Japheth. God promised the spiritual blessings to Shem (ancestor of the Jews), and said that the descendants of Japheth (the Gentiles) would "dwell in the tents of Shem" (Gen. 9:27)—that is, share in the spiritual blessings of Israel. It is through Abraham that all the Gentile nations are blessed (Gen. 12:1–3). This was fulfilled in Christ (Gal. 3:1–18).

PORTER: But why are you so late? The sun has set.[34]

CHRISTIAN: I would have been here sooner, but "wretched man that I am!"[35] I slept in the shelter on the hillside; even with that, I would have been here much sooner, except that in my sleep I lost my evidence and came without it to the brow of the hill; and then looking for it and not finding it, I was forced to go back to the place where I had slept, where I found it, and now I am here.

PORTER: Well, I will call out one of the virgins, who will, if she likes your words, bring you in to the rest of the family, according to the rules of the house.[36]

So Watchful, the porter, rang a bell, and a grave and beautiful young woman, named Discretion, came out of the house and asked why she had been called. [37]

The porter answered, "This man is journeying from the City of Destruction to Mount Zion, but since he is tired and it is dark, he asked me if he might stay here tonight; so I told him I would call you, who, after speaking with him, would decide, according to the law of the house."

Then she asked him where he was from and where he was going, and he told her. She asked him also how he got into the way; and he told her. Then she asked him what he had seen and met with on the way, and he told her. And last she asked his name, and he said, "It is Christian, and I have an even greater desire to stay here tonight, because, from what I

---

[34]Because Christian lost his scroll, he was delayed on his journey. But the statement was also autobiographical. Bunyan was twenty-five years old before he united with the local church in Bedford, pastored by John Gifford.
[35]Another reference to Rom. 7:24. Paul's experience in Rom. 7 parallels Bunyan's own experience of frustration, defeat, and eventual victory in Christ.
[36] The church is a family, and the members of the family interview Christian to discover the reality of his profession. For the Puritans, church membership was not automatic; the candidate had to prove himself. By calling these persons virgins, Bunyan may be referring to Ps. 45:14; Song 1:3; and Matt. 25:1–13, where virgins are closely associated with the church and Christ. The word also symbolizes their moral purity.
[37]Prov. 2:11

can see, this place was built by the Lord of the hill for the relief and security of pilgrims." She smiled, but there were tears in her eyes; and after a little pause she said, "I will call two or three more of the family." So she ran to the door and called out Prudence, Piety, and Charity,[38] who, after talking with him a little more, had him come in to the family; many of them met him at the threshold of the house and said, "Come in, thou blessed of the Lord;[39] this house was built by the Lord of the hill to entertain pilgrims such as yourself."[40] Then he bowed his head and followed them into the house.

When he had entered and sat down, they gave him something to drink, and they agreed that until supper was ready some of them should have spiritual conversation with Christian, to put their time to the best use;[41] and they appointed Piety and Prudence and Charity to converse with him.

PIETY: Come, good Christian, since we have been kind enough to receive you into our house this night, let us talk with you about all the things that have happened to you in your pilgrimage.

CHRISTIAN: I would be happy to.

PIETY: What caused you to take up the pilgrim's life in the first place?[42]

---

[38] These virtues should belong to all Christians. "Charity" means "love," and not merely the giving of aid to the needy.

[39] This is the way Laban greeted Abraham's servant in Gen. 24:31.

[40] The church is often pictured in the New Testament as a house or temple built by the Lord. See Matt. 16:18; 1 Cor. 3:9–17; Eph. 2:19–22; and 1 Peter 2:5–10.

[41] "Spiritual discourse" was a common practice among the Puritans (Mal. 3:16). It was the spiritual conversation of some women in Bedford, overheard by Bunyan, that helped to lead him to salvation. This conversation also pictures the kind of personal examination that was given to candidates for church membership in that day.

[42] Piety asks questions that deal with Christian's outward actions, and Christian tells what he heard, felt, and saw. Later, Prudence asks him about the inner motives of his decision; and Charity focuses on his love for his home.

CHRISTIAN: I was driven out of my native country by something dreadful that I heard; that is, that unavoidable destruction awaited me if I continued to live there.

PIETY: But how did you happen to come out of your country this way?

CHRISTIAN: It was God's doing, for I did not know where to go; but as I was trembling and weeping with fear of destruction, a man named Evangelist happened to come to me, and he directed me to the wicket-gate, which otherwise I should never have found. And thus he set me on the way that has led me directly to this house.

PIETY: But didn't you come past the house of the Interpreter?

CHRISTIAN: Yes, and the memories of the things I saw there will stay with me as long as I live, especially these three things: how Christ, in despite of Satan, maintains his word of grace in the heart; how man's sin is so great that he does not deserve God's mercy; and also the dream of him that dreamed the day of judgment had come.

PIETY: Why, did you hear him tell about his dream?

CHRISTIAN: Yes, and a dreadful one it was. It made my heart ache as he was telling it, and yet I am glad I heard it.

PIETY: Was that all you saw at the house of the Interpreter?

CHRISTIAN: No. He showed me a stately palace, where the people were clad in gold; and while we were there an adventurous man came and cut his way through the armed men who stood in the door to keep him out, and he was told to come in and win eternal glory. I was overcome with joy and delight at the sight of these things and would have stayed at that good man's house a year, except that I knew I had further to go.

PIETY: And what else did you see on the way?

CHRISTIAN: Saw! Why, I had only gone a little further when I saw a man hanging, bleeding, upon a tree, and the

---

Generally speaking, Piety deals with the events of his life, Prudence with the motives, and Charity with how he overcame the obstacles in the way.

very sight of him made my burden fall off my back (for I had been carrying a very heavy burden). I had never seen such a thing before! And while I stood looking up, for then I could not stop looking, three Shining Ones came to me. One of them testified that my sins were forgiven; another stripped me of my rags and gave me this embroidered coat;[43] and the third set the mark that you see on my forehead and gave me this sealed scroll. (And with that he pulled it out of his coat.)

PIETY: But you saw more than this, didn't you?

CHRISTIAN: The things that I have told you were the best; yet there were other things I saw: I saw three men, Simple, Sloth, and Presumption, asleep beside the way, with shackles upon their feet; but do you think I could awake them? I also saw Formality and Hypocrisy come tumbling over the wall, pretending to go to Zion, but they were quickly lost, even as I warned them; but they would not believe. But above all, I found it hard work to get up this hill, and as hard to come past the lions' mouths; and truly if it had not been for the good porter that stands at the gate, I do not know but that I might have turned back after all. But now I thank God I am here, and I thank you for receiving me.

Then Prudence asked him a few questions.

PRUDENCE: Don't you ever think about the country from which you came?

CHRISTIAN: Yes, but with much shame and contempt. If I truly longed for the country I left, I could have returned; but now I desire a better country, that is, a heavenly one.[44]

PRUDENCE: Don't you still bear with you some of the things that concerned you there?[45]

---

[43] The Jewish high priest wore a beautiful embroidered coat (Exod. 28:4). All who have trusted Jesus Christ as Savior are God's priests (1 Peter 2:5, 9). In Ezek. 16:10, 13, 18, the "broidered coat" symbolizes God's love for His people as He covers their shame and forgives them.

[44] Heb. 11:15–16

[45] In other words, "You are not yet perfect, are you?" Salvation does not mean that the Christian is perfect in himself, but only that he is accepted in Christ. There are still areas of weakness and sin that must be overcome.

CHRISTIAN: Yes, but greatly against my will, especially inward and carnal thoughts, with which all my countrymen, as well as myself, were delighted. Now all those things are grievous to me, and if I could I would choose never to think of them again; but when I would do that which is best, that which is worst is with me.[46]

PRUDENCE: Don't you find that sometimes those things can be subdued?

CHRISTIAN: Yes, although seldom. But when it happens, it is precious to me.

PRUDENCE: Can you remember by what means you subdue these things that trouble you?

CHRISTIAN: Yes, when I think of what I saw at the cross, that will do it; and when I look upon my embroidered coat, that will do it; and when I look into the scroll that I carry, that will do it; and when I think about where I am going, that will do it.[47]

PRUDENCE: And what is it that makes you so eager to go to Mount Zion?

CHRISTIAN: Why, there I hope to see him alive who was hanging dead on the cross; and there I hope to get rid of all those things that to this day are an annoyance to me; there, they say, there is no death,[48] and there I shall dwell with the kind of companions I like best. For to tell you truth, I love him, because he relieved me of my burden; and I am weary of my inward sickness. I want to be where I shall die no more, and in the company of those who shall continually cry, "Holy, Holy, Holy!"[49]

---

[46]An allusion to Rom. 7:15–21.

[47]Here Bunyan gives us his views of sanctification, that is, how a Christian can live a godly life. He names four encouragements to godly living: the cross, his justification (the coat), the assurances of salvation (the scroll), and the prospect of heaven. These four encouragements are definitely a part of Puritan theology.

[48] Rev. 21:4; Isa. 25:8

[49] Isa. 6:3; Rev. 4:8

Then Charity said to Christian, "Have you a family? Are you a married man?"

CHRISTIAN: I have a wife and four small children.[50]

CHARITY: Why didn't you bring them along with you?

Then Christian wept and said, "Oh, how willingly I would have done so, but they were all utterly against my going on pilgrimage."

CHARITY: But you should have talked to them and tried to show them the danger of being left behind.

CHRISTIAN: I did. And I told them what God had showed me about the destruction of our city; but I seemed to them "as one that mocked," and they did not believe me.[51]

CHARITY: Did you pray and ask God to bless your advice to them?

CHRISTIAN: Yes, with much love, for you must know that my wife and poor children were very dear to me.

CHARITY: Did you tell them about your own sorrow and fear of destruction?

CHRISTIAN: Yes, over and over and over. They also could see my fears in my expression, in my tears, and in my trembling because of my apprehension about the judgment that hung over our heads; but all that was not sufficient to prevail upon them to come with me.

CHARITY: What did they say for themselves, why they would not come?

CHRISTIAN: Well, my wife was afraid of losing this world, and my children were devoted to the foolish delights of youth; so what with one thing and another, they left me to come this way alone.

CHARITY: Were they perhaps confused because your life did not measure up to your words as you tried to persuade them to come away with you?

---

[50] When *The Pilgrim's Progress* was published, Bunyan had a wife, two sons, and two daughters.

[51] When Lot tried to warn his family that Sodom would be destroyed, he "seemed as one that mocked" (Gen. 19:14).

CHRISTIAN: Indeed, I cannot commend my life, for I am conscious of my many failings, and I know that a man can damage his witness by bad behavior. Yet this I can say, I was very careful, lest by some unseemly action I would cause them to become averse to going on pilgrimage. In fact, they would tell me I was too precise, and that I denied myself things, for their sakes, in which they saw no evil. No, I think I may say that if they saw anything in me that hindered them, it was my great sensitivity about sinning against God or of doing any wrong to my neighbor.

CHARITY: Indeed Cain hated his brother, "because his own works were evil, and his brother's righteous"; and if your wife and children have been offended by you because of this, they cannot be pleased by goodness, and "thou hast delivered thy soul" from their blood.[52]

Now I saw in my dream that they sat talking together until supper was ready and they sat down to eat.[53] Now the table was set with a feast of rich foods and with good wine,[54] and all their talk at the table was about the Lord of the hill; namely, about what he had done, and why he did what he did, and why he had built that house. And by what they said I perceived that he had been a great warrior and had fought with and slain "him that had the power of death," but not without great danger to himself, which made me love him the more.[55]

For, as they said, and as I believe (said Christian), he did it with the loss of much blood; but that which put the glory of grace into all he did was that he did it out of pure love. And besides, some of the household said they had been with him

---

[52] See 1 John 3:12; Gen. 4:1–15; Ezek. 3:19.

[53] This pictures the Lord's Supper, or the Communion, practiced in Puritan churches. It was considered a simple meal, not a ritual or a sacrament. Its purpose was to remember the Lord and glorify Him (Luke 22:19; 1 Cor. 11:24). The Puritans did not teach that participation in the Communion was necessary to salvation.

[54] Isa. 25:6

[55] Heb. 2:14–15

and spoken with him since he died on the cross; and they attested that they had heard from his own lips that he is such a lover of poor pilgrims that the like is not to be found from the east to the west.

They gave an example of this, and that was that he had stripped himself of his glory so he might do this for the poor;[56] and they had heard him say and affirm that he would not dwell in the mountain of Zion alone. They said, moreover, that he had made princes of many pilgrims who had been born beggars and were by nature destined for the dunghill.[57]

Thus they talked together till late at night; and after they had prayed together for their Lord's protection, they went to bed. They put the pilgrim in a large upper chamber,[58] where the windows opened toward the sunrise. The name of the chamber was Peace, and he slept there till break of day, when he awoke and sang:

> *Where am I now? Is this the love and care*
> *Of Jesus for the men that pilgrims are?*
> *Thus to provide that I should be forgiven!*
> *And dwell already the next door to heaven!*

In the morning they all got up, and after some more conversation, they told Christian that he should not depart till they had shown him the various rooms in the palace.[59] First they took him into the study, where they showed him records of great antiquity; in which, as I remember in my dream, they showed him first the genealogy of the Lord of the hill, that he was the son of the Ancient of Days,[60] and came by that eternal generation.[61] Here also the acts that he had done were more

---

[56]An allusion to Phil. 2:5–11.

[57]See 1 Sam. 2:8; Ps. 113:7.

[58]Mark 14:15

[59] The various rooms illustrate various aspects of the Christian life. The visit begins in the study because the knowledge of the Word of God is basic to everything else. Bunyan was a great lover of his Bible.

[60]A name for the Lord. See Dan. 7:9, 13, 22.

[61]A theological term referring to the relationship between Jesus Christ and God the Father. If Jesus is eternal God, then how can He also be the Son of

fully recorded, and the names of many hundreds that he had taken into his service; and how he had placed them in habitations that neither time nor death could destroy.

Then they read to him some of the worthy acts that some of his servants had done: how they had "subdued kingdoms, wrought righteousness, obtained promises, stopped the mouths of lions, quenched the violence of fire, escaped the edge of the sword, out of weakness were made strong, waxed valiant in fight, and turned to flight the armies of the aliens."[62]

They then read, in another part of the records of the house, how willing their Lord was to receive anyone into his favor, even those who in the past had defied him. Here Christian also viewed several other histories of famous things, both ancient and modern, together with prophecies and predictions of things to come, both to the dread and amazement of enemies and to the comfort and solace of pilgrims.

The next day they took him into the armory, where they showed him all the equipment their Lord had provided for pilgrims, such as sword, shield, helmet, breastplate, all kinds of prayers, and shoes that would not wear out.[63] And there was enough here to equip as many men for the service of their Lord as there are stars in the heavens.

They also showed him some of the implements with which some of his servants had done wonderful things. They showed him Moses' rod; the hammer and nail with which Jael slew Sisera; the pitchers, trumpets, and lamps with which Gideon put the armies of Midian to flight. Then they showed him the ox's goad with which Shamgar slew six hundred men, the jawbone with which Samson did such mighty feats, the sling and stone with which David slew Goliath, and the sword with which their Lord will kill the Man of Sin. Besides all this,

---

God? When was He begotten? The orthodox reply is that He was "eternally generated" by the Father, not created; and therefore is both eternal God and God the Son. The Puritans were careful theologians, and Bunyan could debate with the best of them!

[62] Heb. 11:33–34
[63] Deut. 29:5; Eph. 6:13ff.

they showed him many excellent things with which Christian was much delighted. This done, they again went to bed.[64]

On the next day he intended to leave, but they wanted him to stay another day. "If the day is clear," they said, "we will show you the Delectable Mountains, which will add to your comfort because they are nearer your destination than this place." So he consented and stayed.[65]

When morning came they took him to the top of the house and told him to look south; so he did, and he saw at a great distance a beautiful mountainous country, with woods, vineyards, fruits and flowers of all sorts, springs and fountains, wonderful to behold. Then he asked the name of the country, and they said, "It is Immanuel's Land, and it belongs to all pilgrims, as does this hill. And when you get there, you will be able to see the gate of the Celestial City."[66]

Now he thought he should leave, and they were willing that he should. "But first," they said, "let us go again into the armory." So they did, and there they equipped him from head to foot in case he should meet with assaults on the way. Being thus clad, he walked out with his friends to the gate, and there he asked the porter if he had seen a pilgrim pass by. The porter answered, "Yes."

CHRISTIAN: Did you know him?

PORTER: He told me his name was Faithful.[67]

---

[64] Moses' rod (Exod. 4:2ff.); Jael (Judg. 4:18ff.); Gideon (Judg. 6–7); Shamgar (Judg. 3:31); jawbone (Judg. 15:15); David (1 Sam. 17). The "man of sin" is described in 2 Thess. 2; Rev. 13:1–10. He is Satan's future "world dictator," who will fight Christ. The Lord will defeat him with His sword, just as David slew Goliath with a sword (Rev. 19:15). In Bunyan's day, the phrase "man of sin" also referred to the pope, because of Roman persecution of believers. You find this statement in the preface to the King James Bible.

[65] The vision of future blessing encourages the believer in the trials of life.

[66] See Isa. 33:17. "Immanuel" means "God with us" (Matt. 1:23). "Immanuel's Land" refers to the Holy Land (Isa. 8:8), but Bunyan uses it as a name for heaven.

[67] He will be Christian's companion until they reach Vanity Fair. There Faithful will be martyred. It is interesting that Faithful did not stop at the Palace

CHRISTIAN: Oh, I know him. He comes from the place where I was born and was my neighbor. How far ahead is he?

PORTER: By this time he should be at the foot of the hill.

CHRISTIAN: Well, good Porter, the Lord be with you and bless you greatly for the kindness you have showed to me.

Then he began to go forward, but Discretion, Piety, Charity, and Prudence wanted to accompany him down to the foot of the hill. So they went on together, discussing their former conversations, till they started down the hill. Then said Christian, "As it was difficult coming up, so, as far as I can see, it is dangerous going down."

"Yes," said Prudence, "so it is, for it is hard for a man to go down into the Valley of Humiliation, as you are now, and not to slip on the way; that is why we came out to accompany you down the hill."[68] So he began to go down, very carefully; yet he did slip a time or two.

Then I saw in my dream that when Christian had gotten to the bottom of the hill, these good companions gave him a loaf of bread, a bottle of wine, and a cluster of raisins. And then he went on his way.

Beautiful. Bunyan suggests by this that not all Christians unite with local churches.

[68] It is not easy for us to humble ourselves and go "down the hill." Christians must help one another and remind one another of what God has taught them. The Valley of Humiliation represents the special trials and difficulties that come to us from Satan.

When he gets down into the Valley of Humiliation, Christian eats the food that Discretion, Piety, Charity, and Prudence have given him. He will eat some of this food again later after he has defeated Apollyon. The bread and wine remind us of the Lord's Supper; they are symbols of His death. The Christian gets his spiritual strength from "feeding on the Lord."

During this part of his journey, Christian encounters Apollyon, "The Destroyer" (Rev. 9:11), who is the third of the traditional enemies: the world, the flesh, and the Devil. Christian encountered the world at Hill Difficulty, the flesh when he slept at the shelter on the hillside, and now he must battle the forces of Satan.

Here he also enters the Valley of the Shadow of Death. This is not death itself, but the experience of fear and horror that Christians sometimes have in this life. The road to the Celestial City often takes Christian through deep valleys of difficulty.

n the Valley of Humiliation poor Christian faced great difficulty, for he had gone only a short distance before he saw a devilish creature named Apollyon coming across the field to meet him. Then Christian began to be afraid and to wonder whether to go back or to stand his ground. But he realized that he had no armor for his back, and should he turn his back he might give the creature a greater advantage, making it easier for the creature to pierce him with his darts.[1] Therefore he resolved to take a chance and stand his ground. "For," he thought, "if I had no more in mind than the saving of my life, it would be the best way to stand."

So he went on, and Apollyon met him. Now the monster was hideous: he was clothed with scales like a fish (and they were his pride); he had wings like a dragon and feet like a bear; out of his belly came fire and smoke; and his mouth was like the mouth of a lion.[2] He looked at Christian with disdain and began to question him.[3]

APOLLYON: Where did you come from and where are you going?

---

[1]The spiritual armor listed in Eph. 6:13ff. Bunyan saw here the importance of standing against the Devil and not running away. When he was first arrested, Bunyan could have avoided prosecution, but he chose to stand true to the Lord. See also Eph. 6:16.

[2]Bunyan borrowed this composite creature from Job 41:15; Dan. 7:5; 1 Peter 5:8; Rev. 9:17; 12:3ff; 13:2. Christian's song after he defeats Apollyon indicates that Apollyon is not Satan, but was sent by "Great Beelzebub." Rev. 9:11 states that Apollyon is "the angel of the bottomless pit," which suggests that he is Satan.

[3]Apollyon uses every argument he can muster to win back Christian's allegiance. First he claims him as a subject of his kingdom. Then he makes promises to him and asks him to reconsider. When these attempts fail, Apollyon accuses him of being unfaithful to the Lord because of his past failures. Finally, he attacks him physically. First Satan comes as the serpent to deceive (2 Cor. 11:3); then he comes as the dragon and lion to devour (1 Peter 5:8).

CHRISTIAN: I have come from the City of Destruction, which is the place of all evil, and am going to the City of Zion.

APOLLYON: By this I see that you are one of my subjects, for all that country is mine, and I am the prince and god of it.[4] How is it then that you have run away from your king? If I didn't have hopes that you might serve me further, I would strike you down now with one blow.

CHRISTIAN: Indeed I was born in your dominions, but your service was hard, and your wages such that a man could not live on them, "for the wages of sin is death." Therefore, as I got older I did what other thoughtful persons do: I looked for ways to improve myself.[5]

APOLLYON: No prince takes the loss of his subjects lightly, and I do not want to lose you. But since you have complained about your service and the wages, if you are willing to return, I promise to give you whatever our country can afford.[6]

CHRISTIAN: But I have given myself to another, the King of princes. So how can I with fairness go back with you?

APOLLYON: Like the proverb says, you have "gone from bad to worse." But it is common for those who have professed to be his servants to give him the slip and return again to me. If you do so too, all shall be well.

CHRISTIAN: I have given him my faith and sworn allegiance to him. How can I go back and not be hanged as a traitor?

APOLLYON: You did the same to me, and yet I am willing to overlook it if you will turn now and go back.

CHRISTIAN: What I promised you I did out of youthful innocence and immaturity, and I count on the fact that the Prince under whose banner I stand now is able to absolve me and pardon what I did in compliance to you. And besides, O

---

[4] Satan is called the "prince of this world" in John 12:31; 14:30; 16:11; and the "god of this world" in 2 Cor. 4:4.

[5] See Eph. 2:1–3; Rom. 6:23

[6] In Bunyan's day a citizen needed a license in order to leave the realm. No king gives up his people carelessly, for they mean taxes and service to him.

destroying Apollyon! to tell you the truth, I like his service, his wages, his servants, his government, his company, and his country better than yours.[7] Therefore, stop trying to persuade me further; I am his servant, and I will follow him.

APOLLYON: When you are calmer, consider again what you are likely to encounter along the way you are going. You know, for the most part, his servants come to a bad end because they go against me and my ways. How many of them have been put to shameful deaths! You count his service better than mine, and yet he never came and delivered them from that death. But as for me, how many times, as all the world well knows, have I delivered, either by power or fraud, my faithful servants from him and his, and so I will deliver thee.

CHRISTIAN: At present he purposely does not deliver them in order to prove whether they will be faithful to him to the end; and as for the bad end you say they come to, that is a glorious credit to them. For they do not really expect present deliverance; they wait for the glory they shall have when their Prince comes in his glory with the angels.[8]

APOLLYON: You have already been unfaithful in your service to him. How do you think you will receive wages from him?

CHRISTIAN: Where, O Apollyon, have I been unfaithful to him?

APOLLYON: You lost courage when you first set out and you fell into the Swamp of Despond; then you tried to get rid of your burden in the wrong ways instead of waiting till your Prince had taken it off; you sinfully slept and lost your scroll; you were almost persuaded to go back at the sight of the lions; and when you talk about your journey and what you have heard and seen, inwardly you are seeking your own glory in all that you say and do.[9]

---

[7]This list of advantages is reminiscent of the Queen of Sheba's admiration for Solomon and his court (1 Kings 10:1–10).
[8]Matt. 25:31
[9]Satan is the accuser who reminds us of our past sins (Zech. 3:1–5; Rev. 12:10–11).

CHRISTIAN: All this is true, and much more that you have left out; but the Prince whom I serve and honor is merciful and ready to forgive.[10] And besides, these failings possessed me in your country, and I have groaned under them, been sorry for them, and have obtained pardon from my Prince.

Then Apollyon broke out into a terrible rage, saying, "I am an enemy of the Prince; I hate him and his laws and his people; I have come out on purpose to oppose you."

CHRISTIAN: Apollyon, beware what you do, for I am on the King's highway, the way of holiness; therefore, take heed.[11]

Then Apollyon straddled the entire path and said, "I have no fear. Prepare to die. For I swear by all my powers that you shall go no further; here will I shed your blood."

And with that he threw a flaming dart at his breast; but Christian had a shield in his hand, with which he caught it and prevented it from striking him.

Then Christian drew back, for he saw it was time to take action; and Apollyon came at him, throwing darts as thick as hail, which, despite all Christian did to avoid them, wounded him in his head, his hand, and his foot.[12] This made Christian fight back. Apollyon therefore continued his attack, and Christian again took courage and resisted as manfully as he could. This combat lasted for over half a day, until Christian was almost exhausted; for Christian's wounds made him grow weaker and weaker.

---

[10] Ps. 86:5

[11] "The king's highway" was an important trade route mentioned in the Bible (Num. 20:17–19; 21:22; Deut. 2:27). It was the route Israel wanted to use in its wilderness wandering. "The way of holiness" comes from Isa. 35:8. The fact that Christian was on the King's highway meant that he was under the protection of the Lord; therefore, Satan was warned to be careful.

[12] The head is the understanding; the hand is faith in God; the foot is behavior or walk. Perhaps Christian had lost his helmet and shoes so that those areas were vulnerable. Satan wants to attack the believer in those three important areas. See Lev. 8:23–24.

Then Apollyon, seeing his opportunity, began to close in on Christian, and wrestling with him, gave him a dreadful fall, and Christian's sword flew out of his hand. Then said Apollyon, "I am sure of you now." And with that he had almost pressed him to death, so that Christian began to despair of life.[13] But as God would have it, while Apollyon was preparing to take his last blow, thereby making an end of this good man, Christian nimbly reached out his hand and caught his sword, saying, "Rejoice not against me, O mine enemy; when I fall I shall arise"; and with that gave him a deadly thrust, which made him back away, like someone who had received a mortal wound.[14] When Christian saw this, he went at him again, saying, "Nay, in all these things we are more than conquerors through him that loved us."[15] And with that Apollyon spread his dragon wings and sped away, so that Christian saw him no more for a time.[16]

Unless he had seen it and heard it as I did, no one can imagine this combat: what yelling and hideous roaring Apollyon made during the fight—he sounded like a dragon;[17] and on the other side, what sighs and groans burst from Christian's heart. I never saw him give so much as one pleasant look, till he saw that he had wounded Apollyon with his two-edged sword;[18] then he did smile and look upward; but it was the most dreadful sight I ever saw.

A more unequal match can hardly be—
Christian must fight an angel; but you see,
The valiant man by handling sword and shield,
Doth make him, though a dragon, quit the field.

---

[13] 2 Cor. 1:8

[14] See Micah 7:8. The sword is the Word of God (Eph. 6:17). When Satan tempted our Lord, Jesus used the Word to defeat him (Matt. 4:1–11). The great dragon described in Revelation suffered mortal wounds (Rev. 13: 3, 12, 14).

[15] Rom. 8:37–39; James 4:7

[16] See Luke 4:13. Literally it reads "until a season"—that is, until a more appropriate time. Satan patiently waits for the right hour to attack.

[17] Rev. 13:11

[18] Heb. 4:12

So when the battle was over, Christian said, "I will here give thanks to him who has delivered me out of the mouth of the lion, to him who did help me against Apollyon."[19] And so he did, saying:

> *Great Beelzebub, the captain of this fiend,*
> *Designed my ruin; therefore to this end*
> *He sent him harnessed out: and he with rage*
> *That hellish was, did fiercely me engage.*
> *But blessed Michael helped me, and I*
> *By dint of sword did quickly make him fly.*
> *Therefore to him let me give lasting praise,*
> *And thank and bless his holy name always.*[20]

Then there came to him a hand with some of the leaves of the tree of life, which Christian applied to the wounds he had received in the battle and was healed immediately.[21] He also sat down in that place to eat bread and to drink of the bottle that had been given to him earlier. Then being refreshed, he began his journey once more, with his sword drawn; for he said, "Some other enemy may be at hand." But he met with no other attack from Apollyon in this valley.

Now at the end of this valley was another, called the Valley of the Shadow of Death, and Christian had to travel through it because the path to the Celestial City went right through the middle of it.[22] This valley is a very solitary place. Or, as the prophet Jeremiah describes it: "A wilderness, a land of deserts and of pits, a land of drought, and of the shadow of death, a land that no man" (but a Christian) "passed through, and where no man dwelt."

What Christian faced here was worse than his fight with Apollyon, as you shall see.

---

[19] 2 Tim. 4:17

[20] Beelzebub. See page 1 [section 3]. The reference is to a future war in heaven, during which Satan and Michael the archangel will battle. See Dan. 10:13, 21; Rev. 12:7–12.

[21] Rev. 22:2

[22] Ps. 23:4; Isa. 9:2; Jer. 2:6

I saw then in my dream that when Christian got to the borders of the Shadow of Death, he met two men, children of those who brought back an evil report of the Promised Land, and they were hurrying the other way.[23] Christian spoke to them as follows:

CHRISTIAN: Where are you going?

MEN: Back, back! And you should too, if you value either your life or peace.

CHRISTIAN: Why? What's the matter?

MEN: Matter! We were going the same way you are going, and went as far as we dared; and indeed we were almost past the point of no return, for had we gone a little further, we would not be here to bring the news to you.

CHRISTIAN: But what have you met with?

MEN: Why, we were almost in the Valley of the Shadow of Death;[24] but fortunately we happened to looked ahead and saw the danger before we came to it.

CHRISTIAN: But what have you seen?

MEN: Seen! Why, the valley itself, which is as dark as pitch; we also saw there the hobgoblins, satyrs, and dragons of the pit; and we heard in that valley a continual howling and yelling, like people in unspeakable misery, bound in affliction and irons; and over that valley hang the discouraging clouds of confusion.[25] Death always spreads his wings over it. In a word, it is dreadful in every way.

CHRISTIAN: From what you have said, I believe this is my way to the desired haven.[26]

MEN: It may be your way; we will certainly not choose it for ours.

---

[23] Ten of the twelve spies sent into the Promised Land told Israel not to go in because it was too dangerous (Num. 13). This was their evil report.

[24] Ps. 44:19; 107:10

[25] See Isa. 13:21; 34:14; Ps. 107:10; Job 3:5; 10:22. Hobgoblins are impish spirits. Satyrs are lustful men who have the hindquarters of a goat. Of course, such beings are mythical. Isaiah refers to the false gods of the heathen as "satyrs" (he-goats).

[26] See Ps. 107:30; 44:18–19; Jer.2:6. God is able to take His people through the valley.

So they parted, and Christian went on his way, but with his sword drawn, in case he should be assaulted.

I saw in my dream that there was a very deep ditch on the right, running the entire length of the valley; it is that ditch into which the blind have led the blind in every age, and there both have perished miserably.[27] On the left was a dangerous marsh; if even a good man falls into this, he can find no bottom on which to stand. It was into that bog that King David once fell and would have been smothered had not he that is able pulled him out.[28]

The pathway here was also extremely narrow, and Christian had to be more careful than ever; for when he tried to avoid the ditch on one side, he almost slipped into the mire on the other; and when he tried to escape the mire, he had to be careful not to fall into the ditch. I heard him sigh bitterly; for, besides the dangers mentioned above, the pathway was so dark that often when he lifted up his foot to go forward, he did not know where or upon what he should set it next.[29]

> *Poor man! Where art thou now?*
> *Thy day is night.*
> *Good man, be not cast down, thou yet art right,*
> *Thy way to heaven lies by the gates of hell;*
> *Cheer up, hold out, with thee it shall go well.*

Midway through this valley I noticed the mouth of hell close to the pathway.[30] "Now," thought Christian, "what shall I do?" Flame and smoke spewed out continually and in such abundance, with sparks and hideous noises (things that could not be dealt with by Christian's sword, as was Apollyon), that he was forced to sheath his sword and take up another weapon, called *all-prayer*.[31] So he cried, "O Lord, I beg you,

---

[27] Matt. 15:14

[28] Ps. 69:14

[29] 1 Sam. 2:9

[30] Christian will discover several ways to hell as he continues his journey, including one at the very gate of heaven!

[31] See Eph. 6:18. His prayer is from Ps. 116:4. The Christian must use the right weapons in his spiritual warfare.

deliver my soul!" Thus he went on a great while, yet still the flames reached toward him. Also he heard sorrowful voices, and sounds of great movement back and forth, so that sometimes he thought he should be torn in pieces or trodden down like mud in the streets.[32] He saw and heard these frightful sights and dreadful noises for several miles; and reaching a place where he thought he heard a company of fiends coming forward to meet him, he stopped and began to consider what would be the best thing to do. Sometimes he had half a mind to go back; then again he thought he might be halfway through the valley, and he remembered how he had already conquered many dangers, and that the danger of going back might be much worse than going forward; so he resolved to go on. Yet the fiends seemed to be coming straight at him, and he cried out forcefully, "I will walk in the strength of the Lord God!"[33] So the fiends gave way and came no further.

One thing I could not help noticing: by now poor Christian was so confused that he did not know his own voice. I realized this because just as he came up to the mouth of the burning pit, one of the wicked ones got behind him, and stepped up softly and whisperingly suggested terrible blasphemies to him, which he actually thought had come from his own mind. This was a greater trial to Christian than anything he had met with so far, even to think that he should now blaspheme him that he loved so much before; yet if he could have helped it, he would not have done it; but he had not the understanding to either cover his ears or to know where these blasphemies came from.[34]

When Christian had traveled in this disconsolate condition for some considerable time, he thought he heard the

---

[32] 2 Sam. 22:43; Isa. 10:6; Micah 7:10

[33] Ps. 71:16

[34] Bunyan himself experienced times when his mind was filled with blasphemous thoughts. He writes in *Grace Abounding*: "While I was in this temptation, I should often find my mind suddenly put upon it, to curse and swear, or to speak some grievous thing against God, or Christ his Son, and of the Scripture. Now I thought, surely I am possessed of the devil."

voice of a man, going before him, saying, "Though I walk through the Valley of the Shadow of Death, I will fear no evil, for thou art with me."[35]

Then he was glad, and for these reasons:

First, because he gathered from this that he was not alone in this valley. There were others here who feared God as well.

Second, since he perceived that God was with them in this dark and dismal state, then why not with him, even though in the present circumstances it did not seem so.[36]

Third, because he hoped he could overtake them and have company by and by. So he went on and called to the man who was ahead of him; but the man did not know what to answer, for he also thought he was alone. And before long it was daybreak, and Christian said, "He has turned the shadow of death into the morning."[37]

Now he looked back, not out of any desire to return, but to see by the light of day what hazards he had gone through in the dark. So he saw more perfectly the ditch that was on the right and the marsh that was on the left, and how narrow the path was between them; also he now saw the hobgoblins and satyrs and dragons of the pit afar off (for after daybreak they did not come near him), yet they were revealed to him according to that which is written, "He discovereth deep things out of darkness, and bringeth out to light the shadow of death."[38]

Christian was greatly affected by his deliverance from all the dangers of his solitary way; which, though he had feared them more before, he now saw more clearly because the light of day made them conspicuous to him. And about this time the sun was rising, and this was another mercy to Christian; for you must note that though the first part of the Valley of the Shadow of Death was dangerous, this second part, which he

---

[35] Ps. 23:4

[36] Job 9:11

[37] Amos 5:8

[38] See Job 12:22. Christians learn lessons in the valley, and even the darkness brings blessing.

had yet to travel, was far more dangerous. From the place where he now stood to the end of the valley, the way was filled with snares, traps, gins, nets, pits, deep holes, and slopes;[39] had it now been dark, as it was when he came the first part of the way, and had he had a thousand souls, they would have had reason to be cast away. But as I said, the sun was rising, so he said, "His candle shineth on my head, and by his light I go through darkness."[40]

In this light, therefore, he came to the end of the valley. And I saw in my dream that at the end of this valley lay blood, bones, ashes, and mangled bodies of pilgrims who had gone this way before; and while I was wondering about the reason for this, I saw a little ways in front of me a cave, where two giants, Pope and Pagan, had lived, by whose power and tyranny the men whose remains lay there were cruelly put to death.[41] But Christian passed this place without much danger, which I wondered about; I have learned since that Pagan has been dead for some time, and the other, though still alive, has grown so crazy and stiff in his joints because of his age and the many dangerous skirmishes he met with in his younger days that he can now do little more than sit in the mouth of his cave, grinning at pilgrims as they go by and biting his nails because he cannot attack them.

---

[39] A list of various kinds of traps for catching game.

[40] Job 29:3

[41] Since Foxe's *Book of Martyrs* was Bunyan's second Bible, and since England in that day was threatened by Rome through alliances with Roman Catholic nations, it is understandable that Bunyan would take this attitude. Puritan theology had no room for a Pope, traditions, or sacraments. However, Bunyan personally did not refuse to fellowship with true Christians who happened to be in the Church of Rome. In his book *Communion and Fellowship of Christians,* Bunyan wrote: "I hold therefore to what I said at first: That if there be any saints in the anti-christian church, my heart, and the door of our congregation is open to receive them, into closest fellowship with us." Bunyan obviously made a distinction between the Roman system of doctrine and practice, and individual believers. He allies Pagan with Pope because he believed that most of Rome's converts were still pagan, even though they were joined to a religious system.

So Christian went on his way. Yet at the sight of the Old Man who sat in the mouth of the cave, he did not know what to think, especially since the man spoke to him, saying, "You will never change till more of you be burned." But Christian kept quiet and looked cheerful and thus went by without being harmed. Then he sang:

O world of wonders! (I can say no less)
That I should be preserved in that distress
That I have met with here! O blessed be
That hand that from it hath delivered me!
Dangers in darkness, devils, hell, and sin
Did compass me, while I this vale was in:
Yea, snares and pits and traps and nets did lie
My path about, that worthless, silly I
Might have been catched, entangled, and cast down;
But since I live, let Jesus wear the crown.

Now as Christian went on his way, he came to a little hill, which was set there so that pilgrims might see what lay before them. Christian climbed this and, looking ahead, saw Faithful before him upon his journey. Then said Christian aloud, "Ho! Ho! So-ho! Wait, and I will be your companion." At that Faithful looked behind him, and Christian cried again, "Wait, wait until I catch up with you." But Faithful answered, "No, my life depends on it, for the avenger of blood is behind me."[42]

At this, Christian was somewhat moved, and using all his strength, he quickly caught up with Faithful and overtook him, so that the last was first. Then Christian smiled proudly because he had gotten ahead of his brother; but not watching his feet carefully, he suddenly stumbled and fell and could not get up again until Faithful came to help him.[43]

---

[42] There was no police system in Israel. Each family and clan had to avenge the blood of those who were murdered. See Num. 35:9ff.; Deut. 19:6ff. God appointed cities of refuge where the slayer might flee and get a fair trial. Faithful was in a hurry to escape the avenger of blood, which in this case means the consequences of his own sins.

[43] See Matt. 19:30; Prov. 16:18; 1 Cor. 10:12. Keep in mind that Christian was wearing armor. Bunyan is illustrating how much believers need each other as they go through life. See Eccl. 4:9–10; Gal. 6:1.

Then I saw in my dream that they went lovingly on together and had pleasant conversation about all the things that had happened to them on their pilgrimage; and thus Christian began:

CHRISTIAN: My honored and well-beloved brother Faithful, I am glad I have caught up with you and that God has so tempered our spirits that we can walk as companions in this pleasant path.

FAITHFUL: I had thought, dear friend, that I would have your company all the way from our town; but you started before me, so I was forced to come this far alone.

CHRISTIAN: How long did you stay in the City of Destruction before you set out after me on your pilgrimage?

FAITHFUL: Till I could stay no longer; for there was much talk after you were gone that our city would shortly be burned to the ground with fire from heaven.

CHRISTIAN: What! Did your neighbors talk like that?

FAITHFUL: Yes, for a while it was on everybody's tongue.

CHRISTIAN: What! And did no one but you leave to escape the danger?

FAITHFUL: Though there was, as I said, much talk about it, I do not think they really believed it. For in the heat of conversation I heard some of them speak contemptuously of you and your desperate journey (for that's what they called this pilgrimage of yours). But I did believe, and still do, that the end of our city will be with fire and brimstone from above; and therefore I have made my escape.

CHRISTIAN: Did you hear any talk of neighbor Pliable?

FAITHFUL: Yes, Christian, I heard that he followed you till he came to the Swamp of Despond, where, as some said, he fell in. He did not want it known that he had done so, but I am sure he was covered with that kind of dirt.

CHRISTIAN: And what did the neighbors say to him?

FAITHFUL: Since his return he has been greatly ridiculed by all sorts of people; some mock and despise him and scarcely anyone will give him work. He is now seven times worse than if he had never left the city.[44]

CHRISTIAN: But why should they be so set against him, since they also despise the way that he forsook?

FAITHFUL: They say hang him, he is a traitor! He was not true to his profession. I think God has stirred up even his enemies to scoff at him because he has forsaken the way.[45]

CHRISTIAN: Did you talk with him before you left?

FAITHFUL: I met him once in the streets, but he crossed over to the other side, as though ashamed of what he had done. So I didn't speak to him.

CHRISTIAN: Well, when I first set out I had great hopes for that man; but now I fear he will perish in the overthrow of the city, for he is like the true proverb: "The dog is turned to his own vomit again, and the sow that was washed to her wallowing in the mire."[46]

FAITHFUL: Those are my fears for him too, but who can prevent the inevitable?

CHRISTIAN: Well, neighbor Faithful, let us leave him and talk of things that more immediately concern us. Tell me about your experiences on the way, for I know you have encountered some things, or else it will go down as a miracle.[47]

FAITHFUL: I escaped the Swamp that you fell into and got up to the gate without that danger; only I met with one whose name was Wanton, who would like to have done me harm.[48]

---

[44] Jesus uses a similar idea in His parable in Matt. 12:43–45.

[45] Jer. 29:18–19

[46] See 2 Peter 2:22. True Christians are sheep, not dogs and swine. Pliable was not a true believer.

[47] Faithful's experiences were different from Christian's. He escaped some of the trials and faced a different set of temptations. Bunyan shows here that each believer must follow the Lord and not measure himself against other Christians. Faithful met with Wanton, the First Adam, Moses, Discontent, and Shame, none of whom were encountered by his companion.

[48] A temptation to sensual sin. Joseph was tempted by his master's wife and fled from her (Gen. 39:11–13). Bunyan himself was very shy with women, so this particular temptation did not beset him.

CHRISTIAN: It was well you escaped her net. Joseph was tempted by her, and he escaped her as you did; but it almost cost him his life. What did she do to you?

FAITHFUL: You cannot imagine unless you know what a flattering tongue she has. She made every effort to get me to turn aside with her, promising me all kinds of satisfaction.[49]

CHRISTIAN: I bet she did not promise you the satisfaction of a good conscience.

FAITHFUL: You know what I mean; all kinds of carnal and fleshly satisfaction.

CHRISTIAN: Thank God you have escaped her, for the "abhorred of the Lord shall fall" into her trap.[50]

FAITHFUL: Well, I don't know whether I completely escaped her or not.

CHRISTIAN: Why, I trust you did not consent to her desires?

FAITHFUL: No, not to defile myself; for I remembered an old writing that I had seen, which said, "Her steps lead straight to hell." So I shut my eyes so I would not be bewitched by her looks.[51] Then she spoke harshly to me, and I went my way.

CHRISTIAN: Did you meet with any other assault as you traveled?

FAITHFUL: When I came to the foot of the hill called Difficulty, I met a very aged man who asked me who I was and where I was going. I told him that I was a pilgrim going to the Celestial City. Then he said, "You look like an honest fellow; would you be content to live with me for the wages I shall give you?" Then I asked him his name and where he lived. He said his name was the First Adam and that he lived in the town of Deceit.[52] I asked him then what kind of work he had

---

[49] See Prov. 6:24. In Prov. 7 you have a graphic description of this temptation.

[50] Prov. 22:14

[51] Prov. 5:5; Job 31:1

[52] Jesus Christ is the Last Adam; the first man is the First Adam (1 Cor. 15:45). All are born children of the First Adam. Christ by His obedient death on the cross reversed the consequences of Adam's sin and brought salvation

and what wages he would pay. He told me that his work contained many delights and for my wages I should be his heir. I asked him what kind of house he had and what other servants. So he told me that his house contained all the delicious things in the world and that his servants were his children. Then I asked how many children he had. He said he had but three daughters: The Lust of the Flesh, The Lust of the Eyes, and The Pride of Life, and that I should marry them all if I wanted.[53] Then I asked how long he would want me to live with him, and he told me, as long as he lived himself.

CHRISTIAN: Well, what conclusion did you and the old man come to at last?

FAITHFUL: Why, at first I was somewhat inclined to go with the man, for I thought he spoke fairly; but looking at his forehead as I talked with him, I saw written, "Put off the old man with his deeds."[54]

CHRISTIAN: And what then?

FAITHFUL: Then it came burning hot into my mind that whatever he said and however he flattered, when he got me home to his house, he would sell me as a slave. So I told him he could quit talking, for I would not come near the door of his house. Then he reviled me and told me he would send one after me who would make my way miserable. So I turned to leave him; but just as I turned, I felt him take hold of my flesh and give me such a deadly jerk backward that I thought he had pulled part of me after himself. This made me cry, "O wretched man!"[55] and I went on my way up the hill.

(Rom. 5:6–21). The First Adam can still oppose Christians because they have the old nature with them yet. See also Eph. 4:22.

[53]1 John 2:15–17

[54]See Col. 3:9. Just as Jesus left His grave clothes behind at His resurrection, so the Christian leaves "the old man" behind because of his union with Christ in His resurrection. Salvation means the believer now belongs to the Last Adam — Christ — and not the First Adam.

[55]Bunyan's favorite cry again, from Rom. 7:24. He does not want us to forget that the old nature can still cause trouble for the Christian.

Now when I had gotten about halfway up, I looked behind and saw someone coming after me swift as the wind; he overtook me just about where the shelter stands.[56]

CHRISTIAN: Just there did I sit down to rest; but being overcome with sleep, I lost this scroll out of my coat.

FAITHFUL: Wait, good brother, hear me out. As soon as the man overtook me, he knocked me down and I lay there like I was dead. When I came to myself again, I asked him why he had treated me so. He said, "Because of your secret interest in the First Adam." And with that he struck me another deadly blow on the breast and beat me down backward so that I lay at his feet as before. So when I came to myself again, I cried to him, "Have mercy!" But he said, "I don't know how to show mercy," and with that knocked me down again.[57] No doubt he would have killed me, if someone had not come by and told him to stop.

CHRISTIAN: Who told him to stop?

FAITHFUL: I did not know him at first, but as he went by I saw the holes in his hands and his side; then I concluded that he was our Lord.[58] So I went up the hill.

CHRISTIAN: That man who overtook you was Moses. He spares no one, nor does he know how to show mercy to those who break his law.

FAITHFUL: I know it very well; it was not the first time he has met with me. It was he who came to me when I lived securely at home and told me he would burn my house over my head if I stayed there.

CHRISTIAN: But didn't you see the house that stood there on the top of the hill on the side where Moses met you?

---

[56] This is Moses, representing the Law. Because Faithful was interested in the First Adam (the old nature), Moses disciplined him. All of this is an illustration of Rom. 7:7–12. The Puritans believed that the Law had a ministry in the Christian life. It can still convict the believer of his sins.

[57] The Law cannot grant mercy; it can only pronounce judgment. Christ is the only one who can grant mercy and meet the righteous demands of the Law.

[58] The wounds in our Lord's body (John 20:24–29).

FAITHFUL: Yes, and the lions too, before I came to it: but I think the lions were asleep. And because there was so much daylight left, I passed by the porter and came down the hill.[59]

CHRISTIAN: He told me that he saw you go by, but I wish you had stopped at the house, for they would have showed you so many wonderful things that you would never forget. But tell me, did you meet anyone in the Valley of Humility?

FAITHFUL: Yes, I met with Discontent, who tried to persuade me to go back with him; his reason for doing so was that the valley was totally without honor. He told me that to go there was to disobey friends like Pride, Arrogance, Self-conceit, Worldly-glory, and others, who would be offended if I made a fool of myself by wading through this valley.

CHRISTIAN: How did you answer him?

FAITHFUL: I told him that although all these that he named might claim kinship with me—and rightly so, for they were my relatives in the flesh—yet since I became a pilgrim they have disowned me, just as I have rejected them; and therefore it is as though they had never been in my family. I also told him that he had quite misrepresented this valley, for "before honor is humility, and a haughty spirit before a fall."[60] Therefore, said I, I would rather go through this valley to the honor accounted so by the wisest, than choose that which he considered worthy of our affections.

CHRISTIAN: Did you meet with anything else in that valley?

FAITHFUL: Yes, I met with Shame; but of all those I encountered on my pilgrimage, he, I think, bears the wrong name, for he is without shame.[61]

---

[59] Faithful did not fellowship in the local church family as Christian did. Again, each believer's experience is different. While Bunyan strongly believed in the local church, and even pastored one, he did not make it essential to salvation. Note, however, that Christian tells Faithful how much he missed by passing by!

[60] See Prov. 15:33; 16:18; 18:12. Faithful desires the honor that comes only from God.

[61] See Mark 8:38. Shame argues that religion is not a manly thing, that few great people follow it, and that it causes people to act in shameful ways.

CHRISTIAN: Why? What did he say to you?

FAITHFUL: Why he objected to religion itself, saying it was a pitiful, low, sneaking business for a man to care about religion; he said that a tender conscience was an unmanly thing and that a man who watches his words and ways loses the freedom that is rightfully his in this age and makes him look ridiculous. He also objected to religion on the grounds that few mighty, rich, or wise people care about it; they are not foolish enough to risk losing everything for the un- known.[62] He said that most of those who were pilgrims were poor and uneducated. Yes, he went on at this rate about a great many more things: that it was a shame to sit whining and mourning under a sermon, and a shame to come sighing and groaning home; that it was a shame to ask my neighbor's for- giveness for petty faults or to make restitution. He said also that religion made a man seem odd to great people because of its objection to a few vices, which he called by more dignified names, and made a man respect the lower classes because they were in the same religious fraternity. And wasn't this, said he, a shame?

CHRISTIAN: And what did you say to him?

FAITHFUL: Say! I didn't know what to say at first. He kept at me so that my face became red. But at last I began to think about the fact that "that which is highly esteemed among men is abomination in God's sight."[63] And I thought, this Shame tells me what men are, but he tells me nothing about what God or the Word of God is. And then I thought, at the day of judgment we shall not be awarded death or life according to the bullying spirits of this world, but according to the wisdom and law of the Highest. Therefore, thought I, what God says is best, though all the men in the world are against it. Seeing, then, that God prefers a tender conscience; seeing that they who make themselves fools for the kingdom of heaven are wisest;[64] and seeing that the poor man who loves Christ is

---

[62] 1 Cor. 1:26; 3:18; John 7:48; Phil. 3:7–9
[63] Luke 16:15
[64] 1 Cor. 4:10; 1:18–25

richer than the greatest man in the world that hates him, I said, Shame, depart! You are an enemy to my salvation! If I listen to you instead of my sovereign Lord, how can I look him in the face when he returns? If I am ashamed of his ways and servants now, how can I expect his blessing?[65]

But this Shame was a bold villain; I could hardly get rid of him. He kept following me and whispering in my ear about the various things that are wrong with religion. But at last I told him it was futile for him to continue this business; for those things that he disdained, I valued the most. So finally I got past this troublesome one, and when I had gotten rid of him, I began to sing:

> *The trials that those men do meet withal,*
> *That are obedient to the heavenly call,*
> *Are manifold, and suited to the flesh,*
> *And come, and come, and come again afresh;*
> *That now, or sometimes else, we by them may*
> *Be taken, overcome, and cast away.*
> *Oh, let the pilgrims, let the pilgrims then*
> *Be vigilant, and quit themselves like men.*[66]

CHRISTIAN: I am glad, my brother, that you withstood this villain so bravely; for as you have said, I think he has the wrong name. He boldly follows us in the streets and attempts to put us to shame before all men: that is, to make us ashamed of that which is good. But if he was not himself without shame, he would never try to do what he does. But let us still resist him; for despite all his bragging, he only furthers the cause of fools. "The wise shall inherit glory," said Solomon, "but shame shall be the promotion of fools."[67]

FAITHFUL: For help against Shame, I think we must cry to him who would have us be valiant for truth upon the earth.[68]

---

[65] Mark 8:38

[66] See 1 Cor. 16:13. "Quit" is short for "acquit," or "conduct yourselves."

[67] Prov. 3:35

[68] From Jer.9:3. Bunyan used the character Valiant for Truth as one of the most important characters in the second part of *The Pilgrim's Progress,*

CHRISTIAN: You speak the truth. But, tell me, did you meet anyone else in that valley?

FAITHFUL: No, I did not, for I had sunshine all the rest of the way through it, and also through the Valley of the Shadow of Death.

CHRISTIAN: You fared better than I did then. Almost as soon as I entered into that valley, I began a long and dreadful battle with that foul fiend Apollyon; in fact, I thought he was going to kill me, especially when he got me down and crushed me to pieces; for as he threw me, my sword flew out of my hand; he even told me that he had me. But I cried to God, and he heard me and delivered me out of all my troubles.[69] Then I entered into the Valley of the Shadow of Death and had no light for almost half the way through it. Over and over I thought I was going to be killed there, but at last day broke and the sun rose and I went the rest of the way with far more ease and quiet.

Moreover, I saw in my dream that as they went on, Faithful happened to look to one side and saw a man whose name is Talkative walking beside them but at some distance away (for here it was wide enough for them all to walk side by side).[70] He was a tall man and more handsome at a distance than up close. To this man Faithful addressed himself in this manner:

FAITHFUL: Friend, where are you going? To the heavenly country?

TALKATIVE: I am going to that place.

FAITHFUL: Good. Then I hope we may have your company.

TALKATIVE: I will gladly be your companion.

---

published in 1684, telling how Christian's wife and children journeyed to the heavenly city.

[69]Ps. 34:6

[70]See Job 11:2; Prov. 10:19; Titus 1:10, 16. Talkative represents the person who can discuss religious themes but whose personal life is completely without religious character.

FAITHFUL: Come on then, and let us travel together and spend our time discussing things that are profitable.

TALKATIVE: I enjoy talking about worthwhile matters, and I am glad that I have met with those who are inclined the same way; for to tell you the truth, there are only a few who care to spend their time in this manner as they travel; most choose instead to argue about things that don't matter, and that troubles me. [71]

FAITHFUL: That is indeed regretful, for what is more worthy of the use of the tongue and mouth of men on earth than the things of the God of heaven?

TALKATIVE: I like you, for your words are full of conviction. And I will add, what is more pleasant or more profitable than to talk about the things of God? (That is, if a man takes any delight in things that are wonderful.) For instance, if a man enjoys talking about the history or the mystery of things, or if a man loves to talk about miracles, wonders, or signs, where will he find anything more wonderful than that which is recorded in the Holy Scripture?

FAITHFUL: That is true. But our intention should be to profit from such things in our conversation.

TALKATIVE: That is just what I said. For to talk of such things is most profitable; and by doing so, a man may gain knowledge of many things, such as the vanity of earthly things and the benefit of things above. But more particularly, by this a man may learn the necessity of the new birth, the insufficiency of our works, the need of Christ's righteousness, and so forth. By talking, a man may learn what it is to repent, to believe, to pray, to suffer, or the like; he may also learn the great promises and consolations of the gospel, to his own comfort. [72] Further, by this a man may learn to refute false opinions, to confirm the truth, and to instruct the ignorant.

FAITHFUL: I am glad to hear these things from you.

---

[71] 2 Tim. 2:14

[72] Talkative thinks that learning comes primarily from talking. He is ignorant of what Christian and Faithful later call "heart-work": the working of the Spirit of God in the heart, convicting and teaching.

TALKATIVE: Sadly, the lack of such talk is why so few understand the need for faith and the necessity of a work of grace in their soul in order to obtain eternal life; instead, they ignorantly live by the works of the law, which cannot lead a man to the kingdom of heaven.

FAITHFUL: But heavenly knowledge of these matters is the gift of God; no man can attain these things by human means, or only by talking about them.

TALKATIVE: All this I know very well. For a man can receive nothing unless it is given him from heaven; all is of grace, not of works. I could give you a hundred scriptures that confirm this.[73]

FAITHFUL: Well then, what shall we talk about?

TALKATIVE: Whatever you want. I will talk of things heavenly or things earthly; things moral or things evangelical; things sacred or things profane; things past or things to come; things foreign or things at home; things essential or things circumstantial; provided that all this is done to our profit.

Now Faithful began to marvel at what he heard. And stepping to Christian—who had been walking all this time by himself—he said softly, "What a brave companion we have! Surely this man will make an excellent pilgrim."[74]

At this, Christian smiled a little and said, "This man with whom you are so taken could, with his tongue, deceive twenty who don't know him."

FAITHFUL: Do you know him then?

CHRISTIAN: Know him! Yes, better than he knows himself.

FAITHFUL: Who is he?

CHRISTIAN: His name is Talkative, and he lives in our town. I'm surprised that you don't know him, but our town is large.

FAITHFUL: Whose son is he? And where does he live?

---

[73] See John 3:27; Eph. 2:8–9. Note that Talkative is quick to quote the Bible and use the correct language, but he is deficient in personal experience. It is all in his head and not in his heart.

[74] Faithful is deceived by Talkative because he judged him by his words alone (Matt. 7:21).

CHRISTIAN: He is the son of Say-well and lives in Prating Row; all who are acquainted with him know him by the name of Talkative. And despite his fine tongue, he is a contemptible fellow.[75]

FAITHFUL: Well, he seems to be a very handsome man.

CHRISTIAN: He seems so to those who are not thoroughly acquainted with him; for he is best abroad; near home he is ugly. Your saying that he is a handsome man brings to mind what I have observed in the work of artists, whose paintings look best at a distance, while up close they are unpleasing.

FAITHFUL: I think you are joking with me.

CHRISTIAN: God forbid that I should jest about such a matter, or that I should accuse anyone falsely! I will tell you more about him. This man enjoys any company and any talk; as he talks with you now, so will he talk when he is in the tavern; and the more he drinks, the more he talks; religion has no place in his heart, or his home, or his behavior; he is all talk, and his religion is his tongue.

FAITHFUL: You don't say! Then I have been greatly deceived by this man.

CHRISTIAN: Deceived! You may be sure of it. Remember the proverb, "They say and do not"; but "the kingdom of God is not in word, but in power."[76] He talks of prayer, of repentance, of faith, and of the new birth; but he only talks of them. I have been with his family and have observed him both at home and abroad; and I know that what I say of him is the truth. His house is as empty of religion as the white of an egg is of flavor.[77] There is neither prayer there, nor sign of repentance for sin; even the animals serve God far better than he. For those who know him, he brings shame and reproach to the name of the Lord; in that end of the town where he lives, he gives religion a bad name.[78] The folks who know him say, "He's a saint abroad and a devil at home." Certainly his poor

---

[75] "Prating" means idle chatter or empty talk.
[76] See Matt. 23:3. Christ's indictment of the Pharisees. Also see 1 Cor. 4:20.
[77] Job 6:6
[78] Rom. 2:24

family finds it so; he is rude and abusive and so unreasonable with his servants that they never know how to approach him. Men that have any dealings with him say it is better to deal with a Turk than with him; for they will receive fairer treatment at their hands.[79] This Talkative, if it is possible, will outdo them in defrauding, deceiving, and getting the better of others by unscrupulous means. Besides, he brings up his sons to act the same way; and if he finds in any of them a foolish timidity (for that is what he calls a tender conscience), he calls them fools and blockheads and will not employ them or recommend them to others. I believe that his wicked life has caused many to stumble and fall and that he will, if God does not prevent it, cause the ruin of many more.

FAITHFUL: Well, my brother, I have to believe you; not only because you say you know him, but also because you look at men as a Christian. Also, I do not believe you say these things out of malice, but because they are true.

CHRISTIAN: Had I known him no better than you do, I probably would have thought the same of him as you did at first; and had I heard these things about him only from those who are enemies of religion, I would have thought it slander— something that often falls from bad men's mouths about good men's names and professions—but from my own knowledge, I can prove he is guilty of all these things and more. Besides, good men are ashamed of him; they can neither call him brother nor friend; the very sound of his name makes them blush, if they know him.

FAITHFUL: Well, I see that saying and doing are two different things, and from here on I shall be careful to observe this distinction.[80]

CHRISTIAN: They are two different things indeed, and are as diverse as the soul and the body; for as the body without the soul is but a dead carcass, so are words without deeds.[81]

---

[79]"Turk" was a general name for all barbarians and foreigners who could not be trusted.
[80]Matt. 23:1–4
[81]James 2:26

The soul of religion is the practical part: "Pure religion and undefiled, before God and the Father, is this, To visit the fatherless and widows in their affliction, and to keep himself unspotted from the world."[82] This, Talkative is not aware of; he thinks that hearing and saying will make a good Christian, and thus he deceives his own soul.[83] Hearing is but the sowing of the seed; talking does not prove that the heart and life are fruitful; and let us rest assured that at the day of judgment, men shall be judged according to their fruits.[84] It will not be said then, "Did you believe?" but, "Were you doers or talkers only?" and they shall be judged accordingly.[85] The end of the world can be compared to our harvest; and you know that at harvest men are interested in nothing but the fruit.[86] Not that anything can be accepted that is not the result of faith, but I say this to show you how insignificant the profession of Talkative will be at that time.

FAITHFUL: This brings to mind the words of Moses, when he described the beast that is clean.[87] It is one that has a split hoof and chews the cud; not one that only has a split hoof, or one that only chews the cud. The rabbit chews the cud, but is unclean because he does not have a split hoof. And this is what Talkative resembles: he seeks knowledge by chewing upon the word, but he does not split from his sinful ways; so, like the rabbit, he is unclean.

CHRISTIAN: For all I know you have spoken the true gospel sense of those texts. And I will add another thing. Paul calls some men, and those great talkers too, "sounding brass and tinkling cymbals"; that is, as he expounds in another place, "things without life, giving sound."[88] Things without

---

[82] James 1:27

[83] James 1:26

[84] Matt. 7:16; 13:23

[85] James 1:22

[86] Matt. 13:30

[87] See Lev. 11; Deut. 14. This is a fine example of how the Puritans "spiritualized" the Old Testament Scriptures to find practical guidance for daily life.

[88] 1 Cor. 13:1–3; 14:7

life are those things without the true faith and grace of the gospel; and consequently, such things shall never enter the kingdom of heaven among those who are the children of life; even though they sound, by their talk, as if they were the tongue or voice of an angel.

FAITHFUL: Well, I was not overly fond of his company before, but now I am truly sick of it. How can we get rid of him?

CHRISTIAN: Take my advice and do as I tell you and you will find that he will soon be sick of your company too, unless God touches his heart and turns it.

FAITHFUL: What would you have me do?

CHRISTIAN: Go to him and enter into some serious discussion about the power of religion; and when he has agreed with you, for he will, then ask him point-blank whether this power has been established in his heart, house, or behavior.

Faithful stepped forward again and said to Talkative, "How are you doing?"

TALKATIVE: Well, thank you. I thought we would have talked a great deal by this time.

FAITHFUL: Well, if you will, we will go to it now; and since you left it with me to state the question, let it be this: How can you tell when the saving grace of God is in the heart of man?

TALKATIVE: I see that our talk must be about the power of things. Well, it is a very good question, and I am willing to answer you. First, and in brief, when the grace of God is in the heart, it cries out against sin. Second—

FAITHFUL: Wait! Hold on! Let's consider one thing at a time. I think you should say instead that grace evidences itself by causing the soul to abhor its own sin.

TALKATIVE: Why, what difference is there between crying out against and abhorring sin?

FAITHFUL: Oh, a great deal. A man may cry out against sin, as a general policy, but he cannot abhor it unless he has a godly hatred of it. I have heard many cry out against sin in the pulpit, who still live with it in the heart, home, and behavior. Joseph's master's wife cried out with a loud voice, as though she were very holy; but she would willingly have committed adultery with him.[89] Some cry out against sin even as the mother playfully cries out against her child in her lap, calling her a naughty girl, and then begins hugging and kissing her.

TALKATIVE: You lie in wait to catch me, I see.

FAITHFUL: No, I just want to set things straight. Now what is the second thing by which you would prove the existence of a work of grace in the heart?

TALKATIVE: Great knowledge of gospel mysteries.

FAITHFUL: This sign should have been first; but first or last, it is also false; for knowledge, great knowledge, of the mysteries of the gospel may be obtained, and yet there may be no work of grace in the soul. Yes, a man may have all knowledge and still not be a child of God.[90] Christ said, "Do you know all these things?" and the disciples answered, "Yes." Then he added, "Blessed are you if you do them."[91] The blessing is not in the knowing, but in the doing.[92] For knowledge is not always accompanied by actions, like the servant who knows what his master wants but does not do it. [93] A man may have the knowledge of angels and still not be a Christian; therefore your sign is not true. Indeed, to know is a thing that pleases talkers and boasters; but to do is that which pleases God. Not that the heart can be good without knowledge; for without that, the heart is nothing. There is knowledge and there is knowledge: knowledge that knows about things; and knowledge that is accompanied with the grace of faith and love, which causes a man to do the will of God from the heart. The first of these will satisfy the talker; but the true Christian is not content without the other. "Give me understanding, and I shall keep thy law; yea, I shall observe it with my whole heart."[94]

---

[89]Gen. 39:7–23
[90]1 Cor. 13:2
[91]John 13:12–17
[92]Eph. 6:6; James 1:25
[93]Luke 12:41–48
[94]Ps. 119:34

TALKATIVE: You are trying to trip me up again. This is not edifying.[95]

FAITHFUL: Well, if you please, give me another sign of this work of grace for our discussion.

TALKATIVE: No, for I see we shall not agree.

FAITHFUL: If you will not, then will you let me do so?

TALKATIVE: Feel free to do so.

FAITHFUL: A work of grace in the soul is evident both to him who has it and to those standing by.

The one who has it is convicted of sin, especially of the defilement of his nature and the sin of unbelief (for which he is sure to be damned if he does not find mercy at God's hand by faith in Jesus Christ).[96] This conviction causes him sorrow and shame for his sin; moreover, it reveals to him his need to make himself right with the Savior of the world, which makes him hunger and thirst for God; and it is this hungering and thirsting for salvation that God has promised to satisfy.[97] Now, his joy and peace are equivalent to the strength or weakness of his faith in his Savior, as are his love of holiness and his desire to know more of the Savior and serve him in this world. But though it evidences itself to him in this way, seldom is he able to conclude that this is a work of grace, because his corruption and his abused reason make him misjudge this matter; therefore a very sound judgment is required before he can conclude with assurance that this is a work of grace.

To others, it is evident in other ways:

1. By an experiential confession of his faith in Christ.[98]

2. By a life that answers to that confession; that is, a life of holiness—holiness of heart, holiness of family (if he has a family), and holiness of behavior in the world.[99] Such holi-

---

[95]"To build up spiritually" (Rom. 15:2).

[96]Mark 16:16; John 16:8–9; Rom. 7:24

[97]See John 4:42; 1 John 4:14; Ps. 38:18; Jer. 31:19; Matt. 5:6; Acts 4:12; Gal. 1:15–16; Rev. 21:6

[98]That which is experienced in the life personally. "Existential" would be the philosopher's word.

[99]Ps. 50:23; Ezek. 20:43–44; 36:25; Matt. 5:8; John 14:15; Rom. 10:9–10; Phil. 1:27; 3:17–20

ness teaches him to abhor his own sin, and this he does in private; to suppress sin in his family; and to promote holiness in the world—not only in words, as a hypocrite or talkative person may do, but in a practical subjection, in faith and love, to the power of the Word. And now, sir, as to this brief description of the work of grace and the evidence of it, if you have any objection, object; if not, then may I raise a second question?

TALKATIVE: No, it is not for me to object, but to listen. So give me your second question.

FAITHFUL: It is this: Do you experience the first part of this description of the work of grace? And do your life and behavior testify to this? Or is your religion in word or in tongue, and not in deed and truth?[100] And if you do desire to answer me in this, say no more than you know the God above will say "Amen" to and only that which your conscience can justify; "For it is not the one who commends himself who is approved, but the one whom the Lord commends."[101] Besides, it is very wicked to say "I am thus and thus" when my behavior and all my neighbors tell me I lie.

At first Talkative began to blush; but then regaining his poise, he replied thus:

TALKATIVE: You come now to experience, conscience, and God, and to appeal to him to judge what is said. This kind of discussion I did not expect; nor am I disposed to answer such questions, because I do not consider myself bound to do so, unless you are assuming the role of a catechiser; and even if you did that, I might still refuse to make you my judge. But tell me, will you, why you ask me such questions?

FAITHFUL: Because I saw you were eager to talk. Besides, to tell you the truth, I have heard that you are a man whose religion is all talk and that your behavior says that what you profess with your mouth is a lie. They say you bring disgrace to the people of God and that religion fares the worse

---

[100]See 1 John 3:18. To love "in tongue" means to love without sincerity or truth.
[101]2 Cor. 10:18

because of your ungodly behavior;[102] they say that some have already stumbled because of your wicked ways and that more are in danger of being destroyed by them; your religion and the tavern and covetousness and uncleanness and swearing and lying and bad company will be judged together. There is a proverb, said of a whore: that she is a shame to all women. So are you a shame to all professing Christians.

TALKATIVE: Since you are ready to listen to reports and to judge so rashly, I can only conclude that you are an ill-tempered man who is not fit to converse with. Farewell.

Then Christian came up and said to his brother, "I told you what would happen: your words and his lusts could not agree; he would rather leave your company than change his life. But he is gone, and I say, let him go; it is his loss. He has saved us the trouble of leaving him; as he is, he would have been a hindrance to us. Besides, the apostle says, 'From such withdraw thyself.'"[103]

FAITHFUL: I am glad we had this little discussion with him, though, for perhaps he will think of it again sometime. However, I have been forthright with him and so I am innocent of his blood if he perishes.[104]

CHRISTIAN: You did well to talk as plainly to him as you did; there is little of this faithful dealing with men nowadays, and that makes religion distasteful to many;[105] for such talkative fools whose religion is only in word, and whose behavior is corrupt (yet being often admitted into the fellowship of the godly),[106] do puzzle the world, blemish Christianity, and grieve the sincere. I wish that all men would deal with them as you have done. Then they would either be made more

---

[102]See Jude 12–16. Professed Christians who can talk, but who do not obey, bring defilement and disgrace to the people of God.
[103]See 1 Tim. 6:5. The Puritans practiced church discipline and withdrew fellowship from sinning members.
[104]Acts 20:26; Ezek. 33:1–9
[105]The Puritans feared shallow conversions and sham religious experiences.
[106]Christian remembers the interviews at the Palace Beautiful, when he had to give an account of his conversion and Christian life. The Puritans looked with disfavor upon "easy church membership."

conformable to religion or the company of saints would be too hot for them.

Then Faithful said:

How Talkative at first lifts up his plumes!
How bravely doth he speak! How he presumes
To drive down all before him! But so soon
As Faithful talks of heart-work, like the moon
That's past the full, into the wane he goes.
And so will all, but he that heart-work knows.[107]

Thus they went on talking of what they had seen on the way, and so made that part of the journey easy, which would, otherwise, no doubt, have been tedious, for now they went through a wilderness.

When they were almost out of this wilderness, Faithful happened to look back and spied someone coming after them, and he recognized him. "Oh!" said Faithful, "Look who comes yonder!" Then Christian looked and said, "It is my good friend Evangelist." "And my good friend too," said Faithful, "for it was he who told me the way to the gate."[108] Now Evangelist had caught up with them and greeted them:

EVANGELIST: Peace be with you, dearly beloved, and peace be with those who have helped you.

CHRISTIAN: Welcome, welcome, my good Evangelist! The sight of your face reminds me of your former kindness and your work for my eternal good.

FAITHFUL: A thousand times welcome! Your company, O sweet Evangelist, how desirable it is to us poor pilgrims!

EVANGELIST: How have you fared, my friends, since I saw you last? What have you met with, and how have you behaved yourselves?

---

[107]"Heart-work" is the work of God in the human heart. Talkative had the right words on his lips, but he lacked a heart experience of God's grace.
[108]This is the third appearance of Evangelist. He met Christian at the beginning of the pilgrimage to instruct him in the way to the cross. He met him after Christian's failure to correct his errors at the Hill Legality. Now he meets the two pilgrims to prepare them for the trials they will endure in Vanity Fair. Bunyan sees the evangelist not only as one who wins the lost, but also as one who teaches and helps guide believers in the right way.

Then Christian and Faithful told him of all the things that had happened to them along the way, and how, and with what difficulty, they had arrived at that place.

EVANGELIST: I am glad, not that you have met with trials, but that you have been victors and that you have, despite many weaknesses, continued in the way to this very day.[109]

I say, I am glad of this, and that for my own sake as well as yours. I have sowed, and you have reaped; and the day is coming when both he that sowed and they that reaped shall rejoice together; that is, if you hold out, for in due time you shall reap, if you faint not.[110] The crown is before you, and it is an incorruptible one; so run that you may obtain it.[111] Some set out for this crown, and after they have gone far for it, another comes in and takes it from them; hold on to what you have, and let no man take your crown. You are not yet out of the devil's range; you have not resisted with your own blood; let the kingdom be always before you, and believe steadfastly in those things that are invisible.[112] Let nothing that is on this side of the other world become a part of you; and above all, watch out for the lusts of your own hearts, for they are deceitful and desperately wicked; endure with determination, for you have all the power in heaven and earth on your side.[113]

Christian thanked him for his exhortation and told him they would like him to speak further for their help the rest of the way, for they knew he was a prophet and could tell them of things that might happen to them and how they might resist and overcome those things. Faithful seconded this request.

EVANGELIST: My sons, you have heard in the words of the gospel that you must pass through many tribulations to

---

[109]See Acts 26:22. Continuing in the faith is proof of true salvation.

[110]John 4:36; Gal.6:9

[111]In 1 Cor. 9:24–27 Paul compares himself to an athlete who must discipline himself and obey the rules if he is to win the prize. The Greek athletes won an olive branch crown that faded. The obedient Christian wins a crown that will never perish (Rev. 3:11).

[112]Heb. 12:4; 2 Cor. 4:18; Heb. 11:27

[113]Jer. 17:9; Isa. 50:7; Luke 9:51; Matt. 28:18

enter into the kingdom of heaven.[114] And, again, that in every city you face prison and hardship;[115] and therefore you cannot expect to go long on your pilgrimage without them, in one form or other. You have already found some of the truth of these testimonies, and more will immediately follow; for now, as you see, you are almost out of this wilderness, and therefore before long you will enter a town that you will soon see before you; and in that town you will be harshly attacked by enemies who will try to kill you; and you may be sure that one or both of you must seal your testimony with blood; but be faithful unto death, and the King will give you a crown of life.[116] He who shall die there, although his death will be unnatural and his pain perhaps great, will have the better of his fellow—not only because he will arrive at the Celestial City sooner, but because he will escape many miseries that the other will meet with on the rest of his journey. But when you have come to the town and have found fulfilled what I have told you, then remember your friend; behave like men and commit yourselves to your faithful Creator and continue to do good.[117]

---

[114] Acts 14:22
[115] This was Paul's testimony in Acts 20:23.
[116] See Rev. 2:10. This statement all but announces that Faithful is the one who will lay down his life.
[117] 1 Peter 4:19

When Bunyan was a young man, he visited the great fair held at Stourbridge. The Moot Hall, still standing in Bunyan's hometown of Elstow, was also the scene of much buying and selling in Bunyan's day. Vanity Fair represents the world and all its activities—the vanity or emptiness of the human life—apart from God. The merchandise offered at the fair includes all the things that unconverted people live for. And since Satan is the god and prince of this world, he is the originator and the director of Vanity Fair.

In the things that happen at Vanity Fair, Bunyan sees Christian and Faithful sharing the experiences of the first apostles; he also bases some of this section on his own many court trials, as well as the trials of the Puritans in general. For example, Lord Hate-good is probably patterned after the judges who tried Bunyan and the other Puritans. Judge George Jeffreys was one of the worst, and Bunyan himself was tried by Sir John Keelynge. The king's courts were not favorable to the Puritan position.

hen I saw in my dream that when Christian and Faithful had emerged from the wilderness, they soon saw a town ahead of them, and the name of that town was Vanity; and at the town there was a fair, called Vanity Fair, which went on all the year long. It was named Vanity Fair because all that was sold there was vain or worthless, and all who came there were vain. As the wise saying goes, "all that cometh is vanity."[1]

This fair was no newly established business, but a thing of long-standing. I will show you how it originally began.

Almost five thousand years ago there were pilgrims walking to the Celestial City, as these two honest persons were; and Beelzebub, Apollyon, and Legion,[2] with their companions, seeing that the pilgrims always passed through this town of Vanity, decided to set up a fair here that would last all year long, where they would sell all sorts of vanity: houses, lands, trades, places, honors, promotions, titles, countries, kingdoms, lusts, pleasures, and delights of all sorts, such as prostitutes, wives, husbands, children, masters, servants, lives, blood, bodies, souls, silver, gold, pearls, and precious stones.[3]

At this fair one could always see jugglers, cheats, games, plays, fools, mimics, tricksters, and scoundrels of every kind. Here one also could see, without charge, thefts, murders, adulteries, liars, and things of scarlet.[4] *(movies)*

And as in other fairs of less importance where there are several rows and streets with proper names where wares are sold, so here you had rows and streets (namely, countries and kingdoms) where the wares of this fair could be found. Here was the Britain Row, the French Row, the Italian Row, the Spanish Row, the German Row, where several sorts of vanities

---

[1]Ps. 62:9; Eccl. 1:2, 14; 2:11, 17; 11:8; Isa. 40:17

[2]All names for Satan and his helpers. "Legion" comes from Mark 5:9, the "legion" of demons that lived in the man.

[3]Bunyan is drawing upon the apostle John's description of "Babylon the great" in Rev. 18:11–14.

[4]See Rev. 17:3–4; 18:12, 16 for the significance of this color.

were sold. But just as one commodity is the most popular at other fairs, so it was in this fair, for here Rome and her merchandise were greatly promoted; only our English nation and a few others have taken a dislike to it.[5]

Now, as I said, the path to the Celestial City passed right through this town where this fair was kept; and if anyone wanted to go to the city and yet not go through this town, he must "leave this world."[6] The Prince of princes himself,[7] when he was here, passed through this town, and that was on a fair day too; and I believe it was Beelzebub, the chief lord of this fair, who invited him to buy some of his vanities; yes, he said he would make him lord of the fair if he would only worship him as he went through the town. And Beelzebub took him from street to street and showed him all the kingdoms of the world so that he might, if possible, allure the Blessed One to lower himself and buy some of his vanities; but the Blessed One was not interested in the merchandise and left the town without spending one cent on these vanities.

This fair, therefore, was an ancient thing, of long-standing, and a very large fair; and these pilgrims, as I said, had to pass through it. But when they entered the fair, all the people got excited, and the town was soon in an uproar around them. There were several reasons for this:

First, the pilgrims' clothing was different from any worn by those who were trading at the fair.[8] Therefore, the people stared at them rudely: some said they were fools, some said they were madmen, and some said they were outlandish.[9]

---

[5]Bunyan is referring to England's break with Rome during the reign of Henry VIII.

[6]1 Cor. 5:10

[7]Jesus Christ was offered the kingdoms and glory of the world, but refused them (Matt. 4:8–10). Satan promised to make Him "lord of the fair," but He obeyed His Father and resisted Satan. See also Luke 4:5–8.

[8]God's righteousness makes believers stand out from the crowd. See 1 Cor. 4:9–10; Job 12:4.

[9]"Outlandish" means "from outside the land," therefore different from us and not as good as we are!

Second, just as they had doubts about their apparel, so they were uncertain of their speech, for few could understand what they said.[10] Christian and Faithful spoke the language of Canaan, but those who ran the fair were the men of this world; so from one end of the fair to the other they seemed like barbarians to each other.[11]

Third, and this greatly amused the merchants, these pilgrims were not interested in any of their wares;[12] they didn't even want to look at them; and if they called upon them to buy, they would put their fingers in their ears and cry, "Turn away mine eyes from beholding vanity," and look upward, signifying that their business was in heaven.[13]

One, noticing the conduct of the men, said to them mockingly, "What would you buy?" They looked at him gravely and answered, "We buy the truth."[14] This gave them even more reason to despise the men; some mocked them, some reproached them, and some called upon others to attack them. At last this caused a great commotion in the fair, so much so that there was total disorder.[15] Presently word was brought to the governor of the fair, who quickly came down and deputized some of his most trusted friends to take these two men into custody and question them. So the men were brought to trial, and those who examined them asked where they came from, where they were going, and why they were wearing such unusual clothing. The men told them that they were pilgrims and strangers in the world,[16] that they were

---

[10] The "language of Canaan" is the language of God's people. See Neh. 13:24; 1 John 4:5–6.

[11] 1 Cor. 2:7–8; 14:11

[12] The Christian is not attracted by or interested in the things of this world (1 John 2:15–17).

[13] Ps. 119:37; Phil. 3:20–21

[14] Prov. 23:23

[15] The entire scene in the fair is based on the riot in Ephesus caused by Paul's ministry and the opposition of the silversmiths (Acts 19:23–41).

[16] The Old Testament saints and the New Testament believers looked upon themselves as strangers to this world and pilgrims on the way to the heavenly city. See Heb. 11:13–16; 1 Peter 2:11.

going to their own country, which was the heavenly Jerusalem, and that they had given the men of the town and the merchants no reason to abuse them or hinder their journey, except that when one asked them what they would buy, they said they would buy the truth. But those who had been appointed to examine them believed them to be nothing other than madmen or those who had come to cause confusion in the fair. So they beat them and smeared them with dirt and put them into a cage to make a spectacle of them to all who were at the fair.[17]

> Behold Vanity Fair! the pilgrims there
> Are chained and stoned beside;
> Even so it was our Lord passed here,
> And on Mount Calvary died.

There they lay for some time and were the objects of any man's sport, or malice, or revenge, while the governor of the fair laughed at all that happened to them. But because Christian and Faithful were patient and did not return evil for evil,[18] instead giving good words for bad and kindness for injuries done, some men in the fair that were more observant and less prejudiced than the rest began to reprimand and blame the baser ones[19] for their continual abuses to the two men; they therefore flew at them in anger, considering them as bad as the men in the cage and telling them that they seemed to be their confederates and should share their misfortunes. The others replied that for all they could see, the men were quiet and sober and intended nobody any harm, and that there were many who traded in their fair who deserved to be put into the cage more than the two men they had abused.

Thus after various words had been exchanged on both sides (during which the two men behaved wisely and soberly), they fell to fighting among themselves and injuring one another. Then these two poor men were taken to court again

---

[17] 1 Cor. 4:9

[18] They were obeying Rom. 12:17–21 and 1 Peter 3:9.

[19] Just the kind of people to start a riot (Acts 17:5).

and charged with being guilty of causing the latest trouble in the fair. So they beat them mercilessly and led them in chains up and down the fair as an example to others, lest any should speak in their behalf or join them. But Christian and Faithful behaved even more wisely and bore the humiliation and shame with so much meekness and patience that they won several of the men in the fair to their side (though few in comparison to the rest). This made the others so enraged that they decided the two men should die for what they had done and for deluding the men of the fair.

Then they returned the men to the cage and fastened their feet in the stocks, until further orders should be given.[20]

Here Christian and Faithful recalled what they had heard from their faithful friend Evangelist and were strengthened, for their sufferings confirmed what he had told them would happen to them. They also comforted each other that whoever was chosen to suffer should be blessed; therefore, each man secretly wished that he might have that honor; but they committed themselves to the all-wise will of the one who rules all things, content to abide in their present condition until he should will otherwise.

Finally a time was set for their trial, and they were brought before their enemies and arraigned. The judge's name was Lord Hate-good. Their indictment was the same as before, with a slight variation in form, and the basic contents stated:

"That they are enemies of and disturbers of their trade; that they have caused commotion and dissension in the town and have won a certain party to their own dangerous opinions, in contempt for the law of their prince."[21]

---

[20] Paul and Silas experienced this in Philippi (Acts 16:24).

[21] A reference to the revolt of the silversmiths in Ephesus, who were in danger of losing their trade (Acts 19:25). Because the Puritans would not conform to the state church, they were considered heretics and causes of division. Bunyan's indictment in 1661 was that he was a disturber who refused to cooperate with the established religion. But Hopeful was converted through their witness.

Now, Faithful, play the man, speak for thy God:
Fear not the wickeds' malice; nor their rod!
Speak boldly, man, the truth is on thy side:
Die for it, and to life in triumph ride.

Then Faithful began to answer their charges, saying that he had only opposed that which had opposed him who is higher than the highest. "And as for disturbance," he said, "I make none, being myself a man of peace; the parties that were won to us were won by our truth and innocence, and they have only turned from the worse to the better. And as to the king you talk of, since he is Beelzebub, the enemy of our Lord, I defy him and all his angels."

Then it was proclaimed that those who had anything to say for their lord the king against the prisoner at the bar should appear and give their evidence. So three witnesses came in, namely, Envy,[22] Superstition, and Pickthank.[23] They were then asked if they knew the prisoner at the bar, and what they had to say for their lord the king against him.

Then Envy stood up and said, "My Lord, I have known this man a long time and will attest under oath before this honorable bench that he is—"

JUDGE: Hold on a moment! Administer the oath.

So they swore him in.

Then he said, "My Lord, this man, regardless of his name, is one of the vilest men in our country. He does not respect prince or people, law or custom,[24] but does all he can to impress others with his disloyal notions, which he calls principles of faith and holiness. And I heard him once myself affirm that Christianity and the customs of our town of Vanity were diametrically opposed and could not be reconciled. By which, my Lord, he not only condemns all our good deeds, but also us for doing them.

JUDGE: Have you any more to say?

---

[22] Matt. 27:18

[23] "Pickthank" means to win favor by flattery and talebearing.

[24] The early apostles were accused of breaking Roman law and custom (Acts 16:20–21; 17:7).

ENVY: My Lord, I could say much more, only I don't want to weary the court.[25] Yet if, when the other gentlemen have given their evidence, there is not enough to convict him, I will enlarge my testimony against him.

So he was told to stand by. Then they called Superstition and told him to look at the prisoner; they also asked what evidence he had for their lord the king against the man. Then they swore him in and he began.

SUPERSTITION: My Lord, I don't know this man very well, nor do I want to; however, from some conversation I had with him the other day, I do know that he is a troublemaker;[26] for while talking with him, I heard him say that our religion was worthless and by no means pleasing to God. Your Lordship very well knows that by saying this he means that we worship in vain, that we are still in our sins, and finally shall be damned; and that is what I have to say.[27]

Then Pickthank was sworn in and told to state what he knew in behalf of their lord the king against the prisoner at the bar.

PICKTHANK: My Lord, and gentlemen, I have known of this fellow for a long time, and have heard him say things that ought not to be said; for he has reviled our noble prince Beelzebub, and has spoken contemptuously of his honorable friends, the Lord Old Man, the Lord Carnal Delight, the Lord Luxurious, the Lord Desire of Vain-glory, my old Lord Lechery, Sir Having Greedy, along with all the rest of our nobility; and he has said, moreover, that if all men believed as he did, not one of these noblemen would dwell in this town any longer. Besides, he has not been afraid to speak against you, my Lord, who are now his judge, calling you an ungodly villain and many other vilifying terms, with which he has slandered most of the gentlemen of our town.

---

[25] Acts 24:4

[26] Paul was accused of this (Acts 24:5).

[27] When Paul preached at Lystra, he told the people that they should "turn from these vanities unto the living God," and as a result the mob stoned him (Acts 14:8ff.). The result here is that Faithful is slain.

When Pickthank had told his tale, the judge directed his speech to the prisoner at the bar, saying, "You renegade, heretic, and traitor, have you heard what these honest gentlemen have witnessed against you?"

FAITHFUL: May I say a few words in my own defense?[28]

JUDGE: Sir, sir, you deserve to die; yet so that all men may see our fairness to you, let us hear what you, vile renegade, have to say.[29]

FAITHFUL: First, then, in answer to what Mr. Envy has said, I never said anything but this: That any rule, or laws, or custom, or people that are against the Word of God are diametrically opposed to Christianity. If I have spoken amiss in this, convince me of my error, and I am ready to recant before you.[30]

As to the second, Mr. Superstition and his charge against me, I said only this: That a Divine faith is required in the worship of God; but there can be no Divine faith without a Divine revelation of the will of God. Therefore, anything that is done in the worship of God that is not in agreement with Divine revelation must be done by a human faith, which will not bring eternal life.

As to what Mr. Pickthank has said, I say (avoiding terms that would accuse me of reviling and the like) that the prince of this town and his attendants, named by this gentleman, are more fit for hell than for this town and country; and so the Lord have mercy upon me!

Then the judge called to the jury, who had been standing by, listening and observing: "Gentlemen of the jury, you see this man who has caused such a great uproar in this town.[31] You have also heard the testimony of these worthy gentlemen against him. Also you have heard his reply and confession.

---

[28] Paul said this when facing the Jewish mob (Acts 22:1).

[29] This was the mob's sentence on Paul (Acts 22:22). The judge is prejudiced before the trial is ended.

[30] In this trial scene Bunyan combines elements from the trials of Jesus and of Paul (John 18:23).

[31] There was a citywide uproar in Ephesus (Acts 19:28ff.).

You must now decide whether he is to live or die; but first I think it proper to instruct you in our law.[32]

"There was an Act ordered in the days of Pharaoh the Great, servant to our prince, so that those of a contrary religion should not multiply and grow too strong; this provided that their males should be thrown into the river. There was also an Act carried out in the days of Nebuchadnezzar the Great, another of our prince's servants, ordering that whoever would not fall down and worship his golden image should be thrown into a fiery furnace. There was also an Act in the days of Darius that ruled that whoever, at a certain time, called upon any god but him should be cast into the lions' den. Now this rebel has broken the substance of these laws, not only in thought (which is bad enough), but also in word and deed, which is intolerable.

"In the case of Pharaoh, his law was based upon a supposition, to prevent mischief, since no crime was yet apparent; but here a crime is apparent. In regard to the second and third instances, you can see that he argues against our religion; and for the treason he has confessed to, he deserves to die."

Then the jury, whose names were Mr. Blind-man, Mr. No-good, Mr. Malice, Mr. Love-lust, Mr. Live-loose, Mr. Heady, Mr. High-mind, Mr. Enmity, Mr. Liar, Mr. Cruelty, Mr. Hate-light, and Mr. Implacable, went out to deliberate;[33] each one gave his private verdict against Faithful, and afterward they unanimously found him guilty. First, among themselves, Mr. Blind-man, the foreman, said, "I see clearly that this man is a heretic." Then said Mr. No-good, "Rid the earth of the fel-

---

[32] The judge uses the Bible to try to prove his case! Pharaoh ordered the Jewish baby boys drowned (Exod. 1); Nebuchadnezzar commanded a unified worship (Dan. 3); and Darius demanded all prayer to be offered to him (Dan. 6). The Puritans lived at a time when the king wanted a uniform religion, and they refused to conform. The judge uses only those facts that prove his case; he does not mention that in all three examples it was the minority of dissenters who won!

[33] See 2 Tim. 3:4. It is a stacked jury, to say the least!

low!"[34] "I agree," said Mr. Malice, "for I hate the very sight of him." Then Mr. Love-lust said, "I never could stand him." "Nor I," said Mr. Live-loose, "for he was always condemning me." "Hang him, hang him!" said Mr. Heady. "A sorry scrub,"[35] said Mr. High-mind. "My heart rises against him," said Mr. Enmity. "He is a rogue," said Mr. Liar. "Hanging is too good for him," said Mr. Cruelty. "Let us get rid of him," said Mr. Hate-light. Then Mr. Implacable said, "Even if all the world were given to me, I could not accept him; therefore let us immediately bring in a verdict of guilty and a sentence of death." And so they did.

Therefore, Faithful was condemned to the most cruel death that could be invented.

They brought him out then, to punish him according to their law; and first they scourged him, then they buffeted him, then they lanced his flesh with knives; after that they stoned him with stones, then pricked him with their swords; and last of all they burned him to ashes at the stake.[36] And thus came Faithful to his death.

Now I saw that there stood behind the multitude a chariot and a couple of horses, waiting for Faithful, who (as soon as his adversaries had killed him) was taken up into it and immediately carried up through the clouds, with sound of trumpets, the nearest way to the Celestial Gate.[37]

> *Brave Faithful, bravely done in word and deed;*
> *Judge, witnesses, and jury have, instead*
> *Of overcoming thee, but shown their rage;*
> *When they are dead, thou'lt live from age to age.*

But as for Christian, he had some reprieve and was returned to prison. There he remained for a time; but he who overrules all things, having the power of their rage in his own

---

[34] Acts 22:22

[35] An insignificant person.

[36] John 18:31; 19:7; Matt. 26:67; 27:26

[37] This is the way the prophet Elijah went to heaven (2 Kings 2:11). For the Christian, suffering only leads to glory.

hand,[38] enabled Christian to escape them and to continue on his way. And as he went, he sang:

> *Well, Faithful, thou hast faithfully professed*
> *Unto thy Lord; with whom thou shalt be blest,*
> *When faithless ones, with all their vain delights,*
> *Are crying out under their hellish plights:*
> *Sing, Faithful, sing, and let thy name survive;*
> *For though they killed thee, thou art yet alive.*

---

[38] Ps. 76:10

Despite all that has happened at Vanity Fair, Christian sees God at work. Faithful's death praised God and won Hopeful, and God restrained the men so that they did not kill Christian but permitted him to go.

Now Christian has a new and different companion. Again, Bunyan has reminded us that not all conversions are alike and not all Christians are alike. However, the personalities and experiences of the two men are complementary, not contradictory.

On this leg of the journey, Christian and Hopeful will come to Doubting Castle, indicating that even experienced pilgrims like these two can have times of doubt and despair. Bunyan often had his doubts and times of despair when he was seeking the Lord and the assurance of salvation. He wrote in Grace Abounding: *"I found it hard work now to pray to God, because despair was swallowing me up."*

ow I saw in my dream that Christian did not go on alone, for Hopeful, who had been won to the Lord by the words and behavior of Christian and Faithful in their sufferings at the fair, joined him and promised that he would be his companion. Thus one died to bear testimony to the truth and another rose out of his ashes to be a companion to Christian on his pilgrimage. Hopeful also told Christian that there were many more men in the fair who would eventually follow them.

Shortly after they had left the fair, they overtook someone who was ahead of them, whose name was By-ends.[1] So they said to him, "What country are you from, sir, and how far are you going?" He told them that he came from the town of Fair-speech[2] and was going to the Celestial City, but he did not tell them his name.

"From Fair-speech?" said Christian. "Is there anything good there?"

BY-ENDS: Yes, I hope so.

CHRISTIAN: Tell me, sir, what may I call you?

BY-ENDS: I am a stranger to you, and you to me. If you are going this way, I shall be glad of your company; if not, I must be content.

CHRISTIAN: I have heard of this town of Fair-speech, and as I remember, they say it's a wealthy place.

BY-ENDS: Yes, I assure you that it is, and I have many rich relatives there.

CHRISTIAN: Who are your relatives there, if I may be so bold?

BY-ENDS: Almost the whole town; and in particular, Lord Turn-about, Lord Time-server, Lord Fair-speech (from whose

---

[1] By-ends is one who uses base means to achieve his purposes. The end justifies the means. Just as Pliable and Obstinate left the City of Destruction but did not succeed, so By-ends leaves Vanity Fair but fails to reach the Celestial City. Bunyan keeps reminding us that there are "professors" of religion who are not true possessors.

[2] Prov. 26:25; Rom. 16:18

ancestors that town first took its name), also Mr. Smooth-man, Mr. Facing-both-ways, Mr. Anything; and the parson of our parish, Mr. Two-tongues,[3] was my mother's own brother. To tell you the truth, my great-grandfather was only a boatman, looking one way and rowing another, and I got most of my wealth by the same occupation.[4]

CHRISTIAN: Are you a married man?

BY-ENDS: Yes, and my wife is a very virtuous woman, and is the daughter of a virtuous woman. She was Lady Feigning's daughter; therefore, she came of a very honorable family, and has so much breeding that she knows how to deal with anyone, from prince to peasant. It is true that we differ somewhat in religion from those of the stricter sort, yet only in two small points: first, we never go against the wind and the tide; and second, we are always most zealous when religion walks in silver slippers and when the sun shines and the people applaud what we believe.[5]

Then Christian stepped aside with Hopeful and said, "It occurs to me that this is By-ends of Fair-speech; and if it is, we have in our company one of the most deceitful fellows in this land." Then said Hopeful, "Ask him. I should think he wouldn't be ashamed of his name." So Christian went up to him again and said, "Sir, you talk as if you knew more than anybody else, and if I am not mistaken, I believe I know who you are. Isn't your name Mr. By-ends of Fair-speech?"

BY-ENDS: That is not my name, but it is a nickname given me by some who do not like me; and I must be content to bear it as a reproach, as other good men before me have done.

CHRISTIAN: Did you never give men a reason to call you by this name?

---

[3]Church leaders are not to be double-tongued (1 Tim. 3:8).
[4]Bunyan's humor shows up here: the boatman is "looking one way and rowing another," a perfect description of a double-minded person.
[5]By-ends's theology is simple: always take the easy way in religion. Christian and Faithful had just suffered in Vanity Fair, Faithful giving his life; and By-ends counsels compromise and safety.

BY-ENDS: Never, never! The worst I ever did to give them a reason to call me this was that I was always lucky enough to go with the tide, whatever it was, and thereby gain the advantage; and if things go my way, let me count them a blessing; but the malicious should not therefore heap me with reproach.

CHRISTIAN: I thought you were the man I had heard of; and to tell you what I think, I fear this name belongs to you more than you are willing to admit.

BY-ENDS: Well, if you want to think so, I cannot help it; you will find me good company if you will still let me associate with you.

CHRISTIAN: If you want to go with us, you must go against wind and tide, which, I see, is against your beliefs; you must also own religion when it is in rags, as well as when it is in silver slippers, and stand by it when it is bound in irons, as well as when it is applauded in the streets.

BY-ENDS: You must not impose your beliefs on me, nor lord it over my faith;[6] leave me my freedom, and let me go with you.

CHRISTIAN: Do not take a step further, unless you will do as we do.

"I shall never desert my old principles," said By-ends, "since they are harmless and profitable. If I may not go with you, I must go by myself, until someone overtakes me who will be glad of my company."

Now I saw in my dream that Christian and Hopeful left him and kept their distance in front of him; but one of them, looking back, saw three men following Mr. By-ends, and as they caught up with him, he made a very low bow toward Christian and Hopeful, as though dismissing them.[7] The men's names were Mr. Hold-the-world, Mr. Money-love, and Mr. Save-all, all men that Mr. By-ends had formerly been ac-

---

[6] See 2 Cor. 1:24. People who want to go their own way can appeal to the Bible for support.

[7] By-ends was rude to Christian and Hopeful as he welcomed the three new companions.

quainted with; for when they were young they had been schoolmates and were taught by Mr. Gripe-man, a teacher in Love-gain, which is a town in the county of Coveting in the north. This schoolmaster taught them the art of getting, either by violence, cheating, flattery, lying, or by putting on a guise of religion;[8] and these four gentlemen had learned the art of their master so well that they could have conducted such a school themselves.

Well, when they had greeted each other, Mr. Money-love said to Mr. By-ends, "Who are those two in front of us?" (for Christian and Hopeful were still within view).

BY-ENDS: They are a couple of our distant countrymen who are going on pilgrimage.

MONEY-LOVE: Why didn't they wait so that we could enjoy their company? For all of us, I hope, are going on pilgrimage.

BY-ENDS: We are indeed. But the men in front of us are so rigid, and love their own beliefs so much, and think so little of the opinions of others, that even if a man is ever so godly, if he does not agree with them in all things, they do not want him with them.[9]

SAVE-ALL: That is too bad, but we have read of some who are overly righteous;[10] and such men's rigidness causes them to judge and condemn all but themselves. But tell me, what were the things on which you differed?

BY-ENDS: Why, in their headstrong manner, they believe it is their duty to hurry on their journey in all kinds of weather, and I am for waiting until the wind and tide are with me. They think you should risk all for God, and I believe in taking every advantage to make sure my life and worldly goods are secure.[11] They are for holding to their beliefs, though all other

---

[8] 1 Thess. 2:1–6

[9] The Puritans were criticized for their discipline of life and convictions in matters of faith. The average church member in that day did not take his religious faith seriously.

[10] Eccl. 7:16

[11] Acts 15:26

men are against them; but I am for religion as long as the times and my safety will bear it. They are for religion when it is in rags and held in contempt, but I am for it when it walks in golden slippers in the sunshine and with applause.

MR. HOLD-THE-WORLD: Hold fast to that, good Mr. By-ends; for I consider anyone a fool who, having the freedom to keep what he has, is so unwise as to lose it.[12] Let us be as wise as serpents;[13] it is best to make hay when the sun shines;[14] you see how the bee lies still all winter, and stirs only when she can do so with profit and pleasure. God sometimes sends rain and sometimes sunshine; if they are foolish enough to go through the first, then let us be content to take the fair weather. For my part, I like that religion best that represents the security of God's blessings to us; since God has given us the good things of this life, why would he not want us to keep them for his sake?[15] Abraham and Solomon grew rich in religion. And Job says that a good man shall lay up gold like dust.[16] But he must not have been like the men before us, if they are as you have described them.

MR. SAVE-ALL: I think we are all agreed in this matter, and therefore we don't need to discuss it further.

MR. MONEY-LOVE: No, we need no more words about this matter indeed; for he who believes neither Scripture nor reason (and you see we have both on our side) neither knows his own freedom, nor seeks his own safety.

MR. BY-ENDS: My brothers, we are all going on pilgrimage; and to take our minds off such negative things, let me propose this question:

Suppose a man—a minister or a shopkeeper—should have the opportunity to get the good blessings of this life, but only if he, in appearance at least, becomes extraordinarily

---

[12] Matt. 16:25

[13] Matt. 10:16; Gen. 3:1

[14] This familiar proverb was already over a hundred years old when Bunyan quoted it, having been published in England in 1546.

[15] Acts 14:17; 1 Tim. 6:17

[16] Job 22:24

zealous about some points of religion that he has not concerned himself with before; may he not use this means to attain his end and still be an honest man?

MR. MONEY-LOVE: I see the essential meaning of your question; and with these gentlemen's permission, I will endeavor to formulate an answer. First, to speak to your question as it concerns a minister himself: Suppose a minister, a worthy man, possesses a very small benefice[17] and desires a greater one by far; he now has an opportunity of getting it by being more studious, by preaching more frequently and zealously, and, because the nature of the people requires it, by altering some of his principles; for my part, I see no reason why a man may not do this (provided he has a call), and a great deal more besides, and still be an honest man. For

1. His desire for a greater benefice is lawful (this cannot be contradicted), since it is set before him by Providence; so then he may get it, if he can, without raising questions of conscience.[18]

2. Besides, his desire for that benefice will make him more studious, a more zealous preacher, and thus a better man; yes, it makes him improve himself, which is according to the mind of God.

3. Now as for his complying with the desires of his people, to serve them, by altering some of his principles, this shows that he has a self-denying temperament, a sweet and winning manner, and is all the more fit to function as a minister.

4. I conclude, then, that a minister who changes a small benefice for a great should not be judged as covetous for

---

[17]"Benefice" was an Anglican term referring to the economic benefits attached to a ministry, such as lands, a house, and so forth. Ministers with smaller benefices were often anxious to acquire bigger and better ones, and sometimes resorted to devious means to get them. Puritan ministers lived by faith and did not seek for worldly gain. Of course, there were exceptions in both camps.

[18] See 1 Cor. 10:25–27. Mr. Money-love knows how to use the Bible to support his own ideas!

doing so; but rather, since he has thereby improved himself and his work, he should be counted as one who pursues his call and the opportunity given him to do good.

And now to the second part of the question, which concerns the shopkeeper you mentioned. Suppose such a person has had only a small business, but by becoming religious he may increase the size of his shop, perhaps get a rich wife, or bring more and far better customers to his shop; for my part, I see no reason why this may not be lawfully done. For

1. To become religious is a virtue, no matter by what means a man becomes so.

2. Nor is it unlawful to get a rich wife or more customers to his shop.

3. Besides, the man who gets these by becoming religious, gets that which is good from those who are good by becoming good himself; so here is a good wife, and good customers, and good gain, and all these by becoming religious, which is good; therefore to become religious to get all these is a good and profitable plan.

This answer given by Mr. Money-love to Mr. By-ends's question was applauded by all of them; therefore they concluded that it was wholesome and advantageous. And because they thought no man was able to contradict it, and because Christian and Hopeful were still within the sound of their voices, they agreed to throw the question at them as soon as they overtook them because Christian and Hopeful had opposed Mr. By-ends before. So they called after them, and the two men stopped and waited. But the four decided, as they walked, that old Mr. Hold-the-world, not Mr. By-ends, should propose the question, because they figured Christian's and Hopeful's answer to him would not be subject to the strong feelings that had been aroused between them and Mr. By-ends at their earlier parting.

So they came up to each other, and after a short greeting, Mr. Hold-the-world raised the question to Christian and Hopeful and asked them to answer it if they could.

CHRISTIAN: Even a babe in religion may answer ten thousand such questions. For if it is unlawful to follow Christ for loaves,[19] as it is, how much more abominable is it to make him and religion a stalking-horse[20] to promote themselves or their business. Only heathens, hypocrites, devils, and witches think this way.

1. For when the heathens Hamor and Shechem wanted the daughter and cattle of Jacob and saw that there was no way to get them except by becoming circumcised, they said to their companions: If each of our males is circumcised as they are circumcised, will not their cattle, and their substance, and every beast of theirs be ours? They wanted Jacob's daughter and cattle, and Jacob's religion was the stalking-horse they made use of to get them. Read the whole story.[21]

2. The hypocritical Pharisees were also of this religion; long prayers were their pretense, but to get the widows' houses was their intent; and greater damnation from God was their judgment.[22]

3. Judas the devil was also of this religion; he was religious for the bag of money so that he might possess what was therein; but he was lost, cast away, and the very son of perdition.[23]

4. Simon the witch was of this religion too; for he wanted the Holy Ghost in order to get money; and he was sentenced accordingly from Peter's mouth.[24]

---

[19] See John 6:26–27. The crowd followed Jesus to be fed, not to be made holy.

[20] A stalking-horse is something used to hide a real purpose. Hunters used to hide behind horses to go after game.

[21] See Gen. 34. The sons of Jacob offered to let their sister marry the heathen prince if all the men would be circumcised. The men agreed, and while they were healing, two of Jacob's sons, Simeon and Levi, killed them all. They used their religion as a cover-up for murder.

[22] Luke 20:46–47

[23] Judas was treasurer of the disciple band and kept the bag of money (John 12:6). He was in the habit of taking money out of the bag for himself. Of course, he also sold Christ for thirty pieces of silver. See John 6:70–71; 17:12. "Perdition" means "destruction, waste, or ruin."

[24] See Acts 8:1–24. Originally the term "witch" referred to any person who dabbled in the occult. There were he-witches and she-witches. The term

5. The man who takes up religion for the world will throw away religion for the world; for as surely as Judas resigned the world in becoming religious, so surely did he also sell religion and his Master for the same. Therefore, to answer the question affirmatively, as I see you have done, and to accept such an answer as authentic, is heathenish, hypocritical, and devilish; and you will be rewarded accordingly.

Then they stood staring at one another, but had no way to answer Christian. Hopeful also agreed with the truth of Christian's answer; so there was a great silence among them.[25] Mr. By-ends and his company hesitated and lagged behind so that Christian and Hopeful might go ahead of them. Then said Christian to his friend, "If these men cannot stand before the judgment of men, what will they do with the judgment of God? And if they are silent when dealt with by vessels of clay, what will they do when they are rebuked by the flames of a devouring fire?"[26]

Then Christian and Hopeful went ahead of them again and traveled until they came to a pleasant plain called Ease, where they walked with great contentment; but the plain was very narrow, so they crossed it quickly.[27] Now at the far side of that plain was a little hill called Lucre, and in that hill was a silver mine, which some who had previously passed that way had turned aside to see because of its rarity;[28] but when they got too close to the edge of the pit, the ground gave way

---

simony comes from this event: the offering of money to buy religious power and position.

[25] The silence of spiritual conviction (Rom. 3:19).

[26] Heb. 12:29; Exod. 24:17

[27] God balances the difficulties with delights. But note that the plain was narrow. The Puritans did not approve of too much ease!

[28] *Lucre* is from the Latin, meaning "wealth, profit." Samuel's sons "turned aside after lucre" (1 Sam. 8:3). Church officers were to avoid "filthy lucre" (1 Tim. 3:3, 8). False teachers go after filthy lucre (Titus 1:11). Pastors should serve the Lord willingly, not for money (1 Peter 5:2). The Puritans believed in honest pay for honest toil, but they did not encourage the love of money, which is "the root of all evil" (1 Tim. 6:10).

under them and they were killed;[29] some also had been maimed there and were never the same to their dying day.

Then I saw in my dream that a little off the road, beside the silver mine, stood Demas, calling politely for travelers to come and see; he said to Christian and Hopeful, "Hello there! Come over here and I will show you something."[30]

CHRISTIAN: What could be worthwhile enough to make us leave the way?

DEMAS: There is a silver mine here, and some are digging in it for treasure. If you will come, with very little effort you may richly provide for yourselves.[31]

HOPEFUL: Let us go see.

CHRISTIAN: Not I. I have heard of this place before, and how many have been killed here; and besides that, treasure is a trap to those who seek it,[32] for it hinders them in their pilgrimage.

Then Christian called to Demas, "Isn't this place dangerous? Hasn't it hindered many in their pilgrimage?"[33]

DEMAS: Not very dangerous, except to those who are careless (but he blushed as he said this).

CHRISTIAN: Let us not move a step toward it, but keep on our way.

HOPEFUL: I will guarantee you that when By-ends comes up, if he receives this same invitation, he will turn in there to look at it.

CHRISTIAN: No doubt he will, for his principles lead him that way, and a hundred to one he dies there.

Then Demas called again, saying, "But will you not come over and see?"

---

[29] Matt. 13:22

[30] At one time, Demas had been Paul's fellow worker (Philem. 24); but he left Paul, "having loved this present world" (2 Tim. 4:10). He stands for all who abandon their faith in order to get rich.

[31] The danger of getting rich quick! See Prov. 28:20, 22.

[32] 1 Tim. 6:9

[33] Covetousness is idolatry (Col. 3:5). Bunyan here refers to Israel's backsliding because of her idolatry (Hos.4:16–19; 14:8).

Then Christian rebuked him, saying, "Demas, you are an enemy to the right ways of the Lord of this way, and have been condemned already for your own waywardness by one of His Majesty's judges.[34] Why do you try to bring us into the same condemnation? Besides, if we turn aside at all, our Lord the King will certainly hear of it and will put us to shame, and we desire to stand with boldness before him."

Demas cried that he also was one of their brothers, and that if they would wait a little while, he would walk with them.

CHRISTIAN: What is your name? Is it not the name I have called you?

DEMAS: Yes, my name is Demas; I am the son of Abraham.

CHRISTIAN: I know you. Gehazi was your great-grandfather, and Judas your father; and you have walked in their steps.[35] It is a devilish prank that you use; your father was hanged as a traitor, and you deserve no better reward. You may be assured that when we come to the King, we will tell him about your behavior.

Thus they went their way.

By this time By-ends and his companions were again within sight, and I saw that they went over to Demas the first time he called to them. Now whether they fell into the pit by looking over the brink, or whether they went down to dig, or whether they were smothered in the bottom by the poisonous gases, I am not certain; but I did observe that they were never seen again in the way. Then Christian sang:

> *By-ends and silver Demas both agree;*
> *One calls, the other runs, that he may be*
> *A sharer in his lucre; so these do*
> *Take up in this world, and no further go.*

---

[34] Paul's rebuke to Elymas, the sorcerer (Acts 13:10). Paul also condemns Demas in 2 Tim. 4:10.

[35] Gehazi was the prophet Elisha's servant (2 Kings 4–5). He lied to Naaman, whom Elisha had healed, and took some wealth from him against Elisha's will. He was judged by God for this sin. Judas was the disciple who turned traitor and sold Christ (Matt. 26:14–15; 27:3–5).

Now I saw that just on the other side of this plain the pilgrims came to a place where there stood an old monument, right beside the highway, at the sight of which they were both concerned because of its strange form, for it looked to them like a woman transformed into the shape of a pillar; they stood looking at it for a long time but could not tell what it was. At last Hopeful spied something written on the head of it in an unusual script; but he, being no scholar, called to Christian (for he was well-educated) to see if he could figure out the meaning; so he came and finally found that the words said, "Remember Lot's wife."[36] So he read it to Hopeful, after which they concluded that this was the pillar of salt into which Lot's wife was turned when she was fleeing from Sodom and looked back with a covetous heart. This unexpected and amazing sight gave rise to this conversation between them.

CHRISTIAN: Ah, my brother! This sight came at an opportune time, right after the invitation Demas gave us to come over to view the Hill Lucre; and had we gone over as he desired, and as you were inclined to do, my brother, we would have, for all I know, been like this woman ourselves, a spectacle for those who come after us.

HOPEFUL: I am sorry I was so foolish, and it makes me wonder why I am not like Lot's wife now; for what was the difference between her sin and mine? She only looked back; and I had a desire to go look. Let grace be revered, and let me be ashamed that such desires should ever have been in my heart.

CHRISTIAN: Let us take note of what we see here for our help in the future. This woman escaped one judgment, for she did not die in the destruction of Sodom; yet she was destroyed by another, as we see, for she was turned into a pillar of salt.

HOPEFUL: True. And she may be both a warning and example to us: a warning that we should shun her sin, and an example of what judgment will be ours if we do not heed that

---

[36] Lot's wife disobeyed God, turned back toward Sodom, and became a pillar of salt (Gen. 19:26). See also Luke 17:32.

warning, just as Korah, Dathan, and Abiram, with the two hundred and fifty men that perished in their sin, became a sign or example to others to beware.[37] But above all, I marvel at one thing, and that is how Demas and his companions can stand so confidently looking for that treasure for which this woman, who only looked behind her but did not step one foot out of the way, was turned into a pillar of salt; especially since the judgment which overtook her made her an example within sight of where they are; for they cannot help but see her if they only lift up their eyes.

CHRISTIAN: It is something to be wondered at, and it seems to indicate that their hearts are desperately sinful; and I cannot help but compare them to those who pick pockets in the presence of the judge, or that cut purses right under the gallows.[38] It is said that the men of Sodom "were sinners exceedingly" because they were sinners "before the Lord"; that is, in his eyesight and notwithstanding the kindnesses he had showed them; for the land of Sodom was at that time like the Garden of Eden.[39] This provoked him all the more to jealousy, and made their plague as hot as the fire of the Lord in heaven could make it. And it can logically be concluded then that those who sin within sight of and in spite of such examples set continually before them, to caution them to the contrary, shall be judged the most severely.

HOPEFUL: Doubtless you have spoken the truth; but what a mercy it is that neither you nor I, especially I, have been made an example like this. It is an occasion for us to thank God, to fear him, and always to remember Lot's wife.

---

[37] Korah was an Israelite who led a revolt against Moses. Dathan and Abiram assisted him and were also judged (Num. 16; 26:9–10). The earth opened and swallowed them up.

[38] Many people kept their purses hanging on a belt, and thieves would cut the purses and steal them or empty the contents. It was the usual thing for thieves to pick pockets and steal purses in the huge crowds that attended executions. The fear of being caught and hanged themselves did not seem to stop them.

[39] See Gen. 13:10, 13. Men may not consider us sinners, but it is before God that we are judged.

I saw then that they went on their way to a pleasant river, which David the king called "the river of God," but which John called the "river of the water of life."[40] Now their path lay just along the bank of the river, and here Christian and his companion walked with great delight; they also drank the water of the river, which was pleasant and enlivening to their weary spirits. On the banks of this river, on either side, were green trees that bore all kinds of fruit, and the leaves of the trees had healing qualities.[41] They were delighted with the fruit of these trees, and they ate the leaves to prevent illness from overindulgence and other diseases to which travelers are susceptible. On either side of the river was a meadow filled with beautiful lilies, and it was green all the year long.[42] In this meadow they lay down and slept, for here they could rest safely. When they awoke, they again gathered the fruit of the trees, and drank the water of the river, and then lay down again to sleep. This they did for several days and nights. Then they sang:

> *Behold ye how these crystal streams do glide*
> *(To comfort pilgrims) by the highway side;*
> *The meadows green, besides their fragrant smell,*
> *Yield dainties for them: and he that can tell*
> *What pleasant fruit, yea, leaves, these trees do yield,*
> *Will soon sell all, that he may buy this field.*[43]

So when they felt ready to go on (for they were not, as yet, at their journey's end), they ate and drank and departed.

Now I beheld in my dream that they had not journeyed far when the river and the path separated for a time; they were rather sad about this, but they dared not leave the path. Then the path away from the river became rough, and their feet became tender from walking; "so the souls of the pilgrims

---

[40] This river is another brief period of rest and refreshment. Jesus offers the living water to all who will come and drink. See Ps. 46:4; 65:9; Rev. 22:1; John 7:37–39; Ezek. 47.

[41] A reference to the tree of life in heaven (Rev. 22:2).

[42] The green pastures of Ps. 23:2. See also Isa. 14:30.

[43] Matt. 13:44

were much discouraged because of the way."[44] Therefore, they wished for a better pathway. Now a little ahead of them there was on the left-hand side of the road a meadow, and a set of steps by which to cross over the fence into it; and that meadow is called By-path Meadow.[45] Then Christian said to his friend, "If this meadow lies alongside our pathway, let's go over into it." Then he climbed the steps to see, and, behold, there was a path running along the other side of the fence. "It's just what I was wishing for," said Christian. "Here it is much easier going.[46] Come, good Hopeful, let's go over."

HOPEFUL: But what if this path should lead us out of the way?

CHRISTIAN: That's not likely.[47] Look, doesn't it go along parallel to the pathway?

So Hopeful, being persuaded by his friend, followed him over the fence, and they found this path very easy for their feet. Then, looking ahead, they spied a man walking as they did (and his name was Vain-confidence); so they called out to him and asked him where this path led.[48] He said, "To the Celestial Gate." "Look," said Christian, "didn't I tell you so? See, we are right." So they followed, and Vain-confidence went before them. But behold, night came on and it grew very dark and they lost sight of the man ahead of them.

> *The pilgrims now, to gratify the flesh,*
> *Will seek its ease; but oh! how they afresh*
> *Do thereby plunge themselves new grief into!*
> *Who seek to please the flesh, themselves undo.*

---

[44] A description of the feelings of the Israelites when they were wandering in the wilderness (Num. 21:4). Like Israel, the two pilgrims got into trouble because they wanted a different way and did not submit to God's will.

[45] See Prov. 4:25–27. They had been warned about detours.

[46] This had been the philosophy of By-ends! Take the easiest way! The pilgrims were walking by sight, not by faith (Rom. 14:23).

[47] Christian is overconfident and leads himself and his brother astray. Bunyan adds a note: "Strong Christians may lead weak ones out of the way." Even Peter went astray and led Barnabas into sin (Gal. 2:11–21).

[48] Ps. 118:8

Therefore, the one who was ahead of them, not being able to see the pathway, fell into a deep pit, which was put there purposely by the prince of those grounds to catch vainglorious fools, and he was dashed in pieces by the fall.[49]

Now Christian and Hopeful heard him fall. So they called out, asking what had happened, but there was no answer, only a groaning sound. Then said Hopeful, "Where are we now?" But his companion was silent, afraid that he had led him out of the way; and now it began to rain and thunder and lightning in a dreadful manner, and the pathway began to flood.

Then Hopeful groaned in himself, saying, "Oh, I wish I had kept on my way!"

CHRISTIAN: Who could have thought that this path would lead us out of the way?

HOPEFUL: I was afraid of it from the very first, and that is why I was cautious. I would have spoken plainer, except that you are older than I.

CHRISTIAN: Good brother, don't be offended. I am sorry I have brought you out of the way and put you in such imminent danger. Please forgive me, my brother; I did not do it with any evil intentions.

HOPEFUL: Be comforted, my brother, for I forgive you; and I also believe that this shall be for our good.[50]

CHRISTIAN: I am glad I have a merciful brother with me. But we must not stand here like this. Let's try to go back again.

HOPEFUL: Let me walk in front, good brother.

CHRISTIAN: No, if you please, let me go first, so that if there is any danger I will be the first to encounter it, because it is my fault that we have both left the way.

HOPEFUL: No, you shall not go first. You are upset, and this may cause you to lead us astray again.

Then for their encouragement they heard the voice of one saying, "Let thine heart be towards the highway, even the

---

[49] Isa. 9:16; Prov. 14:12

[50] See Rom. 8:28. This is not an excuse for sin, but it is an encouragement in difficulty.

way that thou wentest, turn again."[51] But by this time the waters had risen greatly, making the pathway back very dangerous. (Then I thought: it is easier to get out of the way when we are in it, than to get in when we are out.) Yet they tried to go back; but it was so dark, and the flood was so high, that in going back they were almost drowned nine or ten times.

Neither could they, with all the skill they had, get back that night to the place where they had crossed the fence. At last, finding a little shelter, they sat down to rest until morning; but, being weary, they fell asleep.

Now there was, not far from the place where they lay, a castle called Doubting Castle, owned by Giant Despair,[52] and it was on his land that they were sleeping. Therefore, when he got up early in the morning and walked up and down in his fields, he caught Christian and Hopeful asleep on his property.[53] Then with a grim and surly voice he told them to wake up and asked them where they had come from and what they were doing on his land. They told him they were pilgrims and that they had lost their way. Then said the giant, "You have trespassed on me by trampling in and lying on my grounds, and therefore you must go along with me." So they were forced to go, because he was stronger than they. They also had little to say because they knew they were at fault. The giant prodded them on before him and put them into a dark dungeon inside his castle, a nasty and stinking place to the spirits of these two men. Here they lay from Wednesday morning till Saturday night, without one bite of bread, or drop of water, or light, or anyone to ask how they were; thus they were in this evil situation, far from friends and acquaintances.[54] Now in this place Christian had double sorrow, because it was through his ill-advised haste that they had gotten into this trouble.

---

[51] Jer. 31:21

[52] The apostle Paul "despaired even of life" (2 Cor. 1:8).

[53] This event begins on Wednesday morning and ends on Sunday morning.

[54] See Ps. 88:18. Bunyan's own experiences in jail are certainly seen here.

Now Giant Despair had a wife, and her name was Diffidence.[55] So when he went to bed, he told his wife what he had done; that is, that he had taken a couple of prisoners and cast them into his dungeon for trespassing on his grounds. Then he asked her what he should do with them. So she asked him who they were, where they came from, and where they were going; and he told her. Then she advised him to beat them without mercy in the morning.

So when he arose, he got a heavy club made from the wood of a crab-tree, and he went down into the dungeon to the prisoners. First he scolded them as if they were dogs, although they never spoke a word of complaint to him. Then he beat them so badly that they were unable to move. After this, he left them in their misery. So all that day they did nothing but sigh and moan bitterly. The next night the wife, in talking with her husband about them further and learning they were still alive, advised him to counsel them to kill themselves. So in the morning he went to them in a surly manner as he had before, and seeing they were very sore from the beating he had given them the day before, he told them that since they were never likely to get out of that place, their only escape was to do away with themselves, either with knife, rope, or poison.[56] "For why," said he, "should you choose life, since it is filled with so much bitterness?" But they asked him to let them go. With that he gave them an ugly look and rushed at them and no doubt would have killed them himself, except that he fell into one of his fits (for he sometimes in sunshiny weather fell into fits),[57] and lost the use of his hand for a time;

---

[55] It is logical that Giant Despair would be married to Diffidence (meaning lack of confidence or mistrust), for distrust and despair go together. The wife does nothing to the pilgrims herself, but always tells her husband what to do.

[56] Job's wife counseled him to commit suicide (Job 2:9 –10) just as the giant's wife does with the two prisoners. It is worth noting that John Donne's treatise on suicide was published in 1646, and in it he stated that there were times when suicide was the right course to take. Bunyan would not agree with him.

[57] Doubt thrives in darkness.

therefore he withdrew and left them as before to consider what to do. Then the prisoners discussed whether or not they should take his advice.

CHRISTIAN: Brother, what shall we do? The life we now live is miserable. For my part, I don't know whether it is better to live this way or to die without delay. "My soul chooseth strangling rather than life," and the grave looks better to me than this dungeon.[58] Shall we take the giant's advice?

HOPEFUL: Indeed our present condition is dreadful, and death would be far more welcome to me than to live like this forever. But let us remember that the Lord of the country to which we are going has said, "You shall not kill another person"; much more then are we forbidden to take his advice to kill ourselves.[59] Besides, he who kills another only commits murder upon his body; but one who kills himself kills both body and soul. And moreover, my brother, you talk of ease in the grave; but have you forgotten the Hell where murderers go? For "no murderer has eternal life."[60]

And let us consider again that all the law is not in the hand of Giant Despair. Others, as far as I can understand, have also been captured by him, yet have escaped. Who knows but that God who made the world may cause the death of Giant Despair? Or that at some time or other he may forget to lock us in? Or he may soon have another of his fits and lose the use of his limbs? And if ever that should happen again, I am resolved to take heart and try my utmost to get away from him. I was a fool not to try to do it before; but, my brother, let's be patient and endure for a while longer.[61] In time we may escape. But let us not be our own murderers.

---

[58] See Job 7:15. Christian is giving in to his feelings. It is Hopeful who does the encouraging.

[59] Exod. 20:13

[60] 1 John 3:15

[61] See Heb. 6:15; 12:5. Hopeful realizes that they have gotten themselves into the situation, that the Lord is chastening them, and that all they can do is trust and be patient. He reminds his friend that God has seen him through all the other trials, and that He will see him through this one.

With these words, Hopeful calmed his brother, and they endured the dark together that day, in their sad condition.

Well toward evening the giant went down into the dungeon again to see if his prisoners had taken his advice. But when he got there, he found them alive; and barely alive was all, for what with lack of bread and water and by reason of the wounds they had received when he beat them, they could do little but breathe. But he did find them alive, at which he fell into a terrible rage and told them that since they had disobeyed his counsel, they were going to wish they had never been born.

At this they trembled greatly, and Christian fainted. But after he had revived a little, they once more began to discuss whether or not they had better take the giant's advice. Now Christian again seemed to be in favor of doing this, but Hopeful replied as follows:

HOPEFUL: My brother, don't you remember how brave you have been heretofore? Apollyon could not crush you, nor could all that you heard and saw and felt in the Valley of the Shadow of Death. Think about the hardship, terror, and bewilderment you have already gone through. You see that I am in the dungeon with you, a far weaker man by nature than you are; also, this giant has wounded me as well as you and has also refused me bread and water; and with you I mourn without the light. But let us exercise a little more patience; remember how brave you were at Vanity Fair, and were neither afraid of the chain, nor the cage, nor even bloody death. Therefore let us at least avoid the shame that is unbecoming to a Christian and bear up with patience as well as we can.

Now night had come again, and the giant and his wife were in bed, and she asked him about the prisoners, whether they had taken his counsel. To which he replied, "They are rugged scoundrels. They would rather bear the hardship than kill themselves." Then said she, "Take them into the castle yard tomorrow and show them the bones and skulls of those you have already killed, and make them believe that before the week is out you will also tear them in pieces, as you have done to those before them."

So in the morning the giant went to them again and took them into the castle yard and showed them, as his wife had told him. "These once were pilgrims as you are," said he, "and they trespassed on my property as you have done; and when I thought fit, I tore them in pieces; and so will I do to you within ten days.[62] Go! Get down to your dungeon again!" And with that he beat them all the way there. Therefore, all day Saturday they lay in a deplorable state, as they had before.

Now when night fell and Mrs. Diffidence and her husband Despair had gone to bed, they once more discussed their prisoners; and the old giant marveled that he could neither by his blows nor his counsel bring them to an end. And with that his wife replied, "I fear that they live in hope that someone will come to relieve them, or that they have lockpicks with them, by the means of which they hope to escape." "Do you think so, my dear?" said the giant. "In that case, I will search them in the morning."

Well, on Saturday about midnight they began to pray, and continued in prayer till almost the break of day.[63]

Now a little before daylight, good Christian broke out in this passionate speech: "What a fool I am to lie in a stinking dungeon when I can freely walk away! I have a key in my bosom called Promise, that will, I am persuaded, open any lock in Doubting Castle." Then said Hopeful, "That is good news, good brother; pull it out of your bosom and try."

Then Christian pulled out the key of Promise and began to try the dungeon door; and as he turned it, the bolt slid back and the door flew open with ease, and Christian and Hopeful both came out. Then he went to the outer door that led into

---

[62] Rev. 2:10

[63] This dungeon experience is based on the experience of Peter in Acts 12, and that of Paul and Silas in Acts 16. It is now Sunday, the Lord's Day, when Jesus Christ broke the chains of death and came forth from the tomb in power and glory. The promises of God, when believed, open the prison doors (Rev. 1:18).

the castle yard, and with his key opened that door also. After that he went to the iron gate, for that must be opened too;[64] that lock was very hard to turn, yet the key did open it. Then they threw open the gate to make their escape quickly, but that gate made such a creaking noise as it opened that it roused Giant Despair. He rose hastily to pursue his prisoners, but felt his legs fail, for one of his fits took him again, so that he could not go after them. So Christian and Hopeful went on and came to the King's highway, and thus were safe because they were out of Despair's jurisdiction.

Now when they had gone back over the fence at the stairs where they had originally crossed, they began to consider how they might prevent others from crossing there and falling into the hands of Giant Despair. So they decided to erect a pillar there and engrave this sentence upon the side: "Over these steps is the way to Doubting Castle, which is kept by Giant Despair, who despises the King of the Celestial Country and seeks to destroy his holy pilgrims." Because of this, many who followed after read what was written and escaped the danger. This done, they sang:

> Out of the way we went, and then we found
> What 'twas to tread upon forbidden ground;
> And let them that come after have a care,
> Lest heedlessness makes them, as we, to fare.
> Lest they for trespassing his prisoners are,
> Whose castle's Doubting and whose name's Despair.

---

[64] Acts 12:10

After the ordeal with Despair and Doubting, pilgrims Christian and Hopeful will soon arrive at the Delectable Mountains, which Christian had seen from afar some time ago. Now he actually arrives, learning that suffering is balanced by rest and joy.

The Delectable Mountains are in Immanuel's Land, a name for Palestine. There the pilgrims meet the Shepherds, men who represent pastors (the word "pastor" means "shepherd"). Their names —Knowledge, Experience, Watchful, and Sincere — describe the characteristics of a spiritual pastor. Bunyan himself served as a pastor.

hristian and Hopeful traveled until they came to the Delectable Mountains, which belonged to the Lord of that hill of which we have spoken before; they went up to the mountains to look at the gardens and orchards, the vineyards, and the fountains of water, where they drank and washed themselves and ate freely from the vineyards.[1] Now on the tops of these mountains, near the pathway, were Shepherds tending their flocks. The two pilgrims approached them and, leaning upon their staffs (as weary pilgrims usually do when they stand to talk with anyone by the way), asked, "Who do these Delectable Mountains belong to? And who owns the sheep that graze upon them?"

Mountains delectable they now ascend,
Where Shepherds be, which to them do commend
Alluring things, and things that cautious are,
Pilgrims are steady kept by faith and fear.

SHEPHERD: These mountains are Immanuel's Land, and they are within sight of his city; the sheep are also his, and he laid down his life for them.[2]

CHRISTIAN: Is this the way to the Celestial City?

SHEPHERD: You are just on the path.

CHRISTIAN: How far is it?

SHEPHERD: Too far for any but those who really want to get there.

CHRISTIAN: Is the way safe or dangerous?

SHEPHERD: Safe for those for whom it is to be safe; "but transgressors shall fall therein."[3]

CHRISTIAN: Is there any relief in this place for pilgrims who are weary and faint?

---

[1]Eccl. 2:4–6
[2]Isa. 8:8; Matt. 1:23; John 10:11, 15
[3]Hos. 14:9

SHEPHERD: The Lord of these mountains has ordered us to entertain strangers; therefore the good things of this place are available to you.[4]

I saw also in my dream that when the Shepherds perceived that they were wayfarers, they questioned them (which they answered as they had in other places) with such questions as, "Where did you come from?" and, "How did you get into the way?" and, "By what means have you persevered?[5] For few of those who begin the journey to this place ever show their face on these mountains."[6] But when the Shepherds heard their answers, they were pleased and looked very lovingly upon them and said, "Welcome to the Delectable Mountains."[7]

The Shepherds, whose names were Knowledge, Experience, Watchful, and Sincere, took them by the hand and led them to their tents and made them partake of that which had been prepared for them. They said, moreover, "We would like you to stay here a while so you can get acquainted with us; and more than that, so you can comfort yourselves with the good of these Delectable Mountains." Christian and Hopeful told them that they were content to stay; so they went to rest that night, because it was very late.

In the morning the Shepherds called to Christian and Hopeful to walk with them upon the mountains; so they walked with them for a while, admiring the pleasant view on every side. Then the Shepherds said to one another, "Shall we show these pilgrims some wonders?" When they had agreed to do this, they took them first to the top of a hill called Error, which was very steep on the far side, and told them to look down to the bottom.[8] So Christian and Hopeful looked down and saw at the bottom several men who had been smashed to

---

[4]Heb. 13:2

[5]Again, a time of examination and testimony. See 1 Peter 3:15.

[6]See Matt. 20:16; Luke 13:23–24. Christian and Hopeful will reach the heavenly city, but many whom they meet on the way will not arrive.

[7]Mark 10:21

[8]Another hill! "Error" refers to doctrinal error.

pieces by a fall from the top. Then said Christian, "What does this mean?" And the Shepherds answered, "Have you not heard of those who were caused to err by listening to Hymenaeus and Philetus concerning the faith of the resurrection of the body?"[9] They answered, "Yes." Then said the Shepherds, "They are the ones you see smashed to pieces at the bottom of this mountain; and they lie there to this day unburied, as you see, as an example to others to be careful lest they climb too high or come too near the brink of this mountain."

Then I saw that they led them to the top of another mountain, named Caution, and told them to look off into the distance.[10] When they did, they saw several men walking up and down among the tombs that were there; and they realized that the men were blind, because they stumbled sometimes upon the tombs and could not get out from among them. Then said Christian, "What does this mean?"

The Shepherds answered, "Did you not see a little below these mountains some steps that led into a meadow, on the left side of this way?" They answered, "Yes." Then said the Shepherds, "From those steps goes a path that leads directly to Doubting Castle, which is kept by Giant Despair, and these men (and they pointed to the men among the tombs) were once on pilgrimage, as you are now, until they came to those steps; and because the right way was rough in that place, they chose to leave it and go into that meadow, and there they were taken by Giant Despair and cast into Doubting Castle; where, after they had been kept in the dungeon a while, he at last put out their eyes and led them among these tombs, where he has left them to wander to this very day, so that the saying of the wise man might be fulfilled, 'He that wandereth out of the way of understanding shall remain in the congrega-

---

[9] Two heretics in Paul's day who erred from the truth (2 Tim. 2:17–18).
[10] A vantage point to see where they had been and what could have happened to them had they not escaped Doubting Castle. It is good to look back and learn, and be warned for the future.

145

tion of the dead.'"[11] Then Christian and Hopeful looked at one another with tears pouring down their cheeks, but said nothing to the Shepherds.

Then I saw in my dream that the Shepherds took them to another place, in the bottom of a valley, where there was a door in the side of a hill; and they opened the door and told them to look in. They looked in and saw that it was very dark and smoky; they also thought that they heard a rumbling noise like fire, and a cry of torment, and the scent of brimstone. Then said Christian, "What does this mean?" The Shepherds told them, "This is another road to hell,[12] a way that hypocrites take; like those who sell their birthright, with Esau; like those who sell their master, with Judas; like those who blaspheme the gospel, with Alexander; and like those who lie and dissemble, with Ananias and his wife."[13] Then Hopeful said to the Shepherds, "Every one of these appeared to be on pilgrimage, as we are now, did they not?"

SHEPHERD: Yes, and held to it for a long time.

HOPEFUL: How far did they go on pilgrimage in their day, since they were so miserably cast away?

SHEPHERD: Some went further than these mountains, and some did not get this far.

Then the pilgrims said to each other, "We had better cry to the Strong for strength."

SHEPHERDS: Yes, and you will need to use it when you have it too.

---

[11]Prov. 21:16

[12]And this is not the first one! Christian saw "the mouth of hell" by the wayside when he went through the Valley of the Shadow of Death. He will discover a way to hell even at the gate of heaven!

[13]Esau sold his birthright for a single meal of pottage (Gen. 25:29–34; Heb. 12:16). In Bunyan's day, Christians who opposed the state church, called the prayer book "pottage." People who compromised with the state religion were compared with Esau, who sold the spiritual that he might gain the material. For Alexander, see 1 Tim. 1:20. Ananias and his wife, Sapphira, lied about their gift to God and were slain for their hypocrisy (Acts 5:1–11).

By this time the pilgrims desired to go forward, and the Shepherds desired that they should; so they walked together toward the end of the mountains. Then the Shepherds said to one another, "Let us show the pilgrims the gates of the Celestial City, if they are able to look through our telescope." The pilgrims gratefully accepted the suggestion; so the Shepherds led them to the top of a high hill called Clear and gave them their glass to look through.[14]

Then they attempted to look, but the memory of the last thing the Shepherds had shown them made their hands shake; because of this impediment they could not look steadily through the glass; yet they thought they saw something like the gate and some of the glory of the place. Then they went away singing this song:

Thus by the Shepherds secrets are revealed,
Which from all other men are kept concealed.
Come to the Shepherds then, if you would see
Things deep, things hid, and that mysterious be.

When they were about to depart, one of the Shepherds gave them a map of the way. Another warned them to beware of the Flatterer. The third told them not to sleep upon the Enchanted Ground. And the fourth bid them God-speed. So I awoke from my dream.[15]

Then I slept and dreamed again, and I saw the same two pilgrims going down the mountains along the highway toward the city. Now a little below these mountains, on the left hand, lay the country of Conceit; and a little crooked lane led from this country into the way in which the pilgrims walked.[16] Here

---

[14] Still another hill. From this one Christian and Hopeful could see something of the heavenly city. It is the infirmity of our own nature that keeps us from seeing as we should see.

[15] This sentence really adds nothing to the story. Bunyan scholars think that it represents the author's release from jail and his subsequent completing of the book begun in jail. Or perhaps Bunyan does not want his readers to think that he sleeps too long! The Puritans opposed laziness.

[16] As we make spiritual progress, we are in danger of conceit. Paul joins "ignorance" and "conceit" in Rom. 11:25. See also Prov. 26:12; Rom. 12:16.

they encountered a very energetic lad who had come out of that country, and his name was Ignorance. So Christian asked him where he came from and where he was going.

IGNORANCE: Sir, I was born in the country that lies off there a little on the left, and I am going to the Celestial City.

CHRISTIAN: But how do you plan to get in at the gate, for you may find some difficulty there?

IGNORANCE: I will get in as other good people do.

CHRISTIAN: But what do you have to show at the gate, that may cause the gate to be opened to you?

IGNORANCE: I know my Lord's will, and I have lived a good life. I pay every man what I owe him; I pray, fast, tithe, and give to the poor; and I have left my country to go there.[17]

CHRISTIAN: But you did not come in at the wicket-gate at the beginning of this way; you came in through that crooked lane, and therefore I fear that regardless of what you may think of yourself, when the day of judgment comes you will be charged with being a thief and a robber, instead of being admitted to the city.[18]

IGNORANCE: Gentlemen, you are complete strangers to me; I do not know you. So you follow the religion of your country, and I will follow the religion of mine. I hope all will be well. And as for the gate that you speak of, all the world knows that that is a long ways from our country. I cannot think of anyone in our part of the world who even knows the way to it, nor does it matter whether they do or not since we have, as you see, a fine pleasant green lane that comes down from our country into the way.

When Christian saw that the man was "wise in his own conceit," he whispered to Hopeful, "There is more hope for a fool than for him."[19] And, he added, "'When he that is a fool walketh by the way, his wisdom faileth him, and he saith to every one that he is a fool.'[20] Shall we talk further with him or

---

[17] Luke 18:9–14
[18] John 10:1
[19] Prov. 26:5, 12
[20] Eccl. 10:3

go past him and let him think about what we have told him? Then we can wait for him later and see if we can gradually do him any good." Then Hopeful said:

Let Ignorance a little while now muse
On what is said, and let him not refuse
Good counsel to embrace, lest he remain
Still ignorant of what's the chiefest gain.
God saith, those that no understanding have
Although he made them, them he will not save.

HOPEFUL: It is not good to tell him everything at once; let us pass him by and speak with him later, when he is able to bear it.[21]

So they both went on, and Ignorance followed behind. Now when they were a little ways past him, they entered a very dark lane, where they met a man whom seven devils had bound with seven strong cords and were carrying back to the door they had seen on the side of the hill.[22] Now good Christian began to tremble, and so did Hopeful; yet as the devils led the man away, Christian looked to see if he knew him, and he thought it might be Turn-away, who lived in the town of Apostasy.[23] But he did not see his face clearly, for the man hung his head like a thief who had been caught. But once they were past, Hopeful looked back at the man and saw a paper on his back with this inscription, "Wanton professor and damnable apostate." Then Christian said to his companion, "Now I recall something I was told that happened to a good man around here. His name was Little-faith, but he was a good man, and he lived in the town of Sincere.[24] What hap-

---

[21]John 16:12; 1 Cor. 3:2

[22]Matt. 12:45; Prov. 5:22

[23]Apostasy is the sin of openly turning away from the faith once professed (Heb. 12:25). This is the origin of the name "Turn-away." Bunyan does not think that Turn-away is a true Christian, for he calls him "Wanton professor"— that is, one who professes faith but does not possess it.

[24]Little-faith was one of our Lord's favorite names for His disciples (Matt. 8:26; 14:31; 16:8). Bunyan seems to contrast Little-faith with Turn-away. Though Little-faith suffered and was robbed, he did not lose his certificate

pened was this: At the entrance to this passage, a lane comes down from Broad-way Gate called Dead Man's Lane—so called because of the murders that are commonly committed there—and this Little-faith, who was going on pilgrimage as we are, happened to sit down there and fall asleep. Just then three rogues, three brothers named Faint-heart, Mistrust, and Guilt, came down the lane from Broad-way Gate; and spying Little-faith, they came galloping up rapidly. Now the good man had just awakened from his sleep and was preparing to resume his journey when they came up to him and with threatening language ordered him to stand. At this Little-faith turned as white as a sheet and had neither the strength to fight nor to flee. Then said Faint-heart, 'Give us your purse.' But he did not do it, for he did not want to lose his money. So Mistrust ran up to the man and, thrusting his hand into his pocket, pulled out a bag of silver. 'Thieves! Thieves!' cried Little-faith. With that, Guilt struck him on the head with a large club and knocked him flat on the ground, where he lay bleeding like he would bleed to death. All this while the thieves stood by. But at last, hearing someone coming down the road, and fearing that it might be Great-grace from the city of Good-confidence, they ran away, leaving this good man to shift for himself. After a while Little-faith gained consciousness and managed to get to his feet and stumble along on his way."

HOPEFUL: But did they rob him of all that he had?

CHRISTIAN: No. They did not search him thoroughly enough to discover the place where he kept his jewels, so those he still had. But as I was told, the good man was troubled by his loss, for the thieves got most of his spending money. He had a little loose change left, but scarcely enough to take him to his journey's end;[25] no, if I was not misinformed, he was forced to beg as he went, for he could not sell his jewels. But though he begged and did what he could, he went hungry for most of the rest of the way.

---

that gave him entrance into heaven. God honors even a little faith. Not all Christians are great victors!

[25] 1 Peter 4:18

HOPEFUL: Isn't it a wonder, though, that they did not get his certificate which was to gain him admittance at the Celestial Gate?

CHRISTIAN: It is a wonder, but they missed it, though not through any cunning of his; for he was so dismayed when they attacked him that he had neither the power nor the skill to hide anything; so it was more by divine Providence than by his own effort that they missed that good thing.[26]

HOPEFUL: But it must have been comforting to him that they did not get his jewels.

CHRISTIAN: It might have been a great comfort to him, had he used it as he should; but those who told me the story said that he made little use of it all the rest of the way because of the dismay he felt over losing his money. Indeed he forgot it for most of the rest of his journey; and besides, when it did come to his mind and he began to be comforted by the thought, then fresh memories of his loss would come upon him again and overwhelm him.

HOPEFUL: Alas, poor man! This must have been a great grief to him.

CHRISTIAN: Grief! yes, grief indeed! Would not any of us have been grieved by such treatment: to be robbed and wounded, and that in a strange place, as he was? It is a wonder he did not die with grief, poor man! I was told that he complained bitterly almost all the rest of the way, telling all he met about how he was robbed and beaten, describing where it had happened, who had done it, what he had lost, and how he had barely escaped with his life.

HOPEFUL: It's a wonder he didn't have to sell or pawn some of his jewels to support himself on the rest of his journey.

CHRISTIAN: You talk like one who was just hatched! What could he pawn them for, or to whom could he sell them?[27] His jewels were of no value in that country where he

---

[26]2 Tim. 1:14; 2 Peter 2:9

[27]Like a baby bird just out of the shell. This was an unkind statement on the part of Christian and it almost made Hopeful angry. Can you blame him?

was robbed, nor did he want that kind of relief. Besides, had his jewels been missing at the gate of the Celestial City, he would have been excluded from an inheritance there, and that he knew very well. For him that would have been worse than the appearance and villainy of ten thousand thieves.

HOPEFUL: Why are you so sharp with me, my brother? Esau sold his birthright for a mess of pottage, and that birthright was his greatest jewel; and if he did, why might not Little-faith do so too?[28]

CHRISTIAN: Indeed, Esau did sell his birthright, and so have many others, and by doing so they exclude themselves from the chief blessing, as that vile coward did; but you must see the difference between Esau and Little-faith, and between their conditions.[29] Esau's birthright was typical, but Little-faith's jewels were not; Esau's god was his belly, but Little-faith's was not; Esau was ruled by his fleshly appetite, but not so Little-faith. Besides, Esau could see no further than the fulfilling of his own lusts; "For I am at the point to die (said he), and what good will this birthright do me?"[30] But Little-faith, though he had only a little faith, was kept from such extravagances by that faith, and made to see and value his jewels so that he would not sell them, as Esau did his birthright. You do not read anywhere that Esau had faith—no, not even a little; therefore it is no wonder that he sold his birthright and his very soul to the Devil, for that is what happens when the flesh rules (as it will in men without faith to resist); for they are like the ass who cannot be restrained during her time of heat.[31] When their minds are focused upon their lusts, they will have them, whatever the cost. But Little-faith was of another temperament; his mind was set on things divine and his existence depended upon things that were

---

[28] Heb. 12:16

[29] Christian explains the difference between an unbeliever, like Esau, and Little-faith, who stayed true to the Lord.

[30] Gen. 25:32

[31] The reference is to Jer. 2:24, describing the wild ass in her time of heat. Esau acted like an animal, not a man.

spiritual and from above. Therefore what would he gain in selling his jewels (had there been anyone who would have bought them) and filling his mind with empty things? Will a man give a penny to fill his belly with hay; or can you persuade the turtledove to live upon carrion like the crow? Though faithless ones can pawn or mortgage or sell what they have, including their very souls, for carnal lusts, those who have faith, even though it be only a little, cannot do so. Here therefore, my brother, is your mistake.

HOPEFUL: I acknowledge it. But your severe reproach almost made me angry.

CHRISTIAN: Why, I only compared you to some of the young birds who dash about with the shell upon their heads. But ignore that, and consider the matter under discussion, and all shall be well between us.

HOPEFUL: But Christian, I am convinced that these three fellows were just a bunch of cowards; otherwise, do you think they would have run away, as they did, at the sound of someone coming down the road? Why wasn't Little-faith braver? I would think he could have handled at least one skirmish with them, and only yielded if there had been no other choice.

CHRISTIAN: Many have said they are cowards, but few have found it so in the time of trial. As for a great heart, Little-faith had none; and from what you have said, my brother, if it had been you, you would have yielded after just one encounter. And since this is the height of your bravery when they are at a distance from us, should they attack you as they did him, you might have second thoughts.

But remember, they are only hired thieves who serve the king of the bottomless pit,[32] who, if necessary, will come to their rescue himself, and his voice is like the roaring of a lion.[33] I myself have been trapped as Little-faith was, and I found it a terrible thing. Those three villains attacked me, and when I began to resist like a Christian, they gave only one call for help, and in came their master. My life wouldn't have been

---

[32] Satan (Rev. 9:1–2, 11).
[33] Another picture of Satan (1 Peter 5:8).

worth a cent, as the saying goes, except that, as God would have it, I was clothed with armor of proof. And yet even though I was so equipped, I found it hard work to acquit myself like a man. No man can tell what awaits us in that combat unless he has been in the battle himself.

HOPEFUL: But they ran away, you see, when they only imagined that Great-grace was coming their way.[34]

CHRISTIAN: True. Both they and their master have often fled when Great-grace has appeared; and no wonder, for he is the King's champion.[35] But I believe you will see some difference between Little-faith and the King's champion. All the King's subjects are not his champions; nor can they, when tried, accomplish such feats of war as he. Is it right to think that a little child should handle Goliath as David did? Or that a wren should have the strength of an ox? Some are strong; some are weak. Some have great faith; some have little. This man was one of the weak, and therefore he was temporarily overcome.

HOPEFUL: I wish it had been Great-grace for their sakes.

CHRISTIAN: If it had been, he might have had his hands full; for I must tell you that though Great-grace is excellent with his weapons and can handle such fellows well enough as long as he keeps them at sword's point, yet if Faint-heart, Mistrust, or the other get within him, they will eventually knock him down. And when a man is down, what can he do?

Whoever looks carefully at Great-grace's face will see scars and cuts there that are evidence of what I say. Yes, once I heard that he said when he was in combat, "We despaired even of life."[36] These scoundrels made David groan, mourn, and roar. Yes, and Heman and Hezekiah too, though champions in their day, were forced to fight when assaulted by these fellows—and were beaten up by them.[37] At one point

---

[34] Acts 4:33

[35] Instead of both armies fighting, each king would select a champion, and they would battle (1 Sam. 17:4).

[36] 2 Cor. 1:8

[37] Heman, the author of Ps. 88, certainly a song of despair and trouble. Hezekiah was a godly king of Judah (Isa. 36–38).

Peter went up against them, but of all the apostles, they handled him so skillfully that at last they made him afraid of a weak girl.[38]

Besides, their king is at their beck and call. He is never out of earshot; and if at any time they are getting the worst of it, he, if possible, comes in to help them; and of him it is said, "The sword of him that layeth at him cannot hold: the spear, the dart, nor the [breastplate]. He esteemeth iron as straw, and brass as rotten wood. The arrow cannot make him flee: slingstones are turned with him into stubble. Darts are counted as stubble: he laugheth at the shaking of a spear."[39] What can a man do in this case? If a man could have Job's horse, and had skill and courage to ride him, he might do notable things. "For his neck is clothed with thunder, he will not be afraid of the grasshopper, the glory of his nostrils is terrible, he paweth in the valley, rejoiceth in his strength, and goeth out to meet the armed men. He mocketh at fear, and is not affrighted, neither turneth back from the sword. The quiver rattleth against him, the glittering spear, and the shield. He swalloweth the ground with fierceness and rage, neither believeth he that is the sound of the trumpet. He saith among the trumpets, Ha, ha! and he smelleth the battle afar off, the thundering of the captains, and the shoutings."[40]

But for such travelers as you and I, let us never desire to meet with an enemy, nor brag as if we could do better when we hear of others who have been defeated, nor be delighted by thoughts of our own bravery; for those who do usually come out the worst when they are tried. Look at Peter, whom I mentioned before. He boasted, yes, he did, saying that he would do better and stand more firmly for his Master than all other men; but who was more defeated by these villains than he?

---

[38] Luke 22:54–62 records this apostle's temptation and defeat. The girl is a reference to the servant girl who questioned Peter.
[39] Job 41:26–29
[40] Job 39:19–25

Therefore when we hear of such robberies on the King's highway, there are two things we should do:

1. Go out clad in armor, and be sure to take a shield with us; for it was for lack of that, that he who attacked Leviathan could not make him yield: for indeed, he does not fear us at all if we are without armor and shield.[41] Therefore he who has skill has said, "Above all take the shield of faith, wherewith ye shall be able to quench all the fiery darts of the wicked."[42]

2. We should also ask the King for a protective escort; yes, we should ask that he go with us himself. This made David rejoice when he was in the Valley of the Shadow of Death; and Moses would rather have died where he stood than go one step without his God. [43] Oh, my brother, if he goes with us, why should we be afraid of ten thousand who set themselves against us? But without him, the proud helpers "fall under the slain."[44]

For my part, I have been in the battle before; and though, through his goodness, I am alive, I cannot boast of my own bravery. I shall be glad if I encounter no more of such attacks, but I fear we are not beyond all danger. However, since the lion and the bear have not as yet devoured me, I hope God will also deliver us from the next uncircumcised Philistine.[45] Then sang Christian:

> Poor Little-faith! Hast been among the thieves?
> Wast robbed? Remember this, whoso believes
> And gets more faith; shall then a victor be[46]
> Over ten thousand, else scarce over three.

So they went on, with Ignorance following, until they came to a place where another pathway joined their way, and

---

[41]See Job 41:26–29. This is probably a poetic description of a crocodile. It probably symbolizes Satan.
[42]Quoted from Eph. 6:16. It means "in addition to all the other parts."
[43]Ps. 23:4; Exod. 33:15
[44]Pss. 3:6; 27:1–3; Isa. 10:4
[45]Referring to David's victories (1 Sam. 17:26–36).
[46]1 John 5:4

it seemed to lie as straight as the way they should go; and they did not know which of the two paths to take, for both seemed to lie straight before them. Therefore they stopped to decide what to do.[47] And as they were thinking about the way, a black man dressed in a very light robe came to them and asked them why they were standing there.[48] They told him they were going to the Celestial City, but did not know which way to go. "Follow me," said the man, "for that is where I am going." So they followed him down the path that had just intersected with the road, which gradually turned,[49] and turned them so far that soon their faces were turned away from the city to which they desired to go. Still, they followed him. But by and by, before they realized it, he had led them both into a net, in which they became so entangled that they didn't know what to do; and with that the white robe fell off the black man's back and they saw where they were. Then they lay there crying for some time because they could not free themselves.

CHRISTIAN: Now I see my error. Didn't the Shepherds tell us to beware of the flatterers? As the wise man says, "A man that flattereth his neighbor spreadeth a net for his feet."[50]

HOPEFUL: They also gave us a map of the way, but we have forgotten to read it and have not kept ourselves from the paths of the destroyer. Here David was wiser than we, for he said, "Concerning the works of men, by the word of thy lips, I have kept me from the paths of the destroyer."[51]

Thus they lay sorrowing in the net, until at last they noticed a Shining One coming toward them with a whip of small cord in his hand.[52] When he reached them, he asked

---

[47]Another dangerous detour (Prov. 14:12). Note that this new road seems as straight as the one they were on. As we progress in the Christian life, temptations become more subtle. Previous detours were rather obvious.

[48] This turns out to be the Flatterer they were warned about by the Shepherds.

[49] The enemy leads us astray gradually.

[50] Prov. 29:5

[51] Ps. 17:4

[52] A whip such as Jesus used in the temple (John 2:15).

where they came from and what they were doing there. They told him they were poor pilgrims going to Zion, but had been led astray by a black man dressed in white. "He told us to follow him," they said, "for he was going there too." Then the man with the whip said, "It was Flatterer, a false apostle, who has transformed himself into an angel of light."[53] So he tore open the net and released the men. Then he said to them, "Follow me so that I may set you on your way again." So he led them back to the pathway they had left to follow the Flatterer. Then he asked them, "Where did you stay last night?" They said, "With the Shepherds, upon the Delectable Mountains." Then he asked them if those Shepherds had given them a map of the way. They answered, "Yes." "When you were at a standstill," said he, "did you take out your map and read it?" They answered, "No." He asked them, "Why?" They said, "We forgot." Then he asked them if the Shepherds had warned them to beware of the Flatterer. They answered, "Yes, but we never imagined that this fine-spoken man was he."[54]

Then I saw in my dream that he commanded them to lie down; and when they did, he chastised them severely to teach them that they should walk in the good way; and as he chastised them, he said, "As many as I love, I rebuke and chasten; be zealous, therefore, and repent."[55] This done, he told them to go on their way and to heed carefully the other directions of the Shepherds. So they thanked him for all his kindness and went softly along the right way, singing:[56]

> *Come hither, you that walk along the way;*
> *See how the pilgrims fare that go astray!*
> *They catched are in an entangling net,*
> *'Cause they good counsel lightly did forget:*
> *'Tis true they rescued were, but yet you see,*
> *They're scourged to boot.*
> *Let this your caution be.*

---

[53]2 Cor. 11:13–14; Dan. 11:32
[54]Rom. 16:17–18
[55]Heb. 12:6; Deut. 25:2; 2 Chron. 6:27; Rev. 3:19
[56]1 Kings 21:27; Isa. 38:15

Now after a while they saw someone in the distance, walking leisurely and alone along the highway. Then said Christian to his companion, "Yonder is a man with his back toward Zion, and he is coming to meet us."

HOPEFUL: I see him. Let us be careful now, lest he should prove to be another flatterer.

The man came closer and closer, until at last he came up to them. His name was Atheist, and he asked them where they were going.

CHRISTIAN: We are going to Mount Zion.

Then Atheist began to laugh loudly.

CHRISTIAN: What is the meaning of your laughter?

ATHEIST: I am laughing because I see what ignorant people you are, to make such a tedious journey, when you will probably have nothing but your travel to show for your effort.

CHRISTIAN: Why, man, do you think we shall not be received?

ATHEIST: Received! The place you dream about does not exist anywhere in the world.

CHRISTIAN: But it does in the world to come.

ATHEIST: When I was at home in my own country, I heard about this place, and after hearing about it, I went out to see it. I have been seeking this city for twenty years, and know no more about it than I did the first day I set out.[57]

CHRISTIAN: We have both heard that there is such a place, and we believe it may be found.

ATHEIST: If I had not believed, when I was still at home, I would not have come this far to seek it; but finding nothing (and I should have if there were such a place to be found, for I have gone further than you to seek it), I am going back again, and will seek to refresh myself with the things that I then cast away for hopes of that which I now see is not.

Then Christian said to Hopeful, "Is what this man says true?"

---

[57]Eccl. 10:15; Jer. 17:15

HOPEFUL: Be careful; he is one of the flatterers. Remember what listening to such a fellow has cost us already. No Mount Zion!? Why, did we not see the gate of the city from the Delectable Mountains? And besides, are we not to walk by faith?[58]

Let us move on, lest the man with the whip overtake us again. You should have taught me that which I will whisper in your ear: "Cease, my son, to hear the instruction that causeth to err from the words of knowledge." Stop listening to him, and let us "believe to the saving of the soul."[59]

CHRISTIAN: My brother, I did not put the question to you because I doubted the truth of what we believe, but to test you and draw from you what you honestly think in your heart. As for this man, I know he is blinded by the god of this world.[60] So let us go on, knowing that what we believe is the truth, and that no lie comes from the truth.[61]

HOPEFUL: Now I "rejoice in hope of the glory of God."[62]

So they turned away from the man. And he, laughing at them, went his way.

I saw then in my dream that they walked until they entered a country where the air tended to make strangers drowsy. And here Hopeful began to feel listless and sleepy, and he said to Christian, "I feel so sleepy that I can hardly keep my eyes open. Let's lie down here and take a nap."[63]

CHRISTIAN: No, we cannot, for if we sleep here, we may never wake up again.

HOPEFUL: Why, my brother? Sleep is sweet to the working man. We will be refreshed if we take a nap.[64]

CHRISTIAN: Do you not remember that one of the Shepherds told us to beware of the Enchanted Ground? By that, he meant that we should beware of sleeping. Therefore,

---

[58] 2 Cor. 5:7

[59] Prov. 19:27; Heb. 10:39

[60] 2 Cor. 4:4

[61] 1 John 2:21

[62] Rom. 5:2

[63] Hopeful has forgotten the warning of the Shepherds.

[64] Eccl. 5:12

"let us not sleep, as do others, but let us watch and be sober."[65]

HOPEFUL: I acknowledge my weakness, and had I been here alone, I would have risked the danger of death by sleeping. I see that what the wise man says is true: "Two are better than one." [66] Up to this time, your company has been a fortunate circumstance for me, "and you shall have a good reward for your labor."

CHRISTIAN: Now then, to keep from getting drowsy in this place, let's have some good discussion.[67]

HOPEFUL: I agree wholeheartedly.

CHRISTIAN: Where shall we begin?

HOPEFUL: Where God began with us. But you begin, if you please.

CHRISTIAN: First I will sing you this song:

When saints do sleepy grow, let them come hither,
And hear how these two pilgrims talk together:
Yea, let them learn of them, in any wise,
Thus to keep ope their drowsy slumbering eyes.
Saints' fellowship, if it be managed well,
Keeps them awake, and that in spite of hell.

Then Christian began and said, "I will ask you a question. Why did you first think of doing what you are doing now?"

HOPEFUL: Do you mean, why did I begin to be concerned about my soul?

CHRISTIAN: Yes, that is what I mean.

HOPEFUL: For a long time I enjoyed those things that were seen and sold at our fair; things that, I believe now, would have (had I continued in them) destroyed me.[68]

---

[65] 1 Thess. 5:6

[66] Eccl. 4:9

[67] Christian and Hopeful enter into a lengthy theological discussion in order to stay awake. If you find it is putting you to sleep, keep in mind that such conversation was common to the Puritans. Talking about personal experiences and scriptural truths is an encouragement to believers (Deut. 6:6–9).

[68] 1 Tim. 6:9

CHRISTIAN: What things?

HOPEFUL: All the treasures and riches of the world. I also delighted in debauchery, partying, drinking, swearing, lying, immorality, Sabbath-breaking, and every other thing that tends to destroy the soul. But by hearing and considering divine things, which I learned about from you, as well as from beloved Faithful who was put to death at Vanity Fair for his faith and goodness, I discovered at last that "the end of these things is death."[69] And that for these things "the wrath of God cometh upon the children of disobedience."[70]

CHRISTIAN: Did you immediately come under conviction?

HOPEFUL: No, for I was not willing at first to recognize the evil of sin or the damnation that results from it; instead, when my mind was initially shaken by the Word, I tried to shut my eyes against the light.

CHRISTIAN: But what caused you to maintain this attitude before God's blessed Spirit began working upon you?

HOPEFUL: Well, first, I did not know that this was the work of God upon me. I never realized that God begins the conversion of a sinner by first awakening him to sin. Second, sin was still very enjoyable to me, and I didn't want to leave it. Third, I did not know how to part with my old companions, for their presence and their actions were so desirable to me. And fourth, the times when I was under conviction were such troubling and frightening hours that I could not bear even the memories of them.

CHRISTIAN: Then, there were times when you were not troubled?

HOPEFUL: Oh, yes, but then it would haunt me again, and I was as bad, no, worse, than before.

CHRISTIAN: What was it that brought your sins to mind again?

HOPEFUL: Many things, such as,

1. If I met a good man on the streets; or,

2. If I heard anyone read the Bible; or,

---

[69] Rom. 6:21

[70] Eph. 5:6

162

3. If my head began to ache; or,

4. If I was told that some of my neighbors were sick; or,

5. If I heard the bell toll for someone who had died; or, [71]

6. If I thought of dying myself; or,

7. If I heard that someone else had died suddenly;

8. But especially when I thought of myself and that I must soon face judgment.

CHRISTIAN: And could you ever easily get rid of the guilt of sin when any of these occurrences brought it upon you?

HOPEFUL: No, I could not, for they were gaining a greater hold on my conscience; and if I even thought about returning to sin (though my mind was turned against it), it was doubly tormenting to me.

CHRISTIAN: And what did you do then?

HOPEFUL: I thought I must try to change my life; otherwise, I thought, I would surely be damned.

CHRISTIAN: And did you try to change?

HOPEFUL: Yes. I tried not to sin, and I avoided sinful company; I began performing religious duties such as prayer, Bible reading, weeping over my sins, speaking the truth to my neighbors, and so forth. These things I did, along with many others, too numerous to relate.

CHRISTIAN: And did you then think you were all right?

HOPEFUL: Yes, for a while. But then my trouble came tumbling upon me again, despite all my changes.

CHRISTIAN: How did that come about, since you had now reformed?

HOPEFUL: Several things brought it upon me, especially such sayings as these: "All our righteousnesses are as filthy rags." "By the works of the law no man shall be justified." "When you have done all things, say, We are unprofitable"; [72] and many more like this. From there I began to reason with

---

[71] This reminds us of John Donne's (d. 1631) famous statement: "Any man's death diminishes me, because I am involved in Mankinde; And therefore never send to know for whom the bell tolls; It tolls for thee." Interestingly, Bunyan himself was an accomplished bell-ringer.

[72] Isa. 64:6; Gal. 2:16; Luke 17:10

myself: If all my righteousnesses are like filthy rags; if no man can be justified by obeying the law; and if, when we have done all we can, we are still unworthy, then it is foolish to think we can get to heaven by the law. Furthermore, I thought: If a man runs up a bill of a hundred pounds with a shopkeeper, and after that he pays for everything he buys but still owes his old bill, the shopkeeper can still sue him and send him to prison until he pays the debt.

CHRISTIAN: How did you apply this to yourself?

HOPEFUL: Why, I thought, I have by my sins run up a great charge in God's book, and my reforming now will not pay off that debt. Therefore, I should continue with my present changes; but how shall I be freed from the damnation I have brought upon myself by my former transgressions?

CHRISTIAN: A very good application. But please continue.

HOPEFUL: Another thing that has troubled me, even since the recent changes in my life, is that if I look carefully at the best of what I do now, I still see sin, new sin, mixing itself with the best of what I do;[73] so I am forced to conclude that, even if my former life had been faultless, I have now committed sin enough in one action to send me to hell.

CHRISTIAN: And what did you do then?

HOPEFUL: Do! I did not know what to do, until I shared my thoughts with Faithful, for he and I were well acquainted. And he told me that unless I could obtain the righteousness of a man who had never sinned, neither my own nor all the righteousness of the world could save me.

CHRISTIAN: And did you think he spoke the truth?

HOPEFUL: Had he told me this when I was pleased and satisfied with my own improvements, I would have called him a fool; but now, since I saw my own frailty and the sin that clung to even my best performance, I was forced to accept his opinion.

---

[73] Rom. 7:21

CHRISTIAN: But did you think, when he first suggested it to you, that a man could be found, of whom it could justly be said, "He never committed any sin"?

HOPEFUL: I must confess the words sounded strange at first, but after we talked more and I spent more time in his company, I was totally convinced of it.

CHRISTIAN: And did you ask him who this man was and how you could be justified by him?[74]

HOPEFUL: Yes, and he told me it was the Lord Jesus, who dwells at the right hand of the Most High. "You must be justified by him, by trusting in what he alone has done during his life on earth and his suffering on the cross."[75] I asked him how that man's righteousness could justify another before God. And he told me that the man was the mighty God, and that he had done what he did and died on the cross not for himself, but for me; and if I believed on him, his righteousness would be applied to my account.[76]

CHRISTIAN: And what did you do then?

HOPEFUL: I stated my objections against my believing this, because I didn't think the Lord was willing to save me.

CHRISTIAN: What did Faithful say to you then?

HOPEFUL: He told me to go to Christ and see. I said I thought that was presumptive. But he said, no, it was not, for I was invited to come.[77] Then he gave me a book of Jesus, his authoritative word, to encourage me to come freely; and he said that every jot and tittle of that book stands firmer than heaven and earth.[78] Then I asked him what I must do when I came to him; and he told me I must kneel down and plead with all my heart and soul for the Father to reveal him to

---

[74] Rom. 4:5; Col. 1:14; Heb. 10:12–21; 2 Peter 1:19

[75] Heb. 5:7; 1 Peter 2:24

[76] Christ was not guilty, yet God put our sins on His account when Christ died for us. When the sinner trusts Christ, God's righteousness is applied to his account. The concept is developed in Rom. 4.

[77] Matt. 11:28

[78] See Matt. 24:35; 5:18. A "jot" is a tiny Hebrew letter. A "tittle" is a small projection on a Hebrew letter.

me.[79] Then I asked Faithful how I should approach him, and he said, "Go, and you shall find him upon a mercy-seat, where he sits all year long, to give pardon and forgiveness to those who come to him." [80] I told him that I did not know what to say when I came. And he told me to say, in effect: God be merciful to me a sinner, and help me to know and believe in Jesus Christ;[81] for I see that without his righteousness, and my faith in that righteousness, I am utterly lost. Lord, I have heard that you are a merciful God and have sent your Son Jesus Christ to be the Savior of the world;[82] and moreover, that you are willing to bestow him upon such a poor sinner as I am (and I am a sinner indeed); Lord, take therefore this opportunity, and magnify your grace in the salvation of my soul, through your Son Jesus Christ. Amen.

CHRISTIAN: And did you do as you were told?

HOPEFUL: Yes, over and over and over.

CHRISTIAN: And did the Father reveal his Son to you?

HOPEFUL: Not at the first, nor the second, nor the third, nor the fourth, nor the fifth; no, nor at the sixth time.

CHRISTIAN: What did you do then?

HOPEFUL: Why, I could not tell what to do!

CHRISTIAN: Did you think of not praying anymore?

HOPEFUL: Yes, a hundred times over.

CHRISTIAN: So why didn't you stop?

---

[79] Ps. 95:6; Jer. 29:12–13; Dan. 6:10

[80] The Jewish tabernacle was divided into three parts: an outer court, where the animals were sacrificed; the holy place, where there stood a table, a lampstand, and a golden altar for burning incense; and a holy of holies. In the holy of holies was a wooden chest called "the ark of the covenant." Upon the top of this chest was a golden covering with an image of an angel at each end. This covering was called "the mercy seat." It was the throne of God in the camp of Israel. Once a year, the high priest sprinkled blood on this mercy seat to cover the sins of the people. See Exod. 25:10 –22; Lev. 16; Num. 7:89; Heb. 4:16. Because of Jesus' death for sinners, God's throne is a throne of grace and mercy, not a throne of judgment.

[81] Luke 18:13

[82] 1 John 4:14; John 4:42

HOPEFUL: I believed that what I had been told was true; that is, that without the righteousness of this Christ, all the world could not save me; and therefore I thought that if I quit praying, I would die, so I will die at the throne of grace. And with that, this came to my mind: "If it tarry, wait for it; because it will surely come, it will not tarry."[83] So I continued praying until the Father showed me his Son.[84]

CHRISTIAN: And how was he revealed to you?

HOPEFUL: I did not see him with my earthly eyes, but with the eyes of my understanding;[85] and this is how it was: One day I was very sad, sadder than at any other time in my life, and this sorrow was the result of a fresh glimpse of the magnitude and vileness of my sins. And as I sat there expecting nothing but hell and the everlasting damnation of my soul, suddenly I saw the Lord Jesus Christ look down from heaven at me and say, "Believe on the Lord Jesus Christ, and thou shalt be saved."[86]

But I replied, "Lord, I am a great, a very great sinner." And he answered, "My grace is sufficient for thee."[87] Then I said, "But, Lord, what is believing?" And then, from the verse, "He that cometh to me shall never hunger, and he that believeth on me shall never thirst," I recognized that believing and coming were the same thing; and that he who sought after salvation through Christ with his whole heart, he indeed believed in Christ.[88] Then tears came to my eyes, and I asked, "But, Lord, can such a great sinner as I really be accepted by you and saved by you?" And I heard him say, "Him that com-

---

[83]See Hab. 2:3. Often verses of Scripture came to Bunyan's mind when he was under conviction, assuring him that God would indeed save him.

[84]Matt. 11:27

[85]Eph. 1:18–19

[86]Acts 16:30–31

[87]This is out of Bunyan's own experience. He wrote in *Grace Abounding*: "As I thought my case most sad and fearful, these words did with great power suddenly break in upon me, 'My grace is sufficient for thee,' three times together. O! methought every word was a mighty word for me." See 2 Cor. 12:9.

[88]John 6:35

eth to me, I will in no wise cast out."[89] Then I said, "But, Lord, how should I think of you when coming to you, so that my faith is in you?" Then he said, "Christ Jesus came into the world to save sinners." "He is the end of the law for righteousness to every one that believes." "He died for our sins, and rose again for our justification: He loved us, and washed us from our sins in his own blood." "He is mediator between God and us." "He ever liveth to make intercession for us."[90] And I gathered from all of these Scriptures that I must look for righteousness in his person and for satisfaction for my sins through his blood;[91] that what he did in obedience to his Father's law, submitting to its penalty, was not for himself, but for anyone who will accept it for his salvation and be thankful. And now my heart was filled with joy, my eyes filled with tears, and my heart brimming over with love for the name, people, and ways of Jesus Christ.

CHRISTIAN: This indeed was a revelation of Christ to your soul. But tell me, what effect did this have upon your spirit?

HOPEFUL: It made me see that all the world, regardless of any good it might contain, is in a state of condemnation. It made me see that God the Father, though he is just, can justify the sinner who comes to him.[92] It made me greatly ashamed of the vileness of my former life, and dismayed me with the sense of my own ignorance; for before now, nothing had so clearly showed me the beauty of Jesus Christ.[93] It made me love a holy life and long to do something for the honor and glory of the name of the Lord Jesus; yes, had I now a thousand

---

[89]John 6:37
[90]1 Tim. 1:15; Rom. 10:4; 4:25; Rev. 1:5; 1 Tim. 2:5; Heb. 7:24–25
[91]We cannot satisfy God by our good works, but Christ satisfied the righteous demands of God's law by His death on the cross. The death of Christ was God's payment to redeem sinners and set them free.
[92]See Rom. 3:26. How can God declare sinners righteous and still be righteous Himself? By having Christ pay the penalty for their sins. Thus, God is just (because sin is paid for) and the justifier of those who trust Christ.
[93]Isa. 33:17; Ps. 45

gallons of blood in my body, I would have shed it all for the sake of the Lord Jesus.

I saw then in my dream that Hopeful looked back and saw Ignorance, whom they had left behind. "Look," he said to Christian, "how that youngster lingers far behind."

CHRISTIAN: Yes, yes, I see him. He doesn't care for our company.

HOPEFUL: But it wouldn't have hurt him to have kept up with us.

CHRISTIAN: That's true, but I guarantee you he thinks otherwise.

HOPEFUL: That, I think, he does; however, let's wait for him.

So they did.

Then Christian said to him, "Come on, man, why do you stay so far behind?"

IGNORANCE: I enjoy walking alone, unless I particularly like the company.

Then Christian said softly to Hopeful, "Didn't I tell you he doesn't care for our company? But let's pass the time in this desolate place by talking to him." Then he turned to Ignorance and said, "How are you? And how do things stand between God and your soul now?"[94]

IGNORANCE: Well I hope; for I am filled with good notions that come to mind and comfort me as I walk.

CHRISTIAN: What good notions? Please tell us.

IGNORANCE: Why, I think of God and heaven.

CHRISTIAN: So do the devils and damned souls.[95]

IGNORANCE: But I think of them and desire them.

---

[94] This introduces another section of introspection and doctrinal discussion. Generally speaking, in this conversation Christian represents the orthodox Puritan point of view, while Ignorance defends a theology the Puritans would consider unbiblical. Ignorance bases his confidence on feelings and man-made ideas, while Hopeful seeks to defend his position from Scripture. Ignorance lives up to his name: he is ignorant of himself and of God's truth.

[95] See James 2:19. The devils (demons) were more honest than Ignorance, for they at least trembled when they thought of God!

CHRISTIAN: So do many that are never likely to get there. "The soul of the sluggard desireth, and hath nothing."[96]

IGNORANCE: But I think of them and leave all for them.

CHRISTIAN: That I doubt; for leaving all is a hard thing to do—harder than many realize. But what makes you think you have left all for God and heaven?

IGNORANCE: My heart tells me so.

CHRISTIAN: The wise man says, "He that trusts his own heart is a fool."[97]

IGNORANCE: That applies to an evil heart, but mine is good.[98]

CHRISTIAN: But how do you prove that?

IGNORANCE: Because it comforts me with the hope of heaven.

CHRISTIAN: That may be through its own deceitfulness; for a man's heart may comfort him with hopes of that thing for which he has no grounds to hope.

IGNORANCE: But my heart and life agree, and therefore my hope is well grounded.

CHRISTIAN: Who told you that your heart and life agree?

IGNORANCE: My heart tells me so.

CHRISTIAN: Ask my friend here if I am a thief![99] Your heart tells you so! Unless the Word of God bears witness to this matter, other testimony is of no value.

IGNORANCE: But is it not a good heart that has good thoughts? And is not that a good life that is in accordance with God's commandments?

---

[96] Prov. 13:4

[97] See Prov. 28:26. Christian does not deny the witness of one's innermost feelings. What he says is that we dare not trust our feelings alone, for they may deceive us. The fact that Ignorance claims to have a "good heart" indicates that he has never seen himself a sinner before the eyes of God.

[98] This is why he is called Ignorance. He is ignorant of his own sinfulness and of God's righteousness (Rom. 10:1–13).

[99] Obviously thieves will not tell on each other! Ignorance is reasoning in circles: his heart tells him he lives a good life, and his good life agrees with his heart! Only the Word of God can tell us what we are.

CHRISTIAN: Yes, it is a good heart that has good thoughts, and it is a good life that is in accordance with God's commandments; but it is one thing indeed to have these, and another thing only to think so.

IGNORANCE: Please tell me, what do you consider good thoughts and a life in accordance with God's commandments?

CHRISTIAN: There are good thoughts of various kinds; some regarding ourselves, some God, some Christ, and some other things.

IGNORANCE: What would be good thoughts regarding ourselves?

CHRISTIAN: Those that agree with the Word of God.

IGNORANCE: When do our thoughts about ourselves agree with the Word of God?

CHRISTIAN: When we pass the same judgment upon ourselves which the Word passes. To explain what I mean: The Word of God says of the natural man, "There is none righteous, there is none that doeth good."[100] It says also that "every imagination of the heart of man is only evil, and that continually."[101] And again, "The imagination of man's heart is evil from his youth."[102] Now then, when we think thus of ourselves, having a real sense of it, then our thoughts are good ones, because they are in agreement with the Word of God.

IGNORANCE: I will never believe that my heart is that bad.

CHRISTIAN: Therefore you have never had one good thought concerning yourself in your entire life. But let me go on. As the Word passes a judgment upon our *hearts,* so it passes a judgment upon our *ways;* and when OUR *hearts* and OUR *ways* agree with the judgment which the Word gives on both, then both are good, because they agree with it.

IGNORANCE: Explain what you mean.

CHRISTIAN: Why, the Word of God says that man's ways are crooked ways, not good, but corrupt.[103] It says they are

---

[100]Rom. 3:10–12
[101]Gen. 6:5
[102]Gen. 8:21
[103]Ps. 125:5; Prov. 2:15

171

naturally out of the good way, and they do not know it.[104] Now when a man thinks this about his ways, both realistically and with humility, then he has good thoughts about his own ways, because his thoughts now agree with the judgment of the Word of God.[105]

IGNORANCE: What are good thoughts concerning God?

CHRISTIAN: Just as I have said concerning ourselves, when our thoughts about God agree with what the Word says about him; and that is, when we think of his being and attributes as the Word teaches; which I cannot right now discuss at length. But to speak of him with reference to us: We have right thoughts about God when we think that he knows us better than we know ourselves, and can see sin in us when and where we see none in ourselves; when we think he knows our innermost thoughts, and when our hearts are always open to his eyes; and when we think that all our righteousness stinks in his nostrils, and that therefore he cannot bear to see us stand before him with any confidence, even in our best performances.

IGNORANCE: Do you think I am such a fool as to think God can see no further than I can or that I would come to God in the best of my performances?

CHRISTIAN: So what do you think about this matter?

IGNORANCE: Why, to be brief, I think I must believe in Christ for justification.

CHRISTIAN: What? You think you must believe in Christ when you don't see your need of him! You see neither your original sin nor your actual sin, but have such an opinion of yourself, and of what you do, that you are clearly revealed as one who has never seen a necessity for Christ's personal

---

[104]Rom. 3:17

[105]Assurance of salvation comes when we believe God's Word and receive its witness. Bunyan wrote in *Grace Abounding*: "I saw that it was not my good frame of heart that made my righteousness better, nor yet my bad frame that made my righteousness worse; for my righteousness was Jesus Christ, the same yesterday, today, and for ever." See Heb. 13:8.

righteousness to justify you before God. How then can you say, "I believe in Christ"?

IGNORANCE: I believe well enough.

CHRISTIAN: What do you believe?

IGNORANCE: I believe that Christ died for sinners, and that I shall be justified before God through his gracious acceptance of my obedience to his law.[106] Christ makes my religious works acceptable to his Father by virtue of his merits, and thus I shall be justified.

CHRISTIAN: Let me give this response to your confession of faith:

1. You believe with an imaginary faith, for this faith is described nowhere in the Word.[107]

2. You believe with a false faith, because it takes justification from the personal righteousness of Christ and applies it to your own.

3. This faith makes Christ a justifier of your works, not of your person, and for your works' sake, which is false.

4. Therefore, this faith is deceptive and will leave you under the wrath of God Almighty in the day of judgment; for true justifying faith sends the soul (aware of its lost condition by the law) flying for refuge to Christ's righteousness.[108] And his righteousness is not an act of grace by which he makes your obedience acceptable to God as a justification; but it is his personal obedience to the law in doing and suffering for us that which would be required of us. This is the righteousness that true faith accepts, and under which the soul is covered and presented as spotless before God, and acquitted of condemnation.

---

[106] Ignorance thinks salvation is by works and that all Christ does is make the sinner's works acceptable to God! See Gal. 2:16.

[107] Faith is only as good as the object. To trust in good works is to have imaginary faith, for good works cannot save. Faith in Christ is true saving faith, because the Word of God assures us that this is God's way of salvation.

[108] A reference to the cities of refuge (Josh. 20), a picture of Jesus Christ, our refuge from the judgment of sin (Heb. 6:18).

IGNORANCE: What! Would you have us trust in what Christ in his own person has done without us? This kind of thinking would free us to live however we liked.[109] For why would it matter how we live, if all we have to do is believe we can be justified by Christ's personal righteousness?

CHRISTIAN: Ignorance is your name, and so are you; even this answer demonstrates it. You are ignorant of what justifying righteousness is, and you are ignorant of how to save your soul from the wrath of God through faith in that righteousness. Yes, you also are ignorant of the true effects of saving faith in this righteousness of Christ, which means to yield the heart to God in Christ, to love his name, his Word, his ways, and his people.

HOPEFUL: Ask him if he ever had Christ revealed to him from heaven.[110]

IGNORANCE: What! You believe in revelations! I think that what you and all the rest say about that matter is just the result of disordered minds.

HOPEFUL: Why, man! Christ is so hidden in God from our natural understanding that he cannot be known by any man unless God the Father reveals him to us.

IGNORANCE: That is your faith, but not mine. Yet I have no doubt that mine is as good as yours.

CHRISTIAN: Allow me to interject this word: You should not speak so lightly of this matter. For this I will boldly affirm (even as my good friend has done), that no man can know Jesus Christ except by the revelation of the Father:[111] yes, and faith too, by which the soul lays hold upon Christ, must be

---

[109] Ignorance uses the old argument, "If we are saved only by faith, without good works, then we shall continue to sin." Paul answers this argument in Rom. 6. The true believer is dead to sin and has a new nature within that makes him want to obey God. Hopeful and Christian try to teach Ignorance that there are "true effects" from saving faith, and these change the life.

[110] God the Father reveals His Son to us in our hearts. See Matt. 11:25–27; 16:17; Gal. 1:15–16.

[111] Matt. 11:27; 1 Cor. 12:3; Eph. 1:18 –19

formed by his mighty power; of which, poor Ignorance, you are ignorant.

So wake up! See your own wretchedness, and fly to the Lord Jesus; and by his righteousness, which is the righteousness of God (for he himself is God), you shall be delivered from condemnation.[112]

IGNORANCE: You go so fast, I cannot keep up with you. You go on ahead; I must stay behind for a while.

Then they said:

Well, Ignorance, wilt thou yet foolish be,
To slight good counsel, ten times given thee?
And if thou yet refuse it, you shalt know
Ere long the evil of thy doing so.
Remember, man, in time; stoop, do not fear,
Good counsel taken well, saves: therefore hear.
But if thou yet shalt slight it, thou wilt be
The loser, Ignorance, I'll warrant thee.

Then Christian said to his friend and companion, "Well, come, my good Hopeful, I see that you and I must walk by ourselves again."

---

[112] See Rev. 3:17. Ignorance was well named!

*And so we reach the last segment of the pilgrims' jour-
ney. In this section is found one of the best analyses of
spiritual decline you will ever read, when Christian cites
the nine reasons to Hopeful. Bunyan, like most Puritan
ministers, was a master at examining his own heart and
the hearts of others. Note in this discourse that secret
failures always precede public sins.*

*Before Christian and Hopeful reach the gate, they must
cross a river. Bunyan borrows this image from Israel
crossing the Jordan and entering into the Promised
Land (Josh. 3). However, nowhere in the Bible is "the
crossing of the Jordan" used as a symbol of death. The
image of crossing a river, meaning death, is used in
Christian hymns and poems and in the writings of
Dante and Virgil, but it is not a Bible image. Israel's Jordan experience pictures the believer dying to self, leaving
a life of wandering in unbelief, and entering into his inheritance in Christ in this life. After all, Canaan cannot
be a picture of heaven because Israel fought battles
there! We must confess, however, that Bunyan's handling of this event is masterful.*

*From the City of Destruction to the gates of heaven, this
is the scope of* The Pilgrim's Progress, *and Christian has
made the journey. But Bunyan closes with a dramatic
warning that a person may be near and yet so far from
God's salvation. Ignorance is self-deluded, and at the
end of the journey he is bound hand and foot and cast
into hell —at the very gate of heaven.*

May this not be true of us.

o I saw in my dream that Christian and Hopeful walked on quickly, while Ignorance came hobbling behind. Then said Christian to his companion, "I pity this poor man, for he will certainly have a hard time at the end."

HOPEFUL: Sadly, there are many in our town in the same condition; whole families, yes, whole streets, and some are pilgrims too. And if there are that many in our part of the world, how many must there be in the place where he was born?

CHRISTIAN: Indeed the Word says, "He hath blinded their eyes lest they should see."[1] But now that we are by ourselves, tell me, what do you think of such men? Have they never been convicted of sin and consequently have no fears about the dangerous conditions of their souls?

HOPEFUL: You tell me what you think, for you are the elder.

CHRISTIAN: I think that sometimes they may come under conviction, but being naturally ignorant, they do not understand that such convictions are for their good; and therefore they desperately seek to stifle them, and continue to flatter themselves that their own hearts are right.

HOPEFUL: I believe, as you say, that fear often works for men's own good when they begin to go on pilgrimage.

CHRISTIAN: Without any doubt it does, if it is the right kind of fear; for the Word says, "The fear of the Lord is the beginning of wisdom."[2]

HOPEFUL: How would you describe the right kind of fear?

CHRISTIAN: True or right fear can be discerned by three things:

---

[1]See John 12:40. God gives men the light of salvation, but if they persistently refuse that light, they become spiritually blinded.

[2]See Prov. 9:10; Job 28:28; Ps. 111:10. "Fear" means reverence and respect, a proper attitude toward God. It is not the cringing fear of a slave, but the respectful fear of a son to a father.

1. By its origin: it is caused by the conviction that one needs salvation for sin.

2. It drives the soul to cling to Christ for salvation.

3. It creates within the soul a great reverence for God, his Word, and his ways, keeping the soul sensitive to all of these and making it afraid to turn from them, to the right hand or to the left, to anything that might dishonor God, destroy the soul's peace, or grieve the Spirit.

HOPEFUL: I believe you have spoken the truth. Are we almost past the Enchanted Ground now?

CHRISTIAN: Why? Are you weary of this conversation?[3]

HOPEFUL: No, not at all, but I would like to know where we are.

CHRISTIAN: We have no more than two miles to go. But let us return to the matter we were discussing. Now the ignorant do not know that convictions that tend to make them fearful are for their good, and therefore they seek to stifle them.

HOPEFUL: How do they do this?

CHRISTIAN: 1. They think those fears are the work of the devil (though indeed they are caused by God), so they resist them as though they are things that will lead to their defeat.

2. They also think these fears tend to spoil their faith, when, sadly enough, they have no faith at all! And so they harden their hearts against these fears.

3. They assume they ought not to fear, and therefore, in spite of the fears, they grow presumptuously self-confident.

4. They see that those fears tend to destroy their pitiful self-righteousness, and they resist them with all their might.

HOPEFUL: I know something about this myself, for that is the way I used to be.

CHRISTIAN: Well, we will leave our neighbor Ignorance by himself for now and find another worthwhile question to discuss.

---

[3]Christian never tires of discussing spiritual truths! He wants to keep Hopeful awake and alert as they cross the Enchanted Ground. See Heb. 12:3.

HOPEFUL: I agree totally, but you shall still begin.

CHRISTIAN: Well then, were you acquainted with a fellow named Temporary, who lived in your area about ten years ago and was opposed to religion?

HOPEFUL: Know him! Yes indeed. He lived in Graceless, a town about two miles from Honesty, and he lived next door to Turnback.

CHRISTIAN: Right. Actually they lived under the same roof. Well, at one point I believe that man had some awareness of and insight into his sinful state and the punishment it deserved.

HOPEFUL: I think the same thing, for my house was no more than three miles from his, and he would often come to me in tears. Truly I pitied the man, and was not altogether without hope for him. But from this one may see that not everyone who cries, "Lord, Lord," will enter the way.[4]

CHRISTIAN: He told me once that he was resolved to go on pilgrimage, as we are now; but all of a sudden he made the acquaintance of Save-self, and then he became a stranger to me.[5]

HOPEFUL: Since we are talking about him, let us investigate the reason for his sudden backsliding, and that of others like him.[6]

CHRISTIAN: That could be very profitable. Why don't you begin?

HOPEFUL: Well, in my judgment there are four reasons for it:

---

[4]Matt. 7:21–22

[5]Save-self represents those who think they can save themselves by good works and character.

[6]Backsliding is an Old Testament term that describes the believer who is not growing and going forward in his faith. Jeremiah uses it thirteen times, and Hosea four times, to describe the sad spiritual condition of the Jewish nation. Hopeful explains why professed Christians backslide: their repentance was emotional but not sincere; they fear what people say; they want to avoid shame; and they do not honestly face their sins and God's judgment. Bunyan seems to suggest that the backslider is, by his backsliding, proving that he was never genuinely converted at all.

1. Though the consciences of such men are awakened, their minds are not changed; therefore, when the guilt passes, they cease to be religious. They return to their old ways again, just as the dog returns to its vomit.[7] Thus they are eager for heaven only because they fear the torments of hell; and as soon as their sense of hell and their fears of damnation chill and cool, so does their desire for heaven and salvation. When their guilt and fears are gone, their desires for heaven and happiness die, and they return to their old course again.

2. Another reason is that they are slaves to certain fears that overpower them; particularly the fear of men, for "the fear of men bringeth a snare."[8] So although they seem eager for heaven as long as the flames of hell are about their ears, when that terror abates, they begin to have second thoughts: namely, that it is good to be wise and not run the risk of losing all, or at least not bringing themselves unnecessary trouble. And so they fall in with the world again.

3. The stigma that surrounds religion is also a stumbling block to them. They are high and mighty, and they consider religion low and common; therefore, when they have lost their sense of hell and the wrath to come, they return to their former ways.

4. They do not even like to think about guilt and fear, or the possibility of future misery; if they did, perhaps the foresight might make them flee to where the righteous flee and are safe. But because they shun even the thoughts of guilt and fear, when once they are rid of their awakenings about the terrors and wrath of God, they gladly harden their hearts and choose ways that will harden them more and more.

CHRISTIAN: You are near the truth, for at the bottom of it all is the need for change in mind and will.[9] They are like the felon who stands before the judge: he shakes and trembles and seems to repent; but at the bottom of it all is his fear of

---

[7] See 2 Peter 2:22. A sinner can reform outwardly, but this does not change his heart. Eventually he will go where his heart is.

[8] Prov. 29:25

[9] The fundamental cause is lack of true repentance.

punishment, not any regret for his crime. Let this man have his freedom, and he will still be a thief and a scoundrel, whereas if his mind were changed, he would be otherwise.

HOPEFUL: I have pointed out the reasons for their backsliding; now you tell me how it happens.

CHRISTIAN: So I will, willingly.

1. As much as they can, they turn their thoughts away from any reminder of God, death, and judgment to come.

2. Then they gradually cease their private duties, such as devotional prayer, curbing their lusts, being vigilant, being repentant for sin, and the like.

3. Then they shun the company of lively and sincere Christians.

4. After that they grow indifferent to public duties such as hearing and reading the Word, gathering together for worship, and the like.

5. Then they begin to find fault with some of the godly, and the devilish purpose behind this is to find some alleged reason for turning away from religion.

6. Then they begin to associate with worldly, immoral, and sensual men.

7. Then they secretly indulge in worldly and lewd conversations; and they are happy if they can find any who are considered honest doing the same, so they may use their example as an excuse to indulge more boldly.

8. After this they begin to play with little sins openly.

9. And then, being hardened, they show themselves as they really are. Launched again into the gulf of misery, they are lost forever in their own deception, unless a miracle of grace prevents it.

Now I saw in my dream that by this time the pilgrims had crossed the Enchanted Ground and entered the country of Beulah, where the air was very sweet and pleasant;[10] the pathway lay directly through it, and they found comfort and res-

---

[10]*Beulah* means "married" in Hebrew. When God restores Israel to her land, she will no longer be called "Forsaken," nor the land "Desolate." Israel will be called "Hephzibah," which means "My delight is in her." The land will be

toration there for a time. In this land the flowers bloomed every day, and the pilgrims continually heard the singing of birds and the voice of the turtledove in the land. Here the sun shone night and day, for this was beyond the Valley of the Shadow of Death and out of the reach of Giant Despair; in fact, they could not even see Doubting Castle from this place. Here they were within sight of the city to which they were going, and here they met some of the inhabitants of that place; for the Shining Ones frequently walked in this land, because it was upon the borders of heaven. In this land also the contract between the bride and the bridegroom was renewed; yes, here, "As the bridegroom rejoiceth over the bride, so did their God rejoice over them."[11] Here they had no lack of corn and wine;[12] for in this place they found an abundance of that which they had sought during all their pilgrimage. Here they heard voices from the Celestial City, loud voices, saying, "Say ye to the daughter of Zion, Behold, thy salvation cometh! Behold, his reward is with him." Here all the inhabitants of the country called them "the holy people, the redeemed of the Lord, sought out."[13]

As they walked in this land, they rejoiced more than they had in those places that were more remote from the kingdom to which they were going; and as they drew near to the city, they had a more perfect view of it.[14] It was built of pearls and precious stones, and the street was paved with gold; and the natural glory of the city and the reflection of the sunbeams

---

called "Beulah" because Israel and her God shall be "married" again. See Song 2:10 –12; Isa. 62:4 –12 for the imagery in this section.

[11] Isa. 62:5

[12] Corn and wine were the two chief crops of Israel, mentioned together some twenty-six times in the Old Testament. See Gen. 27:28, 37. "Plenty of corn and wine" was a mark of God's favor on the land.

[13] Isa. 62:11–12

[14] See Rev. 21–22. Because there is no need for the sun in heaven, the reflections the pilgrims see may be caused by the sun in their world shining on the heavenly city. Bunyan is suggesting that saints on earth can have a foretaste of the glory of heaven.

upon it made Christian sick with desire;[15] Hopeful also had a spell or two of the same disease. Because of this, they lay down for a while, crying out, "If you see my beloved, tell him I am sick of love."[16]

Then, when they had gained a little strength and were able to bear their sickness, they walked on, getting closer and closer to the city, where there were orchards, vineyards, and gardens, and their gates opened onto the highway. As they came up to these places, they noticed the gardener standing in the path, and they asked him, "Whose vineyards and gardens are these?" He answered, "They are the King's, and are planted here for his own enjoyment and for the consolation of pilgrims."

So the gardener led them into the vineyards and told them to refresh themselves with the delicious fruit.[17] He also showed them where the King walked and where his favorite arbors were; and here they stopped and slept.

Now I noticed in my dream that they talked more in their sleep at this time than they ever had during the rest of their journey; and as I was wondering about this, the gardener said even to me, "Why are you marveling at this?[18] The fruit of the grapes of these vineyards goes down so sweetly that it causes the lips of those who are asleep to speak."[19]

Then I saw that when they awoke, they prepared themselves to go up to the city. But, as I said, the reflection of the sun upon the city (for "the city was pure gold") was so glorious that they could not look at it directly, but had to view it through an instrument made for that purpose.[20] As they

---

[15] Prov. 13:12

[16] See Song 2:5; 5:8. There are times when the glories of heaven overwhelm the Christian.

[17] The Law permitted pilgrims to eat from a neighbor's field or vineyard (Deut. 23:24–25).

[18] The gardener speaks to the author!

[19] Song 7:9

[20] See Rev. 21:18; 2 Cor. 3:18; Exod. 34:29–35. When Moses saw the Lord, he received some of God's glory on his face, and he had to wear a veil so that the people would not see the glory fade.

went on, they were met by two men in garments that shone like gold; also their faces shone like light.[21]

These men asked the pilgrims where they had come from, and Christian and Hopeful told them.[22] They also asked them where they had lodged, and what difficulties and dangers, what comforts and pleasures they had encountered on the way, and Christian and Hopeful told them. Then the men said, "You have only two more difficulties to deal with, and then you will be in the city."[23]

Christian and his companion asked the men to go along with them; so they told them they would. "But," they said, "you must reach the city by your own faith." So I saw in my dream that they went on together until they came within sight of the gate.

Now I noticed that between them and the gate was a river, but there was no bridge across it, and the river was very deep. At the sight of this river, the pilgrims were stunned; but the men who were with them said, "You must go through, or you cannot get to the gate."

The pilgrims then asked whether there was any other way to get to the gate, to which the men answered, "Yes, but since the foundation of the world, only two, Enoch and Elijah, have ever been permitted to take that path, and that shall be the case until the last trumpet sounds."[24] The pilgrims then, especially Christian, began to despair, looking this way and that; but they could find no way by which they might escape the river. Then they asked the men if the waters were all the same depth. They said, "No," but they could not help them

---

[21]Not only did Moses have a shining face, but so did Jesus when He was transfigured (Matt. 17:1–8), and Stephen when he preached (Acts 6:15).

[22]Another interrogation!

[23] The two difficulties are crossing the river (a picture of death) and gaining access at the gate of the city.

[24] Enoch was "translated" to heaven without dying (Gen. 5:21–24; Heb. 11:5). Elijah was taken to heaven in a chariot of fire (2 Kings 2:1–11). The last trumpet signals the return of Christ and the changing of the believer to be like Christ (1 Cor. 15:51–54).

with that either, "for," they said, "you will find it deeper or shallower, according to your faith in the King of the place."[25]

They then waded into the water, and Christian began to sink, crying out to his good friend Hopeful, "I sink in deep waters; the billows go over my head, all his waves go over me! Selah."[26]

Then Hopeful said, "Have courage, my brother, for I feel the bottom, and it is solid." Then said Christian, "Ah! my friend, the sorrows of death surround me; I shall not see the land that flows with milk and honey."

And with that a great darkness and horror fell upon Christian so that he could not see before him.[27] Also he became so distraught that he could neither remember, nor speak reasonably about those blessings he had encountered on his pilgrimage. Everything he said focused on his terrible fears of heart and mind and that he should die in that river and never enter the gate. He was also greatly troubled with thoughts about the sins he had committed, both since and before he began to be a pilgrim. Also, his words revealed that he was troubled by visions of demons and evil spirits.

Hopeful therefore had all he could do to keep his brother's head above water; in fact, at times Christian almost disappeared, only to rise up again half dead. Hopeful also tried to comfort him, saying, "Brother, I see the gate, and there are men waiting to receive us." But Christian would answer, "It is you, it is you they wait for; you have been hopeful ever since I knew you." "And so have you," said Hopeful to Christian. "Ah! brother!" he said, "surely if I was right he would

---

[25]See Matt. 9:29. Again, Bunyan teaches us that no two believers have the same experiences. Christian almost gives up and drowns, while Hopeful encourages him to continue crossing the river. The enemy attacks us at the time of death just as during life.

[26]See Ps. 69:2. "Selah" ends Christian's quotation. It is a Hebrew word that was probably a musical direction or notation for the temple singers.

[27]Christian encourages himself by quoting from the Psalms; here it is Pss. 18:4–5; 116:3. Jonah prayed in a similar way (Jonah 2). Abraham experienced a "horror of great darkness" the night God made His covenant with him (Gen. 15:12).

now come to help me; but because of my sins he has led me into this trap and deserted me."[28]

Then said Hopeful, "My brother, you have forgotten the text where it is said of the wicked, 'There is no band in their death, but their strength is firm. They are not troubled as other men, neither are they plagued like other men.'"[29] These troubles you are going through in these waters are not a sign that God has forsaken you, but are sent to try you, testing whether you will remember all his previous mercy to you and rely upon him in your distress.

Then I saw in my dream that Christian seemed to be in deep thought for a while, during which Hopeful added, "Be of good cheer, Jesus Christ maketh thee whole." And with that Christian cried out with a loud voice, "Oh! I see him again, and he tells me, 'When thou passest through the waters, I will be with thee; and through the rivers, they shall not overflow thee.'"[30]

Then they both took courage, and after that the enemy was as silent as a stone, until they had crossed over. Presently Christian found ground to stand upon, and then the rest of the river was shallow. Thus they crossed over.

Now on the bank of the river on the other side they saw the two Shining Men again, waiting for them. "We are ministering spirits," they said, "sent to minister to those who are heirs of salvation."[31] And thus they went along toward the gate.

Now the city stood upon a great hill,[32] but the pilgrims climbed that hill with ease because they had these two men to

---

[28] The memory of past sins can burden and frighten the believer at the hour of death. Christian forgets all the blessings he had received from God along his pilgrimage. It is dangerous to trust our feelings.

[29] Hopeful reminds Christian of the Word of God, which is the only source of assurance. Here he quotes Ps. 73:4–5.

[30] See Acts 9:34. Christian finally gets his assurance from God's Word and quotes Isa. 43:2.

[31] See Heb. 1:14; Luke 16:19–22. The angels escort God's people to heaven at death.

[32] See Matt. 5:14. Christian climbs his last hill!

lead them and to lean upon; also they had left their mortal garments behind them in the river.[33] Therefore they went up
with much agility and speed, though the foundation upon
which the city rested was higher than the clouds. They
climbed up through the air, talking happily as they went, comforted because they had safely crossed the river and had such
glorious companions to accompany them.

> *Now, now look how the holy pilgrims ride,*
> *Clouds are their chariots, angels are their guide:*
> *Who would not here for him all hazards run,*
> *That thus provides for his when this world's done?*

They talked about the magnificence of the place with the
Shining Ones, who told them that the beauty and glory of it
was inexpressible. "There," they said, "is Mount Zion, the
heavenly Jerusalem, the company of angels, and the spirits of
just men made perfect.[34] You are going now to the paradise
of God, where you will see the tree of life and eat of its never-
fading fruits; and there you will have white robes given you,
and you will walk and talk every day with the King, all the
days of eternity.[35] There you will never again see such things
as you saw when you were upon the earth, such as sorrow,
sickness, affliction, and death, 'for the former things are
passed away.'[36] You are now going to Abraham, to Isaac, and
Jacob, and to the prophets — men whom God has 'taken
away from the evil to come,' and who are now resting upon
their beds, each one walking in his righteousness."[37]

Christian and Hopeful then asked, "What shall we do in
the holy place?" And the answer was, "There you shall receive
comfort for all your toil and joy for all your sorrow; you shall

---

[33] The body is like a garment, and at death it is shed so that we can receive
the new, glorified body (1 Cor. 15:53 –57). 2 Cor. 5:1–10 pictures the body
as a soldier's tent, taken down to make room for a permanent and glorious
building.
[34] Heb. 12:22–24
[35] Rev. 2:7; 3:4 –5; 22:5
[36] Isa. 65:16 –17; Rev. 21:4
[37] Isa. 57:1–2

reap what you have sown—the fruit of all your prayers, tears, and sufferings for the King along the way.[38] You shall wear crowns of gold and enjoy the constant sight of the Holy One, for 'there you shall see him as he is.'[39] There also you shall serve continually, with praise, shouting, and thanksgiving, him whom you desired to serve in the world, though with much difficulty, because of the weakness of your flesh.[40] There your eyes shall be delighted with seeing, and your ears with hearing the pleasant voice of the Mighty One.[41] There you shall enjoy your friends again who have gone before you; and there you shall with joy receive every one who follows into the holy place after you. There you shall be clothed with glory and majesty, and shall ride out with the King of Glory. When he comes with the sound of trumpets in the clouds, as upon the wings of the wind, you shall come with him; and when he sits upon the throne of judgment, you shall sit beside him; and when he passes sentence upon all the workers of iniquity, be they angels or men, you shall have a voice in that judgment, because they were his enemies and yours.[42] Also, when he returns to the city, you shall return too, with the sound of trumpets, and be with him forever."

Now as they drew near the gate, a company of the heavenly host came out to meet them; and the other two Shining Ones said to this company, "These are men who have loved our Lord when they were in the world, and who have left all for his holy name; and he has sent us to fetch them, and we have brought them thus far on their desired journey, so that they may go in and look their Redeemer in the face with joy." Then the heavenly host gave a great shout, saying, "Blessed are they which are called into the marriage supper of the Lamb."[43]

---

[38] Gal. 6:7–8

[39] Rev. 4:4; 1 John 3:2

[40] Rev. 7:15; Rom. 6:19; Gal. 4:13

[41] Isa. 64:4; 1 Cor. 2:9

[42] These statements about the return of Jesus Christ for His people come from 1 Thess. 4:13 –18; Jude 14 –15; Dan. 7:9 –10; 1 Cor. 6:2–3.

[43] Rev. 19:9

At this time several of the King's trumpeters also came out to meet them; they were clothed in white and shining raiment and made even the heavens echo with their loud, melodious sounds. These trumpeters saluted Christian and Hopeful with ten thousand welcomes; and this they did with shouts and the sound of trumpets.

This done, they surrounded the two companions; some went before and some behind, some on the right hand and some on the left (to guard them through the upper regions);[44] it was as if heaven itself had come down to meet them. Thus they walked on together. And as they walked, these trumpeters, by mixing their joyful and continual music with looks and gestures, signified to Christian and his brother how welcome they were into their company, and with what gladness they had come to meet them; and now the two men were in heaven before they even came to it, caught up in the sight of angels and the sounds of their melodious notes. They could see the city itself now, and they thought they heard all the bells ringing to welcome them.[45] But above all were their warm and joyful thoughts about their own dwelling there, with such company, for ever and ever. What tongue or pen can express their glorious joy! And thus they came up to the gate.

Now when they reached the gate, they saw written over it in letters of gold, "Blessed are they that do his commandments, that they may have right to the tree of life, and may enter in through the gates into the city."[46]

---

[44] They are guarding them against Satan, prince of the power of the air (Eph. 2:2), who seeks to prevent the saints from arriving at the heavenly city.
[45] Bunyan had enjoyed bell-ringing very much. During the time he was under conviction of sin, he felt that this activity was a sinful practice, so he stopped. However, it was impossible for him to stay away when the bells were being rung. He carefully positioned himself lest one of the bells fall on him in judgment. How suitable that all the bells of heaven should welcome the pilgrims to their new home!
[46] Rev. 22:14

Then I saw in my dream that the Shining Men told them to call at the gate; and when they did, Enoch, Moses, Elijah, and others looked from above over the gate, to whom it was said, "These pilgrims have come from the City of Destruction because of their love for the King of this place." And then each of the pilgrims handed in his certificate, which he had received in the beginning;[47] these were then carried in to the King, and when he had read them, he said, "Where are the men?" When he was told, "They are standing outside the gate," the King commanded that the gate be opened, "That the righteous nation," said he, "which keepeth the truth, may enter in."[48]

Now I saw in my dream that Christian and Hopeful went through the gate; and as they entered, they were transfigured, and they had garments put on them that shone like gold. They were also given harps and crowns—the harps to praise and the crowns as tokens of honor.[49] Then all the bells in the city rang again for joy, and they were told, "Enter ye into the joy of your Lord."[50] I also heard the men themselves singing with a loud voice, "Blessing, honor, glory, and power, be to him that sitteth upon the throne, and to the Lamb, for ever and ever."[51]

Now just as the gates were opened for the men, I looked in after them, and I saw that the city shone like the sun; the streets were paved with gold, and on them walked many men with crowns on their heads, palms in their hands, and golden harps with which to sing praises.[52]

There were also those who had wings, and they answered one another without ceasing, saying, "Holy, holy, holy, is the Lord."[53] And after that they shut the gates, and with what I had seen, I wished myself among them.

---

[47]The certificate was the scroll they carried proving they were believers.
[48] Isa. 26:2
[49] Rev. 4:4; 5:8
[50] Matt. 25:23
[51] Rev. 5:13
[52] Rev. 7:9
[53] Isa. 6:3; Rev. 4:8

Now while I was gazing upon all these things, I turned my head to look back, and I saw Ignorance come up to the river; but he soon got across without half the difficulty which the other two men had encountered. For it happened that there was then in that place one called Vain-hope, a ferryman, who helped him over with his boat.[54] So Ignorance ascended the hill to the gate, only he came alone, for no one met him with the least encouragement.

When he arrived at the gate, he looked up at the writing above it, and then he began to knock, assuming that he would quickly gain entrance. But the men who looked over the top of the gate asked, "Where did you come from?" and "What do you want?" He answered, "I have eaten and have drunk in the presence of the King, and he has taught in our streets."[55] Then they asked him for his certificate, so that they might show it to the King; so he fumbled in his coat for one, and found none.[56]

Then they said, "Have you none?" And the man answered not a word.[57] So they told the King, but he would not come down to see the man. Instead, he commanded the two Shining Ones, who had conducted Christian and Hopeful to the city, to go out and bind Ignorance hand and foot and take him away.[58] Then they carried him through the air to the door that I had seen in the side of the hill and put him in there.

Then I realized that there was a way to hell even from the gates of heaven, as well as from the City of Destruction. And I awoke, and behold it was a dream.

---

[54] Ignorance has an easy time getting over the river simply because he is ignorant. Vain-hope helped him get over. Ease in death is no assurance of entrance into the city. Note that Ignorance is not escorted by the angels.

[55] See Luke 13:26. Jesus warns in that passage that spiritual privileges are no guarantee of salvation. If anything, they make for greater judgment, unless they result in salvation.

[56] Ignorance had no certificate; he was not a true believer. All his professions and arguments were in vain.

[57] 1 Kings 18:21; Matt. 22:12; Rom. 3:19

[58] See Matt. 22:13. Jesus minced no words when it came to warnings about judgment.

The Conclusion

Now, READER, I have told my dream to thee;
See if thou canst interpret it to me,
Or to thyself; or neighbor; but take heed
Of misinterpreting; for that, instead
Of doing good, will but thyself abuse:
By misinterpreting, evil ensues.

Take heed, also, that thou be not extreme,
In playing with the outside of my dream:
Nor let my figure or similitude
Put thee into a laughter or a feud.
Leave this for boys and fools; but as for thee,
Do thou the substance of my matter see.

Put by the curtains, look within my veil,
Turn up my metaphors, and do not fail,
There, if thou seekest them, such things to find,
As will be helpful to an honest mind.

What of my dross thou findest there, be bold
To throw away, but yet preserve the gold;
What if my gold be wrapped up in ore?
None throws away the apple for the core.
But if thou shalt cast all away as vain,
I know not but 'twill make me dream again.

The Author's Apology for His Book

When at the first I took my pen in hand
Thus for to write, I did not understand
That I at all should make a little book
In such a mode; nay, I had undertook
To make another; which, when almost done,
Before I was aware, I this begun.[1]

And thus it was: I, writing of the way
And race of saints, in this our gospel day,
Fell suddenly into an allegory
About their journey, and the way to glory,
In more than twenty things which I set down.
This done, I twenty more had in my crown;
And they again began to multiply,
Like sparks that from the coals of fire do fly.
Nay, then, thought I, if that you breed so fast,
I'll put you by yourselves, lest you at last
Should prove ad infinitum, *and eat out*
The book that I already am about.

Well, so I did; but yet I did not think
To show to all the world my pen and ink[2]
In such a mode; I only thought to make
I knew not what; nor did I undertake

---

[1]Bunyan felt it necessary in this poetic preface to explain how his book was written and why it was published. He did not want anyone to think he was being careless either in writing or in publishing. When he refers to "such a mode," he refers to the fact that it is an allegory, a form of literature in which persons, events, and objects have a deeper meaning than what is apparent in the story. His reference to "another" work probably refers to *The Heavenly Footman,* which was published after Bunyan's death. Based on 1 Cor. 9:24, this book has several ideas in it that parallel *The Pilgrim's Progress.* Some scholars think it was *The Strait Gate,* published in 1676.

[2] Not only did he not intend to write this book, but he also did not intend to publish it. Bunyan had published at least a dozen books by 1678, when *The Pilgrim's Progress* came out, including *Grace Abounding to the Chief of Sinners* (1666). He was not sure that his allegory, quite unlike his other works, would be accepted or do any good.

Thereby to please my neighbor: no, not I;
I did it my own self to gratify.

Neither did I but vacant seasons spend
In this my scribble; nor did I intend
But to divert myself in doing this[3]
From worser thoughts which make me do amiss.

Thus I set pen to paper with delight,
And quickly had my thoughts in black and white.
For, having now my method by the end,
Still as I pulled, it came; and so I penned
It down: until it came at last to be,
For length and breadth, the bigness which you see.

Well, when I had thus put mine ends together,
I showed them others, that I might see whether
They would condemn them, or them justify:
And some said, Let them live; some, Let them die;
Some said, John, print it; others said, Not so;
Some said, I might do good; others said, No.

Now was I in a strait, and did not see
Which was the best thing to be done by me:
At last I thought, Since you are thus divided,
I print it will, and so the case decided.

For, thought I, some, I see, would have it done,
Though others in that channel do not run:
To prove, then, who advised for the best,
Thus I thought fit to put it to the test.

I further thought, if now I did deny
Those that would have it, thus to gratify;
I did not know but hinder them I might
Of that which would to them be great delight.

For those which were not for its coming forth,
I said to them, Offend you I am loath,
Yet, since your brethren pleased with it be,
Forbear to judge till you do further see.

---

[3] Writing the book kept him occupied with spiritual thoughts while he was in jail.

If that thou wilt not read, let it alone;
Some love the meat, some love to pick the bone.
Yea, that I might them better palliate,
I did too with them thus expostulate.

May I not write in such a style as this?[4]
In such a method, too, and yet not miss
My end, thy good? Why may it not be done?
Dark clouds bring waters, when the bright bring none.
Yea, dark or bright, if they their silver drops
Cause to descend, the earth, by yielding crops,
Gives praise to both, and criticizes neither,
But treasures up the fruit they yield together;
Yea, so commixes both, that in her fruit
None can distinguish this from that: they suit
Her well when hungry; but, if she be full,
She spews out both, and makes their blessings null.

You see the ways the fisherman doth take
To catch the fish; what devices doth he make![5]
Behold! how he engageth all his wits;
Also his snares, lines, angles, hooks, and nets;
Yet fish there be, that neither hook, nor line,
Nor snare, nor net, nor device can make thine:
They must be groped for, and be tickled too,
Or they will not be catched, whate'er you do.

How doth the fowler seek to catch his game
By divers means! all which one cannot name:
His guns, his nets, his lime-twigs,[6] *light, and bell;*
He creeps, he goes, he stands; yea, who can tell
Of all his postures? Yet there's none of these

---

[4] Now he defends his style of writing by presenting several arguments. (1) Dark clouds in nature bring rain and fruitfulness. (2) Fishermen and hunters use "bait" to catch their game, and so must he if he is to catch the reader's interest. (3) Nature often puts jewels in unlikely places, and there are jewels in his book. (4) Other writers have used the same approach, including Bible writers, who present types, symbols, and metaphors. (5) Life itself often brings the light out of the darkness.

[5] An allegory is merely a device to "catch" his prey.

[6] Twigs that were smeared with bird lime, a sticky substance that held the birds fast.

Will make him master of what fowls he please.
Yea, he must pipe and whistle to catch this;
Yet, if he does so, that bird he will miss.

If that a pearl may in a toad's head dwell,[7]
And may be found too in an oyster-shell;
If things that promise nothing do contain
What better is than gold; who will disdain,
That have an inkling of it, there to look
That they may find it? Now, my little book
(Though void of all these paintings that may make
It with this or the other man to take)
Is not without those things that do excel
What do in brave but empty notions dwell.

"Well, yet I am not fully satisfied,
That this your book will stand, when soundly tried."

Why, what's the matter? "It is dark."[8] *What though?*
"But it is feigned."[9] *What of that? I trow*
Some men, by feigned words, as dark as mine,
Make truth to spangle and its rays to shine.
"But they want solidness." Speak, man, thy mind.
"They drown the weak; metaphors make us blind."[10]

Solidity, indeed, becomes the pen
Of him that writeth things divine to men;
But must I needs want solidness, because
By metaphors I speak? Were not God's laws,
His gospel laws, in olden times held forth
By types, shadows, and metaphors? Yet loath
Will any sober man be to find fault

---

[7]An ancient superstition that there was a jewel (the "toadstone") hidden on, or in, the toad's head; that is, beauty in the midst of ugliness. Shakespeare mentions this in *As You Like It:* "Which, like a toad, ugly and venomous, wears yet a precious jewel in its head." He was wrong on both counts, for toads do not have jewels, nor are they poisonous.

[8] Difficult to understand. See Prov. 1:6.

[9] Made up, imaginary.

[10]A kind of figurative language that uses one idea to suggest another. The purpose is to convey a much broader idea by using such a comparison. Eph. 4:14 is an example. An allegory is actually an extended metaphor.

With them, lest he be found for to assault
The highest wisdom. No, he rather stoops,
And seeks to find out what by pins and loops,
By calves and sheep, by heifers and by rams,
By birds and herbs, and by the blood of lambs,
God speaketh to him; and happy is he
That finds the light and grace that in them be.

Be not too forward, therefore, to conclude
That I lack solidness, that I am rude;[11]
All things solid in show not solid be;
All things in parables despise not we,
Lest things most hurtful lightly we receive,
And things that good are, of our souls bereave.
My dark and cloudy words, they do but hold
The truth, as cabinets enclose the gold.

The prophets used much by metaphors
To set forth truth; yea, who so considers
Christ, his apostles too, shall plainly see,
That truths to this day in such garments be.

Am I afraid to say that holy writ,
Which for its style and phrase puts down[12] *all wit,*
Is everywhere so full of all these things —
Dark figures, allegories. Yet there springs
From that same book that lustre, and those rays
Of light, that turn our darkest nights to days.

Come, let my carper to his life now look,[13]
And find there darker lines than in my book
He findeth any; yea, and let him know,
That in his best things there are worse lines too.

May we but stand before impartial men,
To his poor one I dare adventure ten,
That they will take my meaning in these lines
Far better than his lies in silver shrines.

---

[11] Lacking solid truth and doctrine.

[12] Luke 1:52

[13] The "carper" is the one finding fault with him, carping at him.

Come, truth, although in swaddling clouts,[14] *I find,*
Informs the judgment, rectifies the mind;
Pleases the understanding, makes the will
Submit; the memory too it doth fill
With what doth our imaginations please;
Likewise it tends our troubles to appease.

Sound words, I know, Timothy is to use,[15]
And old wives' fables he is to refuse;[16]
But yet grave Paul him nowhere did forbid
The use of parables; in which lay hid
That gold, those pearls, and precious stones that were
Worth digging for, and that with greatest care.

Let me add one word more. O man of God,
Art thou offended? Dost thou wish I had
Put forth my matter in another dress?
Or that I had in things been more express?
Three things let me propound;[17] *then I submit*
To those that are my betters, as is fit.

1. I find not that I am denied the use
Of this my method, so I no abuse
Put on the words, things, readers; or be rude
In handling figure or similitude,
In application; but, all that I may,
Seek the advance of truth this or that way.
Denied, did I say? Nay, I have leave
(Example too, and that from them that have
God better pleased, by their words or ways,
Than any man that breatheth now-a-days)
Thus to express my mind, thus to declare
Things unto thee that excellentest are.

---

[14] Swaddling clothes, such as babies were wrapped in. You do not reject the precious baby because the garments are humble.

[15] 2 Tim. 1:13

[16] These were superstitions that only ignorant old women would accept. See 1 Tim. 4:7.

[17] The three things: (1) I am not forbidden by God to use this approach, so long as I am telling truth. (2) If God so guided me, then let us accept His leading and "let truth be free." (3) The Bible uses this approach, and I am seeking to tell Bible truth.

2. I find that men (as high as trees) will write
Dialogue-wise; yet no man doth them slight
For writing so: indeed, if they abuse
Truth, cursed be they, and the craft they use
To that intent; but yet let truth be free
To make her sallies upon thee and me,
Which way it pleases God; for who knows how,
Better than he that taught us first to plough,
To guide our mind and pens for his design?
And he makes base things usher in divine.

3. I find that holy writ in many places
Hath semblance with this method, where the cases
Do call for one thing, to set forth another;
Use it I may, then, and yet nothing smother
Truth's golden beams: nay, but this method may
Make it cast forth its rays as light as day.

And now before I do put up my pen,
I'll show the profit of my book, and then
Commit both thee and it unto that Hand
That pulls the strong down, and makes weak ones stand.

This book it chalketh out [18] *before thine eyes*
The man that seeks the everlasting prize [19]
It shows you whence he comes, whither he goes;
What he leaves undone, also what he does;
It also shows you how he runs and runs,
Till he unto the gate of glory comes.

It shows, too, who set out for life amain [20]
As if the lasting crown they would obtain;
Here also you may see the reason why
They lose their labour, and like fools do die.

This book will make a traveller of thee, [21]

---

[18] Marks out, outlines a course to follow.

[19] Phil. 3:14

[20] To begin suddenly, with great vigor. Several people in *The Pilgrim's Progress* made good beginnings but did not reach heaven.

[21] This book will convert you and make you a pilgrim on the way to the Holy City. Bunyan's aim was not to entertain, but to evangelize.

If by its counsel thou wilt ruled be;
It will direct thee to the Holy Land,
If thou wilt its directions understand:
Yea, it will make the slothful active be;
The blind also delightful things to see.

Art thou for something rare and profitable?
Wouldest thou see a truth within a fable?
Art thou forgetful? Wouldest thou remember
From New Year's day to the last of December?
Then read my fancies; they will stick like burrs,[22]
And may be, to the helpless, comforters.

This book is writ in such a dialect
As may the minds of listless men affect:
It seems a novelty, and yet contains
Nothing but sound and honest gospel strains.

Wouldest thou divert thyself from melancholy?
Wouldest thou be pleasant, yet be far from folly?
Wouldest thou read riddles, and their explanation?
Or else be drowned in thy contemplation?
Dost thou love picking meat? Or wouldest thou see
A man i' the clouds, and hear him speak to thee?
Wouldest thou be in a dream, and yet not sleep?
Or wouldest thou in a moment laugh and weep?
Wouldest thou lose thyself and catch no harm,
And find thyself again without a charm?
Wouldest read thyself, and read thou knowest not what,
And yet know whether thou art blest or not,
By reading the same lines? Oh, then come hither,
And lay my book, thy head, and heart together.[23]

---

[22] By using imaginative pictures in his book, he helps us remember what he has said. We can easily forget sermons and lectures, but stories stick with us, like burrs.

[23] Bunyan believed in a balanced Christian life, with the mind and the emotions involved. Truth ought to enlighten the mind, stir the emotions, and motivate the will. The Puritans did not believe in empty emotionalism; they wanted light as well as heat.

The Life and Times of John Bunyan

"My descent was of a low, inconsiderable generation, my father's house being of that rank that is meanest and most despised of all the families in the land."

So wrote John Bunyan, Puritan preacher and author of *The Pilgrim's Progress,* the most popular Christian classic ever produced in the English-speaking world.

Bunyan was born in November 1628 in Harrowden, Bedfordshire, and was baptized at the parish church in Elstow on the thirtieth day of that month. Bunyan's family lived in Elstow, a village one mile southwest of Bedford. His father was a brazier, or tinker, who traveled from town to town mending pots and pans.

Bunyan's childhood was tempestuous. For some reason, he was plagued by frightening dreams and blasphemous thoughts. In later years he interpreted those experiences as the work of God to bring him to a saving knowledge of Jesus Christ. He attended a local school for poor children, but his education was interrupted so he could assist his father and help support the family.

Life was not easy, but it was not without its simple joys. Like many of the youths of his day, Bunyan enjoyed games on the village green, dancing, and music. If he read at all, it was the Bible or Foxe's *Book of Martyrs.*

The year 1644 was a crisis year for Bunyan. In June, his mother died; then his beloved sister died a month later. In August, his father married again, an event that greatly hurt young John. In November, when he turned sixteen, Bunyan was taken into the army to help fight the civil war that had begun in August 1642. He was probably happy to leave home. It is not clear whether Bunyan fought with the Royalists or the parliamentary army, but he was probably with the latter. Many of the military images in his books were gathered during his three years in the army.

One interesting incident in his military career made a great impression on the youthful Bunyan. At the siege of Leicester a friend asked permission to take Bunyan's place;

during the battle, the man was shot in the head and killed. Bunyan had experienced several narrow escapes in childhood, and that additional one convinced him that God had a special purpose for him to fulfill, although at that time he was not a believer.

Back in Elstow, Bunyan worked as a tinker and enjoyed life as a sinner. "I had but few equals for cursing, swearing, lying, and blaspheming the holy Name of God," he later wrote. There is no evidence that he was ever guilty of drunkenness or immorality, even though in his later writings he painted those years very black.

Bunyan married in 1649. His wife was as poor as he, but she came from a godly home and brought with her two religious books: *The Plain Man's Pathway to Heaven* by Arthur Dent and *The Practice of Piety* by Lewis Bayly. "In these two books I would sometimes read with her," Bunyan wrote, "but all this while I met with no conviction." However, he did try to reform his life, and he began to attend the Bedford church where John Gifford was pastor.

The next three years saw Bunyan struggling against sin and with God. He wanted to escape hell, yet he enjoyed his sins and found them difficult to give up. One Sunday when he was playing tipcat on the village green, he "heard" a voice in his soul that said, "Wilt thou leave thy sins, and go to heaven? or have thy sins, and go to hell?" He was momentarily stunned, but then decided to go on with his game. After all, if he was going to hell, he might as well enjoy himself along the way!

While working in Bedford one day, he saw a group of poor women sitting in the sun and talking. Wondering what their conversation was about, he drew near to listen. "I heard but understood not," he later confessed, "for they were far above, out of my reach. Their talk was about a new birth, the work of God in their hearts, and also how they were convinced of their miserable state by nature."

As a result of hearing this, a deep conviction gripped his own heart, and he struggled desperately to please God. He took a keen interest in the church and regarded the ministers, the vestments, and the services with almost a superstitious awe. "Their Name, their Garb, and Work, did so intoxicate me and bewitch me," he wrote. People noticed his radical self-reformation and wondered how long it would last. One day the pastor preached against Sabbath-breaking, a bitter blow to Bunyan's new self-image, and that was the end of his self-reformation. He returned to the village green and his favorite games, at the same time trying to quiet the voice within.

One day he was standing at a neighbor's shop window "cursing and swearing ... after my wonted manner" when the woman of the house openly rebuked him. The fact that her own reputation was not too savory only made her words sting his conscience that much more. He resolved again to do better, and he succeeded for a time. "I was proud of my Godliness," he wrote. But still he had no peace or joy in his heart, and the more he tried to reform on the outside, the more miserable he was on the inside. Of course, many of those experiences found their way, in one form or another, into *The Pilgrim's Progress*.

It was the ministry and personal friendship of Pastor John Gifford that God used to bring John Bunyan to the place of assurance as His child. Bunyan was baptized by Gifford in 1653 and became a member of the Bedford church. "Conversion to God is not so easy and so smooth a thing as some would have men to believe it is," he wrote. And all of *The Pilgrim's Progress* testifies to that fact.

In 1654 or 1655, the Bunyan family (by then he had two sons and two daughters) moved to Bedford, and Bunyan became more active in the church. But 1655 was another crisis year for him: both his wife and Pastor Gifford died. That same year the church members encouraged Bunyan to start preaching, and before long it was recognized that God's hand was upon this simple tinker. In 1656 Bunyan published his first book, *Some Gospel Truths Opened*. It was the first of sixty titles he would publish, the greatest of which would be *The Pilgrim's Progress*.

In May 1660, the Commonwealth ended, and Charles II was recalled and put on the throne. At first, Charles gave evidence of wanting to cooperate with all the religious faiths in England; but it was not long before his policies changed, and he began to move against the independents in favor of the established church. On November 12, 1660, Bunyan went to preach thirteen miles from Bedford. He had been warned that he was in danger of arrest, and the next day he was arrested and put into the town jail. In spite of pleas from his wife (he had married again) and friends, he was imprisoned for twelve years.

One should not picture Bunyan as a prisoner languishing in a dungeon, however, for he did have a certain amount of freedom and was occasionally permitted to visit his family. While in jail he studied his Bible, wrote books, tried to minister to the other prisoners, and made lace, which he sold to help support his family. He wrote eleven books during that period, including the autobiographical *Grace Abounding to the Chief of Sinners*.

In 1670 the Bedford church wanted to call Bunyan as its pastor, and when he was released in 1672, the call was made effective. On May 9, 1672, Bunyan was licensed to preach. On September 13 he was officially pardoned.

But in 1675 the Declaration of Indulgence was repealed, and Bunyan was returned to jail for six months. It is likely that he completed *The Pilgrim's Progress* during that time. The book was licensed for publication on February 18, 1678. Nathaniel Ponder of London was the publisher, and the book was an immediate success, calling for three editions during the first year alone.

After his final release from jail, Bunyan continued his pastoral and preaching ministry, and God's blessing was upon him in a singular way. He drew huge crowds wherever he preached, and (as with his Lord) the common people heard him gladly. In August 1688, while riding to London, he was caught in a rainstorm and became ill. He preached his last sermon on August 19, and died on August 31. He is buried in

Bunhill Fields, the Nonconformist cemetery located across from Wesley's Chapel on City Road in London.

The Puritans

It is unfortunate that today the word *Puritan* conjures up the picture of a stern man in a black hat, a humorless individual who goes about stopping people from having a good time. Quite the opposite ought to be true. The Puritans were a disciplined people, to be sure, but they knew that their discipline enabled them to enjoy the blessings of God. They delighted in the simple joys of life, especially their homes and children. They worked hard, "doing all to the glory of God," and believed in using their opportunities to provide for themselves and for others who were less fortunate.

The history of Puritanism is woven into the fabric of English political and religious history.

In 1534 Henry VIII separated the English church from the authority of the Pope. No major changes were made in doctrine except in those matters related to papal supremacy. When Henry died in 1547, his heir Edward VI was only ten years old, so the government was controlled by a "protectorate council." Edward and his associates were strongly Protestant and brought about church reforms that strengthened the Protestant position.

When Edward died in 1553, his half sister Mary Tudor was crowned queen. A devout Roman Catholic, she sought to restore "the true faith" to her realm, even to the point of persecuting Protestants. It was under her authority that Latimer and Ridley were burned at the stake. Then in 1558 Mary died, and Elizabeth I ascended to the throne.

In 1559 Parliament passed two laws that permanently settled the Protestant character of the English church: The Act of Supremacy made the reigning monarch the supreme governor of the church, and The Act of Uniformity defined the worship and the doctrines of the church. In 1562 a church convocation accepted the Thirty-Nine Articles as the official doctrinal confession of the Church of England.

For the most part, Elizabeth was lenient with the Roman Catholics, but she had serious problems with certain Protestants who had been influenced by the Reformers on the continent. These men, many of whom were devout scholars, wanted to see the church purged of the Roman Catholic elements that were still evident, especially in the liturgy. The name "puritan" was attached to this school of thought as early as 1563, and it was definitely a term of reproach.

In 1556 Matthew Parker, Archbishop of Canterbury, published his "Advertisements," requiring all clergy to follow a standard rule in wearing vestments. Of course, the Puritans opposed this ruling and asked again for a purifying of the church. Some of the Puritans became impatient and withdrew from the church, thus becoming known as "separatists." Many of them fled to Holland or to the New World.

When Elizabeth died in 1603 the Privy Council named James VI of Scotland as the new monarch. We know him as James I of England, the man who authorized the King James translation of the Bible. During his reign in Scotland, James had experienced problems with the Presbyterians and their Calvinistic doctrines. He carried his prejudices with him to England and transferred them to the Puritans.

Soon after James I ascended to the throne, he was presented with a Puritan petition signed by one thousand clergymen, asking again for reforms in the church. In response, James called a conference at Hampton Court, at which the Puritans and the Church of England bishops could confront each other. It is unfortunate that James confused the Puritans with the Presbyterians, for the Puritan divines had no desire to change church government; it was primarily the liturgy that they wanted the king to reform. But James was not about to make any changes. His reply was, "No bishop, no king!"

One of the results of the conference was the formation of the Scrooby Manor congregation of Puritans, many of whom finally emigrated to America on the *Mayflower* in 1620.

Another result was the authorization of a new translation of the Bible, the one we now know as the King James Version.

The Puritans were not a denomination, nor did they have any desire to divide or destroy the Church of England. The bonds that held them together were doctrinal, not political. The only spiritual authority they recognized was the Bible, the Word of God. They emphasized the preaching and reading of the Bible, not only in the churches but also in their families. They believed in an educated clergy, dedicated pastors who could expound the Scriptures, win the lost, discipline church members, and be personal examples to the flock. Unfortunately, at that time there were many ministers in the established church who were unconverted, untrained, and unconcerned about the needs of the people.

The Puritans were basically Calvinistic in doctrine, following the teachings of the Geneva Reformer, John Calvin (1509–64). They believed in election by the Father and redemption through faith in Jesus Christ. They saw the work of the Holy Spirit as one of convicting sinners, giving sinners new life when they trusted Christ, sealing converts, and empowering them for life and service. The Puritans believed in a personal experience of conversion. It was not sufficient for a person to be baptized as an infant, enrolled as a member of the church, and asked to give assent as an adult to a certain set of doctrines.

The Puritans looked upon their beloved England as God's "covenant nation." If the people would only repent of their sins and trust Christ, God would do for England what He had done for Israel: defeat her enemies, establish her kingdom, and bless her people. God was their King, and their supreme allegiance was to Him.

When Charles I came to the throne in 1625, three years before John Bunyan's birth, the Puritans again requested reform of the liturgy and the clergy, but to no avail. Charles attacked the Puritans, inflicting heavy fines, physical punishment (he cut off the ears of their leaders), and jail sentences. When William Laud became Archbishop of Canterbury in

1633, the pressures against the Puritans grew even greater as Laud sought to create a uniform church.

Meanwhile, King Charles had come into conflict with Parliament; he desperately needed money, and members of Parliament would not grant it. The result was a polarized nation: persons were either for or against the king.

Such polarization inevitably led to civil war (1642–46), and Charles and his forces were defeated. Oliver Cromwell emerged as the leader of the anti-Royalist forces. Charles was beheaded January 30, 1649, and Cromwell was named Lord Protector of the Commonwealth. (It is worth noting that the Puritans did not present a united front against the king, for some of them fought on the Royalist side.)

During the years of Cromwell's leadership, England's standing in Europe grew considerably. He was tolerant of the Jews and Quakers and sought to make England a place where the Word of God was faithfully preached by men of God. But this situation was not to last. Cromwell died on September 3, 1658, and his son Richard was named Lord Protector. Unfortunately, Richard lacked the charisma and stature of his distinguished father, and Parliament asked him to resign. A military government took command, and forces were set in motion to bring the exiled Charles II back home.

On May 8, 1660, Charles II was proclaimed king. The regency was restored, but the Puritans did not look to it for any spiritual encouragement. In spite of his early promises to give liberty of conscience to his subjects, Charles II soon took steps to strengthen the state church. A new Act of Uniformity (May 19, 1662) required all clergymen to accept the Book of Common Prayer and to take an oath of obedience to the king as leader of the church. It also required the reordination of those clergymen who had not been ordained by the established church. More than two thousand conscientious pastors refused to submit and were ejected from their churches. (From then on they would be called "nonconformists.") The Conventicle Acts (May 1664) prohibited Nonconformist meetings of more than five persons, unless the meetings were held in a private house. The Five-Mile Acts (October 1665) prohibited dissenting ministers from going within five miles of any town where they had served a church.

During that time of intense religious persecution, many Puritan pastors faithfully and sacrificially served their congregations; and some, like John Bunyan, were arrested and imprisoned. However, their churches grew both in purity and power.

Charles II died on February 6, 1685, and his Roman Catholic brother James II took the throne. James sought to do what Mary Tudor had failed to do, namely, restore the Roman Catholic faith to the realm, and he authorized extensive arrests. It was at that time that the infamous Judge Jeffreys was in power, arresting devout Christians, trying them illegally, and giving them terrible sentences.

By June 1688 the people were ready for a change. William of Orange of Holland, who was married to the daughter of James II, was invited to "bring over an army and secure the infringed liberties." In 1689 William and Mary were crowned joint monarchs, and that same year the Toleration Act gave religious freedom to all groups, with the exception of the Roman Catholics and the Unitarians. For the most part, the Nonconformists were now free to minister the Word of God without fear of persecution.

Puritan theology and the Puritan spirit of discipline and devotion still enrich the church. The United States in particular owes a great deal to the Puritan fathers who established that nation. The dignity of honest labor, the sanctity of the home, the living of all of life to the glory of God (making no distinction between "secular" and "sacred"), the honoring of the Bible as the Word of God, and the desire to see national leaders fear God and obey His law, are all principles that we have learned from the Puritans.

Scripture Index

Other Discovery House books that will feed your soul with the Word of God:

Broken Things: Why We Suffer
by *M. R. De Haan, M. D.*
　　To those seeking reasons for their suffering and disappointments, this book offers hope and peace through the healing principles of God's Word.

The Christian Salt and Light Company
by *Haddon W. Robinson*
　　A powerful application of the Sermon on the Mount principles as the path to true happiness.

The Solid Rock Construction Company
by *Haddon W. Robinson*
　　Writing on Matthew 6 and 7, the author illustrates how Christians can build their lives on the right foundation, how to pray wholeheartedly, serve devotedly, and trust completely.

Daniel: God's Man in a Secular Society
by *Donald K. Campbell*
　　Intriguing, contemporary perspective and helpful application of the prophecies in Daniel. A call to radical dependence on God.

Our Daily Times With God: *Favorite selections from Our Daily Bread*
　　A powerful devotional book featuring the best from *Our Daily Bread*, organized by themes and the great events of Scripture. Also available in a Large Print edition.

The Strength of a Man
by *David Roper*
　　Fifty short, easy-to-read chapters that explore topics such as money, failure, humility, fear, and prayer. A biblical look at true manhood.

My Utmost for His Highest
by *Oswald Chambers*

The classic devotional bestseller. These powerful words will refresh those who need encouragement, brighten the way of those in difficulty, and strengthen personal relationships with Christ. A book to use every day for the rest of your life.

The Oswald Chambers Library

Spiritual guidance from the author of *My Utmost for His Highest.* Powerful insights on topics of interest to every believer:

If You Will Ask

Reflections on the power of prayer.

The Love of God

An intimate look at the Father-heart of God.

The Place of Help

Thoughts on daily needs of the Christian life.

Not Knowing Where

Keen spiritual direction through knowing and trusting God.

Baffled to Fight Better

Job and the problem of suffering.

Order from your favorite bookstore or from:

DISCOVERY HOUSE PUBLISHERS
Box 3566
Grand Rapids, MI 49501
Call toll-free: 1-800-283-8333